EARTH
TO
EARTH

EARTH
TO
EARTH

**A
Ludington - van der Berg
Novel**

M. M. Lindvall

LEVEL
BEST BOOKS

To our spouses, Terri and Tom, who held down the forts while we retreated to our word processors.

"But, as in ethics, evil is a consequence of good, so, in fact, out of joy is sorrow born."

—Edgar Allan Poe

Praise for Earth to Earth

"This is a beautifully written account of a highly unusual trip to Scotland and strange goings-on in the Orkney Islands. There is enough local detail to satisfy anybody who is interested in Scottish history, and enough suspense to keep the rest on the edge of their metaphorical seats. A well-researched and intriguing novel. A lovely book in every respect."—Alexander McCall Smith, author of the Ladies' No. 1 Detective Agency and Scotland Street Mystery Series

"As detective stories go, this is a truly exceptional one because of its intelligence and completely unexpected twists. But it is much more... It considers love and loyalty when severely tested, various human weaknesses, bottled-up anger and a bold attempt to redirect it. Set in Scotland, it builds to a climax in the Orkney Islands. It is a profound and enthralling novel addressing our human condition. I highly recommend it."—Iain Torrance, former President of Princeton Theological Seminary and Pro-Chancellor of the University of Aberdeen

"If you seek a taste of Scotland in your crime novels, this tale from a father-daughter writing team is for you. From Edinburgh to Orkney, history braids into mystery as a minister-sleuth and his sidekick follow a twisted trail to expose a calculating killer. A satisfying read with a surprise ending."—Katherine Ramsland, award-winning author of *I Scream Man* and *How to Catch a Killer*

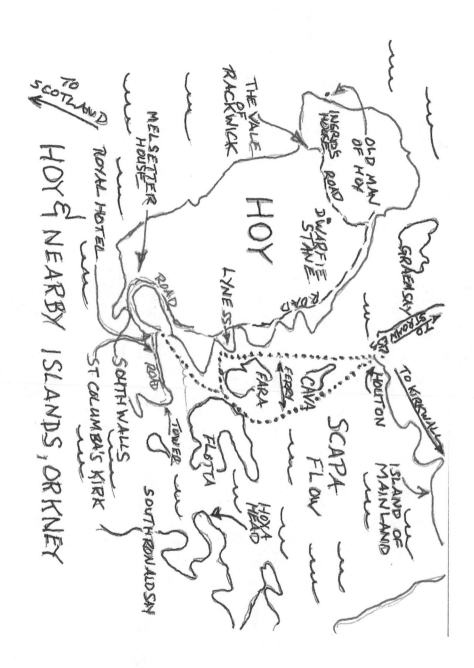

HOY & NEARBY ISLANDS, ORKNEY

TO SCOTLAND

OLD MAN OF HOY

INGRIDS HOUSE

INGRIDS HOUSE ROAD

THE VALE OF RACKWICK

MELSETTER HOUSE

ROYAL HOTEL

HOY

DWARFIE STANE

DWARFIE STANE ROAD

LYNESS

ROAD

ROAD

TOWER

ST COLUMBA'S KIRK

SOUTH WALLS

FARA

FERRY

FLOTTA

HOXA HEAD

SOUTH RONALDSAY

CAVA

SCAPA FLOW

HOUTON

ISLAND OF MAINLAND

GRAEMSAY

A TO STROMNESS

TO KIRKWALL

Chapter One

"Seth, ye ken I dinna' fancy a fortnight in a damn motor coach rambling about the Highlands with a gaggle on auld yins." Fiona Ludington sometimes drifted into colloquial Scots, though it was never really her language, when upset. Product of middle-class Edinburgh and the Mary Erskine School that she was, Fiona Ludington usually spoke a Scottish iteration of the Queen's English.

"Auld yins?" her husband asked.

"Old people," she grumbled back. "Well, anyone older than you and me."

June 14

Nine months later, Seth looked at his wife of more than a decade, a lovely woman, fair and freckled, but presently two shades greener than she had yet been with morning sickness. And they were about to board a six-hour transatlantic flight to embark on the very journey she did not fancy. And she was three months along, with twins no less. A woman accustomed to being in control of her life, she had ached for children even as her husband hesitated. He had pleaded a troubled world with an uncertain future for the next generation, a polite mask for his secret insecurities about his worthiness to be a fit father. The pregnancy had surprised them both. But it had pulled them together, both now delighted with the prospect of children, even if two in one pass. But "delighted" was not Fiona's present humor at Gate 67 at JFK's Terminal 2.

"I'm off to the loo, Seth. First time for nausea like this."

"I'll go with you."

"Now that's not going to work, is it?" This was said over her shoulder as she dashed to the women's room just beyond one of the terminal's several Croque Madame franchises.

Her husband understood that Fiona Ludington was a tenacious woman. She was a human rights lawyer at the U.N., not a calling for frail hearts. But merest nausea can best even the stoutest constitution. She had experienced several bouts of milder morning sickness during her first trimester, but this looked to be a more formidable iteration. It worried Seth, probably more than it did her.

He knew that she had not been enthusiastic about the group tour of Scotland when he had first proposed it the previous fall. She, a daughter of the manse, understood that ministers frequently led such tours for their congregants—often enticed by the free ride it offered them as organizers and leaders—even if they found it tiresome. But Seth Ludington, who was as wealthy as most parish clergy were not, needed no free ride. He had been subtly but insistently cajoled into arranging such a tour by several members of the Old Stone Presbyterian Church, the small and struggling congregation in New York's Yorkville neighborhood that he had served as minister for almost two years. They had started in on him as soon as he had arrived, happily and pointedly remembering trips that had been organized by his predecessors in the pulpit. They had even stooped to showing him photos from past trips., pointing out their smiling faces lined up in front of the Tower of London or the Uffizi. He finally yielded, largely due to the entreaties of his part-time and unpaid church secretary, Harriet van der Berg, and the church's Clerk of Session, Harry Mulholland. Like most ministers, he wanted to please, and he actually liked both of them very much, though his relationship with the latter had been wounded, then healed, by what had unfolded over the previous Lent and Easter. Those same events had only strengthened his affection for the former, the formally formidable Miss van der Berg.

The trip had been planned well before the unhappy events that had preceded Easter just two months earlier. He had at last convinced Fiona to go along with a promise that the itinerary would include the cluster of islands called Orkney. Scotland is a natural destination for Presbyterian types. Not only is it perceived to be the mother country of the denomination, but it is a stunningly beautiful place to ramble about, Presbyterians or no. Orkney was a less obvious destination. The cluster of windswept islands to the north of Britain is closer to Bergen than London and as Norse as it is Scottish. But it is home to a trove of Neolithic archeological sites, tourist magnets all, as well as the 12th Century St. Magnus Cathedral, the northernmost cathedral in Britain. And, of course, St. Magnus is Church of Scotland—Presbyterian, that is to say. All these details Seth had noted when he presented the itinerary to a handful of interested members of the congregation of Old Stone. Fiona was sold simply because the maternal grandmother whom she adored was Orcadian, and the woman had sung the mysteries and wonders of the islands to her granddaughter growing up in Edinburgh. Fiona had long ached to go to Orkney. And that grandmother, who kept a summer cottage on the island of Hoy, would be there when they visited. Seth had phoned Ingrid Gunn to make certain of that.

Anxiously waiting for Fiona's return from her fit of nausea, he surveyed the assembled tour group sitting in the waiting area of Gate 67. Well, he thought to himself, they're not all auld yins. He and Fiona were still both in their thirties, he barely, she comfortably. And there were the three seminary students, all even younger. When it became apparent by February that the only Old Stone members who were actually going to sign up for the tour were Harriet, Harry Mulholland, and his wife, Georgia, Ludington had decided to underwrite a few tour "scholarships" for students at both Princeton and Philadelphia Theological Seminaries. The tour company had set the minimum at 12 participants. Seth had hoped that the scholarships would nudge them to the quota and lower the average age of the group by several decades. But only three students had been enticed to travel with a gaggle of their elders.

The younger two of the three were both Master of Divinity students at Princeton. They were a fetching pair and seemed to already know each other. Ted Buskirk, backpack at his feet, sandy-colored hair in a man bun, legs in skinny jeans, gold stud in his nose but none in his ear, was nice-looking in his avant way. He smiled a lot and addressed Seth as "Reverend Ludington" even after he'd asked him to please call him "Seth." Hope Feely was pretty and petite, raven hair cut in a page boy, clad in a peasant blouse and a long denim skirt for travel. They were seated side-by-side directly opposite him. Ted was looking up at the Delta flat screen that was posting flight upgrades, sipping something from a Venti Starbucks cup. Hope was staring at him. She quickly glanced away when he turned to her, then looked back at him, offering a coy smile as he handed her the cup. She drank from it without hesitation.

The third scholarship student was a PhD candidate from Philadelphia Theological Seminary. Sarah Mrazek's application had noted her age as 34, though she looked older. She was seated alone, a small carry-on set on the floor, guarded anxiously between her knees. She was medium height and stout, on the cusp of overweight, with features that could have been attractive were they not so fretful. Her hair was died the purple of Lenten vestments. She was dressed in what appeared to be vintage clothing, the Goodwill chic popular with many in her age cohort. She was wearing rather too much jewelry—costume vintage, Seth guessed. She had told Ludington when they met at a get-to-know-the-group gathering a month earlier that she was "ABD"—"all but dissertation." Her dissertation, she told him, was on "erotic metaphor in the Song of Solomon," the protracted love poem that had somehow slithered into the Old Testament canon. She said she'd been working on it for nineteen months. "I'm getting there," she had smiled and added, "but barely," as if she dreaded its completion.

His back to Ludington, the other singleton on the tour had just removed his horn-rimmed glasses and run a hand through his thinning and graying hair. Albert McNulty, in his mid-50s, was a member of the Board of Trustees of Philadelphia Theological Seminary who had signed up when he had heard that the seminary's president was going. This had rather surprised Ludington, but it had surprised that same about-to-retire president, Philip Desmond, even more. Desmond later told him that McNulty was divorced, a litigator in a mid-sized Philadelphia corporate law firm, and chair of the board's investment committee. He lived alone in the faux-Tudor pile on the Mainline that he had managed to snag in the divorce.

Ludington had hinted at this question about motivation when he had met McNulty at the May gathering of the tour group at the manse in New York. "I've always wanted to explore my Scottish roots, all those McNultys over there." He pronounced "roots" so that it rhymed with "puts." "I've been doing the Ancestry.com thing. There are scads of McNultys in County Antrim." Ludington had managed not to note the obvious—that Antrim, though indeed peppered with Scots names, was in Northern Ireland. He was unsure whether McNulty knew this or not.

The two even more surprising tour group members were sitting alone under the waiting area's expanse of glass windows overlooking the runway. Ludington had been flabbergasted when Philip Desmond had phoned him in April, just days after they had first met, and asked if there was still space for him and his wife Penny on the tour. The Desmonds—urbane and seasoned travelers, consummately world-wise—seemed to Ludington to be a pair who would much prefer to travel on their own. But Ludington had been pleased, if not a bit flattered, that the Rev. Dr. Philip Desmond and his charming wife, Penny, would be along on the trip. In fact, he had been worried that he was going to have to cancel it for want of enough participants. And he liked and respected Phil Desmond. Decades before he had been called to lead the most liberal seminary in the denomination, a younger Desmond had served Old Stone as its much-loved and ever more fondly-remembered pastor of nearly twenty years. Long-time Old Stone members still recalled the Desmond era as the congregation's Golden Age, in spite of the fact that it spanned the '70s and '80, decades when both church-going and New York City living were tumbling from favor. They were a handsome pair of seniors, he tall with chiseled features, blond hair still peeking through the gray, she slender and a classic blue-blood, meticulously coifed and made up, but not too much, of course. He was reading a small book. Seth recognized the cover. It was one of the endless editions of John Baillie's classic little volume of daily prayers. "Scottish prayers on the way to Scotland, how fit," Ludington thought to himself. But he was surprised that Desmond would choose a collection of devotions that was so insistently confessional, sometimes on the cusp of verbal self-flagellation. As he watched Desmond, he saw the man pull a felt-tip pen from the inside pocket of his beige cashmere sport coat and jot something in the little book.

What Philip Desmond did not know was that for a few uncomfortable days in the previous Lent, Ludington had suspected him of complicity in the long-ago death of an infant, a child whose bird-like bones he had discovered in the ash pit of the manse's fireplace, the home in which Desmond and his family had once lived for two decades. As he watched the sun preparing to set behind them, Ludington prayed that they would never know—neither of the death nor that he had once suspected them of involvement in it.

That Phil Desmond was quite innocent was due in some measure to two other people seated at Delta Gate 67. Harry Mulholland was a retired NYPD homicide detective who now served Old Stone as its Clerk of Session. He sat next to his wife, Georgia, his balding head hidden behind the morning's *Wall Street Journal.* He was predictably dressed in one of his closetful of Harris tweed sport coats, a regimental tie about his neck. Ludington did not think he had ever seen the man without a necktie. Georgia was in a lavender pantsuit. Seth guessed it lived in the back of her closet and found its way out only for the occasional travel adventure she and Harry enjoyed. Her reddish hair was cut short and framed a round and unlined face. She was one of those sweet souls who almost always wore a smile. If Georgia Mulholland was not smiling, you knew that something in her world was amiss.

After Fiona, Harry Mulholland was the first person Ludington had told about his discovery of the fifty-year-old infant bones in the manse. Together, they had agreed that some private investigation might be undertaken before making a call to the Sixteenth Precinct. Harry had assured him that cold cases a half-century old were not going to get much, if any, official attention. The Rev. Seth Ludington had then become a sleuth in a dog collar, while his Clerk of Session had served as his under-the-table conduit to the NYPD forensic lab, passing along DNA samples that Ludington purloined in an attempt to discover who might be related to the bones. But Harry

Mulholland had betrayed Ludington's trust, neglecting to forward one sample, the one sample of DNA that Harry feared could prove disastrously incriminating. Seth later learned that Mulholland had dreaded the very real possibility that the dead child might possibly have been his, or if not his, that of an old friend. The crisis had nearly caused the man to fall off the sobriety wagon he had been riding for decades. As it turned out, that instantiation of duplicity, later confessed and lamented, was irrelevant to the case. But it had been a betrayal nonetheless.

Ludington had been furious. But his anger had been eviscerated by what the man had done in the days after Easter, especially what he had dared at a meeting of the congregation's board, the Session. Ludington had called the meeting after sending the congregation an email in which he confessed to an act of consummate callousness in his youth, an event that ended in a needless death, a death he did not cause but might have prevented. He spared no incriminating details—the fact that the incrimination was moral and not legal was beside the point. He had sanded none of the tale's rough grain smooth. He knew it had too long been held secret. He had also come to understand that it threatened to corrode his soul.

After that Easter confession, he announced that the church's Session would meet in two days' time and that at that meeting, he would ask that the board call a congregational meeting so that the church could accept his resignation. The congregation's reaction to the Easter bombshell had been as diverse as one might expect. There were some emails of support, three resignations from church membership, but mostly, Easter had been followed by awkward glances and too-discreet silence.

It was Harry Mulholland, Clerk of Session, who had turned the tide of opinion. He had volunteered to offer the board meeting's opening prayer—something the minister usually did. He began by straightening his tie as he often did before he spoke. Then he cleared his throat and said, "Hi, I'm Harry, and I'm an alcoholic. Some of you have probably guessed that, but I've never said it to you before. When I was drinking—and doing drugs, by the way—I did lamentable things. I did things of which I am very, very ashamed. I lied, lied left and right. I messed up my own life and the lives of people I cared about. Now I'm sober—not perfect, just sober. Day before yesterday, pastor preached that people can change. Well, you're looking at it. Now, I'm going to offer the Serenity Prayer. We use it at AA meetings. Will you pray with me?"

After offering Niebuhr's famous prayer, speaking the words alone as no one else on the Session seemed to know it, he concluded with an emphatic "AMEN." Then he said, "This is what they call a special meeting of the Session, so there's only one thing to talk about. Pastor Ludington wants us to call a meeting of the congregation so he can resign."

Seth felt he had to speak. All six members of the Session had been in church on Easter when he had confessed to what he had done twenty years earlier, and all had read the email he had sent the congregation. Again, he told them that he thought it rendered him unfit to be their minister.

The silence that followed had been finally broken by Winifred Grimes, of all people. She was one of the few people of color among the Old Stone membership. She was an immigrant from the Virgin Islands, a grandmother of seven; she had once told Ludington, "Three here, four in the islands." She seldom spoke at Session meetings, so when she did, people listened more closely than they might to someone who spoke too frequently.

In a voice that was half whisper, she looked directly at Ludington and spoke, more to him than the other members of the Session. Her Caribbean English had lost none of its sweet lilt, though her words bore an edge, "How can you preach to us about people changin' their ways and not apply it to yourself? I make a motion"—here she hesitated and looked at Harry to make sure she was within the compass of Robert's Rules. He nodded, and she said, "I make a motion that we reject the pastor's request for a meeting of the congregation and that we tell him to forget this resignation nonsense." There was a chorus of seconds and a motion to end debate. Winifred's motion passed by a voice vote, six to zero.

The story of the Session meeting made the rounds in the congregation over the next week. As he looked back on it, Seth had come to see that the litany of the tragedies laid bare during those weeks of Lent—his own secret and the silent lies that had long hidden it, the death of the child in the ash pit of his house, Harry's self-serving dissembling—all of it had ached for a forgiveness. It came, but forgiveness, he now understood only too well, does not come cheap. It often has to be paid for in the dear currencies of candor and time.

Seth looked at Georgia Mulholland, seated at Gate 67, as he remembered Harry's words at the meeting. She had known about her husband's addiction, of course, but knew nothing of his more recent trespass into perfidy. She would have already forgiven him if she had. He watched as Harry lowered his newspaper and his wife lay her head on his tweedy shoulder and closed her eyes. The easy grace of their long and childless marriage had always beguiled Ludington. He hoped that his and Fiona's was tacking toward such a harbor.

His musings were interrupted by Harriet van der Berg, who had been sitting next to Fiona's now empty seat and had risen to her considerable height and moved to stand directly before him.

"Seth, she said, "I think it would be wise for me to check on Fiona. I could not but observe that she appeared unwell and has taken herself in haste to the ladies' lounge."

As she said this, she glanced toward the Croque Madame and the woman's room just beyond. Ludington had often said to Fiona that listening to Harriet van der Berg speak was like reading a Thackeray novel. In response to her unaccustomed informality, he now called her "Harriet," something very few people did. She had retired a decade earlier after a successful career as an executive secretary to a string of shiny-shoe Wall Street lawyers, all of whom she had outlasted and outlived, doubtless by dint of constitution, will, and a dogged but generally unspoken faith.

In addition to serving as what she insisted on naming a "secretary, not an admin, God forbid," Harriet van der Berg had also become the unlikely Watson to his Holmes in the Lenten case of the hidden bones, though he knew that, unlike that pair of detectives a century gone, her Watson was at least as keen as his Holmes, perhaps more so. Their mutual trust and regard had grown deep in the course of their shared, and finally successful, search for a long-buried truth.

The woman had been barely fazed by his Easter confession and failed attempt to resign. He had found her in her tiny office at church the Wednesday after Easter, the morning after the Session meeting. Before he had had a chance to even offer a "good morning," she said to him, an edge to her voice, "Pastor, I do assume you are bright enough to eventually recognize the moral and theological incongruity between the sermon you preached regarding the human capacity for change and your own ill-advised self-recrimination. And I know this church. The Session would never have let it happen." Then she offered him a mischievous smile, "In fact, they'll probably love you all the more for it. Nothing like a chink in the minster's shiny armor."

He looked up at this woman standing before him at JFK and said, "Yes, Harriet, would you go with her? You're right; she was feeling a bit off."

Ludington stood and walked with her to the door of the women's room and waited by the hungry line in front of the Croque Madame. The two women emerged a moment later, arm-in-arm, Fiona throwing Seth a grin and offering him her free arm.

"Much better, my dear. Very much better. It's off to lovely Alba for us." Seth adored his wife for everything, but for nothing more than for her Scots pluck. The three of them strode toward Gate 67 to board Delta Flight 409 to Edinburgh as if they were off to see the Wizard.

Chapter Two

F iona was feeling more herself by the time they landed, though the flight over had been less than comfortable for her, involving as it did two dashes to the tiny toilet four rows up from their business class seats. She had insisted she was feeling quite well by the time they arrived in Edinburgh, and had planted her feet on solid Scottish ground. Seth watched her later that morning at breakfast, a copy of the morning's issue of *The Scotsman* on the table before her, twisting a red-blond ringlet hanging over her forehead as she munched dry toast in the Caledonian Hotel's restaurant called the Peacock Alley. Curious name for a hotel dining room in a Scottish hotel, Ludington had mused as they were being seated. His father-in-law had recommended the "Caly," as the venerable red sandstone Victorian behemoth was fondly called by locals and hotel cognoscenti, for their nights in Edinburgh. The tour company had booked the group in pedestrian accommodations near the airport. When Seth had mentioned where they were to stay to Fiona's father in a March phone call, the man had hesitantly suggested they might want to see if there were rooms available at the Caledonian. "It'll be pricier, Seth, but it's just at the end of Princes Street, a bit of a walk to the Royal Mile, but I think you'll find it worth the hike and the extra cost." The Rev. Graham Davidson knew the depth of his son-in-law's pockets; Ludington knew that their tour bus would carry them to all the Old Town sites that peppered their over-seasoned itinerary in the

Athens of the North. Upon arrival that morning, the Americans had indeed been charmed by the grand old railroad hotel, even when they learned that it had morphed into yet another Hilton.

"Crivvens, Seth, look at this." Fiona tapped a brief story on the bottom of page two with the pointer finger of her toast-free hand. She read him the headline, *"Orkney Anxious as Date of Prior Murders Approaches."* She turned the compact newspaper ninety degrees toward her husband so that they could read it together.

"Many in the Orkney islands find themselves watchful, even fearful, as the third week of June approaches. On the twenty-first of the month in the two prior years, Orkney clergymen have been found murdered in the islands. In both cases, the victims were discovered in Neolithic archeological sites, each with sod stuffed into their mouth, suggesting the possibility of a serial killer who has come to be named "The Sod-Stuffer." The first victim, The Rev. Duncan Taylor, was minister of the Stromness Bible Church, a small independent congregation in Stromness, the second town in the island group. The second victim, The Rev. Halston Hughes of Kirkwall, Orkney, was also an ordained minister, though he was not serving a charge at the time of his death. The first body was discovered at the center of the Ring of Brodgar, the famous stone circle located on Mainland, the largest and most populated of the islands. The body of Rev. Hughes was discovered on the same date, exactly a year later, inside the nearby tomb known as Maeshowe. Both are popular tourist sites visited by thousands each year. The deaths have been ruled homicides. No arrests have been made in connection with either. Chief Inspector Magnus Isbister, Police Scotland's Area Commander for Orkney, issued a press release yesterday assuring the public that 'all necessary precautions are being taken.'"

"The twenty-first, Seth. That's when we'll be in Orkney."

Seth Ludington leaned back in his chair, raised the dark eyebrows of his handsome face, and said, "I have to talk to Harry." He pushed back his chair and pointed at the newspaper.

"May I take this?"

She nodded a yes as Ludington rose and reached into the pocket of his blue blazer for his cell phone. He had arranged for international service before the trip and had recommended that all in the tour group do the same. He found Harry Mulholland's name in his contacts and punched his cell number. Seth could hear Mullholland's voice as his Clerk of Session picked up the call—both through the phone and in person. The man was seated alone at a table not twenty feet away in the Peacock Alley, his back to him, cell phone pressed to his ear.

"Seth, that you? First call on my mobile over here. That's what they call them in the U.K. Actually, makes more sense than 'cell.'"

Ludington walked over to Mulholland and sat in the empty chair next to him.

"Georgia okay?" he asked.

"Fine, fine, decided that tea in the room was plenty. Beautiful place this is. Said she might just enjoy her room for a bit. What's up?"

Ludington set the copy of *The Scotsman* next to the full Scottish breakfast that lay before Mulholland in all its culinary excess—fried egg, Lorne sausage, streaky bacon, tatty scones, black pudding, and fried tomato.

He saw his pastor examining what he was about to eat and said, "When in Rome."

"Eat while it's warm, Harry, and read this."

Seth knew that Harry Mulholland was the right person to talk to, having retired a few years earlier after a long and celebrated career with the New York Police Department, the last of those years as a homicide detective. After Mullholland had sampled his way through his cholesterol bounty and read through the article about the murders in Orkney, he asked a question he knew the answer to, "That's when we'll be up there, isn't it?"

"Yes, exactly when we'll be there. What do you think? I mean, it looks like a clergy serial killer, right?"

"Technically, a serial killer is someone who's killed three or more times in separate acts. Two doesn't make him a serial killer. Not yet, at least not in the U.S. But you do have to worry about another one. I'm sure the cops up there are plenty worried. They're probably having the kind of sites where the murders took place watched. And I can guarantee you that they've warned every minister, priest or rabbi on the islands, as if they needed to. Probably having all of them watched over as well, if they've got the resources, that is.

"Harry, we'll be in Orkney on June 21, and our group includes two ministers—me and Phil—plus three seminarians. They're almost ministers. I feel responsible. I really can't ignore this.

Well, the guy must hate clergy for some reason. And them ending up in—what do you call them—Neolithic sites with dirt in their mouths. Dark stuff. The details make it look like he's sending some sort of message. Or maybe he's punishing ministers for some reason or wants to make them suffer. If he wants to do that, well, there are other ways to hurt people you hate. Guys like this sometimes change their MO."

"What do you mean, Harry?"

The man looked away and then back at Seth, "Well, harm their families, for instance."

This horrific thought had not occurred to Ludington. It only heightened his anxiety. He thought immediately of Fiona, both the wife and daughter of clergymen. Harry read the concern on his pastor's face and quickly said, "Remember, Seth, nobody there knows anything about any visiting American ministers. Except for your wife's grandmother, I suppose. Fiona told me how excited they were about seeing each other, but she's on that remote island of hers. Maybe the hotels, though… Do the places we're staying at know we're a church group? That might be a question to follow up on."

"I honestly don't know, Harry. I mean, the agency that set up the trip does a lot of church tours, but I know they do other kinds of groups. But they might have used the "Reverend" in front of names on our room reservations. We're only staying at two hotels in Orkney, the one in Kirkwall, the other on Hoy. I can check my paperwork and see how they listed our names, I mean, me and Phil."

Ludington paused to think while Harry considered the fried tomato on the plate in front of him.

"So, what do you think, Harry?"

"You gotta tell the group, of course. Best thing is to tell everybody to be extra careful. Don't go anywhere alone, not ever. Always be with somebody else, in pairs at least. And no talking to strangers, as they say. Simple

14

precautions. I wouldn't worry over it too much, Seth. We're not locals. Nobody knows we're there. I mean that we're there with some clergy types."

Ludington left him to the cooling remains of his first Scottish breakfast and returned to the table where he and Fiona had been sitting. She was gone, off to their room he assumed, as there was nothing on their itinerary until a one o'clock visit to the Scottish National Gallery, another of Fiona's "must visits." She had told him she wanted him to see "The Reverend Robert Walker Skating on Duddingston Loch" for himself. After the visit to the museum, it would be a bus drive down the Royal Mile to the manse of the Canongate Kirk, where her parents were hosting a late afternoon drinks party for the group.

Seth found Fiona in their room, dressing for the day's adventures, insisting that she was feeling "quite human again." He rummaged through the outside pocket of his roller bag for the folder containing the tour's detailed itinerary, including the various hotel, dining, and tourist site reservations and vouchers. He looked through them to see if they had prefaced his or Desmond's names with "Reverend." They had not, which was some relief. And the name of the group noted on all the documents was "Old Stone Tour Group." Not "Old Stone Church." Even better. No revealing words, no "church," "minister," "clergy," nor "reverend" appeared in any of the paperwork.

He breathed his relief and noted the phone numbers of the two hotels where they were to stay in Orkney. He told Fiona what he was going to do. He phoned the Royal on Hoy and asked if they could accommodate the group for an additional couple of nights. When the answer was yes, he phoned the Lynnfield Hotel in Kirkwall on the island oddly called Mainland, and cancelled their reservations. He turned to his smiling wife, who was freshly dressed in a Davidson plaid skirt for visiting the Skating Minister and her parents. He smiled and said, "Well, my dear, I think we'll be quite safe in Orkney. We'll be tucked away every night on remotest Hoy."

Chapter Three

June 15—16

Seth struck the predictable pose while standing in front of Scotland's most famous painting. He crossed his arms before him, leaned forward with this right leg raised behind, and drew a sober face, gracefully imitating the Rev. Walker in the painting behind him. I can be a playful minister as well, he thought to himself.

Fiona snapped a picture with her phone and said, "Okay, Seth, enough of that."

He could ice skate himself and knew the pose was actually a challenging one, on or off skates. He said, "People love the painting because they think it's ironic—a dour clergyman having fun in spite of himself. It would be hidden in the museum's vaults if it were merely "*Mr.* Robert Walker Skates on Duddingston Loch.""

"Probably true. You do know that he was my father's predecessor. He was minister of the Canongate just three hundred years ago."

Seth raised a surprised eyebrow and looked down at the Shinola Runwell Fiona had given him for Christmas. "It's nearly time to muster the troops at the omnibus." He was still feeling playful, now with words. "Two-and-a-half hours in this place was nowhere near long enough. It's quite the remarkable museum."

Penny Desmond and Harriet van der Berg arrived at the van together, having left Phil Desmond to rest on a bench in front of the museum, which he had left well before the two women. As Seth counted heads to make sure all his charges had returned to the bus, he saw that Sarah Mrazek had sat herself down next to Desmond. They seemed to be having an animated conversation, from which Desmond suddenly excused himself by rising and walking swiftly away from her. As he came nearer to the bus, he heard the man call back over his shoulder, "Sarah, I have told you before. It simply will not work. We have to rethink this."

Their twelve-passenger omnibus was hardly "omni," just large enough for the eleven of them, but small enough to worm its way through the narrower streets of the city and manage the tight lanes of rural Scotland. At last, most of the troops gathered, including Sarah Mrazek, who boarded red-eyed and clearly distraught. Ted Buskirk and Hope Feely were the last to arrive, jogging up to the bus five minutes late.

"Sorry, Rev. Ludington," Hope smiled as she panted from their dash.

After they had boarded and found their seats, Ludington asked Lewis, the driver who had been assigned to them for the entire tour, if he could remain parked for a minute before heading to the Royal Mile and the planned drive-bys of Edinburgh Castle, the Scottish Parliament Building and Holyrood Palace. Seth told him he had an announcement to make.

Seth Ludington and Lewis Ross were both expected to fulfill tour guide duties, and it looked as though there might be some rivalry between them over the matter. Seth had dutifully boned up on all the places they were to visit, but both his local knowledge and his larger grasp of Scottish history were thin. Fiona's was not. He had asked her if she wanted take over tour guide duties, but she had wisely demurred, "They expect it from you. I'll coach you, love."

Lewis Ross' historical knowledge, he had assured Ludington, was thick, though Seth feared it might also be a bit suspect. Ross was a lowland Scot from Hawick, and when he spoke to his wife on his mobile, which he did often and loudly, he was utterly incomprehensible. He could just as well have been speaking Greek, though Fiona said that she could understand much of it. Yet on the several occasions since their arrival when the man had spoken into his microphone to offer some tour guide comment, he had lapsed into bespoke BBC English.

He nodded to Ludington in response to his request, offering him the floor.

"Afternoon, everyone. Lewis is going to drive us by some of the sites we'll be visiting tomorrow after church—Edinburgh Castle, St. Giles Cathedral, where Knox preached the Reformation, and down to the Palace of Holyrood House and the Scottish Parliament. He'll point these sights out as we pass by, and then it's back up the Royal Mile, as they call it, to the manse of the Canongate Kirk, where Fiona's parents will be hosting us for a wine and cheese party."

He almost said, 'drinks party.' One quickly falls into local idiom. There was a happy murmur in the bus at this news; the event had not been noted in the printed itinerary.

"But before we set off, I have an announcement. We've altered our plans a bit for the days we're to be in Orkney. Instead of changing hotels, we'll spend our nights in Orkney at the same one, the Royal, on the island of Hoy. We'll still visit all the sites as planned, but we'll return to the Royal on Hoy every day."

He hesitated before offering the reason for this change. "I've made this alteration out of an abundance of caution. Orkney is a remarkably safe place to visit. The islands are nearly crime-free, but last year and the year prior have seen two tragic deaths, murders it would seem, both occurring on the twenty-first of June." He winced at speaking the "m-word." Of course, the twenty-first is one of the days we'll be there." He hesitated again before telling the rest of the story. "As it happens, the victims of these crimes were both clergy." He waited for a gasp that never came.

Georgia Mulholland, sitting in the second row next to Harry, explained, "Seth, we all know about it. Read it in the paper this morning."

Ted Buskirk, last on the bus and seated in the front row beside Hope opposite himself and Fiona, said, "And it was on TV too, on the morning news. Totally creepy." He seemed more excited than frightened. Seth should hardly have been surprised that the news had already filtered through his little flock.

"Well, Harry and I have talked—you all know that Mr. Mulholland is a retired police detective—and we agree that we'll be quite safe. If, indeed, clergy are vulnerable, there is no way that it could be known that we are a church-sponsored group or one that includes clergy, for that matter. Both these tragic events occurred on the island called "Mainland," which is by far the most populated. We feel that spending all our nights on Hoy, which is quite remote and very thinly populated, will ensure our security. Harry and I will have some suggestions for you when we get to Orkney, but for now, I don't want you to worry. I simply want us to be completely safe."

Ludington turned to Lewis Ross and nodded. The driver slipped the little bus into gear and drove down The Mound to Princes Street so he could hold forth on the Scott Monument as they passed it, then they rounded the grand old Balmoral Hotel to turn onto the Waverly Bridge. Once on the Royal Mile, Lewis slowed down to point out the house of the Reformer John Knox, declaiming, "such a doll-like house for such a fierce man." A few blocks farther down the street, he noted—even less approvingly—the modernist Scottish Parliament. He turned the bus around at the Palace of Holyroodhouse, the residence of the Queen when in the capital of Scotland, narrating scraps of history as he navigated, and headed back up the Royal Mile.

He pulled to a graceful stop in front of the Canongate Kirk. Fiona's father, the Rev. Graham Davidson, was waiting in front of the church, standing by the striding bronze statue of the poet Robert Fergusson. Davidson waved happily at the bus while craning his neck, obviously looking for his daughter and only child, now pregnant with his grandchildren. The group filed off the bus to stand on the sidewalk and gawk at the curious Dutch-gabled facade of the church. All heads turned to Davidson when he spoke.

"Welcome, welcome," he intoned in the honeyed baritone that had surely helped him land his prestigious position. He addressed them all but had eyes only for Fiona. He had embraced her as she got off the bus, offering the merest glance at Seth, and then held his daughter's shoulders at arm's length, looking her first in the face and then in the belly. They had seen each other nine weeks earlier when Fiona had flown over for his birthday, but she had not known she was pregnant then. All he said was, "Fiona, Fiona."

He turned at last to Seth, shook his son-in-law's hand, and said, "I am so very happy for both of you, and I am so pleased you are here. Welcome back to Edinburgh, Seth. Perhaps the group would fancy a quick look at the kirk and then a ramble about the kirkyard before we go on to the manse?"

Davidson was accustomed to conducting kirk and kirkyard tours, both being tourist sites of some interest. The kirkyard attracted visitors because of who was buried in it. The interior of the kirk was not typically Scottish, in fact, it was not typically anything. It was a great block with a center aisle and pair of side aisles. Its generous windows made it brighter than most old churches. It was bravely painted the blue and white of the Saltire. The group politely explored the sanctuary, hushed and careful of movement, as are most people when inside churches. Ted Buskirk managed to find the Queen's Pew, marked as it was with a small carved crown. He sat himself down in it and attempted to appear regal. Davidson, alarmed at this infraction, went to him and said softly, "Apologies, but only Her Majesty is permitted in this seat." After Ted sheepishly rose and retreated to the aisle, Davidson turned to the group, "When the Queen is in residence at Holyrood, she generally worships with us here at the Canongate. In fact, when in Scotland, she always worships in a Church of Scotland congregation." Then, with a sly grin, "You could say she becomes a Presbyterian when she crosses the border."

The kirkyard nearly surrounded the kirk itself, the saints of the past encircling those of the present, not threateningly, but surely reminding them of their like mortality. Davidson led them to the grave of Adam Smith, the "Father of Economics," as he named him. Smith's remains were surely there, unlike the gravestone he pointed out next, that of David Rizzo, the murdered lover of Mary Queen of Scots, whose bones were probably not there, Italian Roman Catholic that he was.

The manse was only a few weaving steps from the kirk. It was a rambling early eighteenth-century affair, large but not ostentatious, hidden discreetly in Reid's Court behind several newer buildings that faced the Royal Mile. When they arrived, they found Astrid Davidson stationed at the front door, smiling and obviously the source of her daughter's beauty. She greeted each as the group filed into the house and through to the parlor. That room was large and tastefully decorated, if economically so, and now a bit tired. No member of the congregation could critique it for being too showy for a minister.

Second to the last through the door, Fiona was swallowed up in a rolling embrace and blessed with her mother's tears. Even Seth earned a tear and a double kiss as he followed his wife through the door.

"So good to see you, Astrid," he said, disentangling himself.

Astrid Davidson led her daughter and son-in-law into the parlor, an arm draped over each, "Be at home, all of you. We've got wine here, and we'll fix tea if you'd like, and there are cucumber sandwiches and biscuits of all sort."

"And some fine single malt," her husband added.

After Fiona had left for the kitchen to help make tea, her mother pulled Seth into a corner of the room, "You've doubtless seen what's in the news about Orkney, Seth. Those murders."

"I have, we all have. And we've taken precautions, Astrid. I've checked, and there's no way for anybody up there to know we're a church group or that there are ministers in the group. And we're going to be staying at the Royal Hotel on Hoy the whole time, just day trips to Mainland. We'll stick together. Strict instructions on that to everyone. I'll pound it home to them."

"A mother worries, Seth. You'll watch Fiona, will you? And Seth, she does look a bit peely-wally. Pale she is."

"Well, she has had some bouts of morning sickness, but you know Fiona. Not about to let it get the best of her."

"Just keep an eye, Seth, please, a close eye. She's a risk taker, always was. I spoke to my mother; she assured me you'll be safe on Hoy. She'll be happy to hear you'll be tucked away each night on the island. Well then, I need to see to the tea."

As Astrid Davidson retreated to the manse's kitchen, Seth turned to her husband and Phil Desmond, locked in conversation in front of the unlit fireplace. As he approached, he heard them discussing details for the worship service at the Canongate the next morning. Desmond was to be the guest preacher. His father-in-law had asked Seth to preach, but he had suggested the well-known and recently retired seminary president in his stead.

"I've brought along my clerics," Desmond was saying, "the whole kit, collar and tabs included."

Having himself once preached at the Canongate some years earlier, Seth knew that "the whole kit" was expected of preachers.

"Seth, my boy," his father-in-law greeted his approach and lay a hand on his shoulder, "my wife has pressed our worries on you, I assume."

"Yes, but we've taken steps to be doubly safe on the islands. I was just telling her."

"And Phil has been telling me. Retreating to Hoy every night. Probably not necessary, but wise, I suppose."

Ludington turned to Desmond, the only other ordained clergy person about to travel to Orkney, and said, "Phil, are you okay with this? You and I are the ministers in this crew."

Desmond smiled and pointed to Ted Buskirk, who was approaching them boldly, doubtless for an introduction to Graham Davidson. The young man had unzipped his hoodie in the warmth of the room to expose the gray t-shirt underneath. In bold print it proclaimed, "NO FEAR." "No fear," Desmond read to Seth."

* * *

Come Sunday morning, the capacious sanctuary of the Canongate Kirk was hardly full. The crowd—members of the congregation, the American tour group, and a few other tourists who had wandered in—were scattered about the blue pews. The Queen was not in residence, so hers was empty. When it came time for the sermon, the beadle led Desmond to the pulpit and opened the door to the narrow stairs that led up to it, set as it was some six feet above the floor of the church. Seth knew that tradition insisted the beadle escort the preacher in and then out of the pulpit and that he would not open the door to let the preacher free until he judged that the gospel had been faithfully proclaimed.

Phil Desmond did not preach a sermon based on the official lectionary reading from Scripture designated for the day. Rather, he had chosen to preach on the Ninetieth Psalm, familiar words often read at funerals. Graham Davidson had read the Psalm to the congregation in its entirety, in the old King James translation at Desmond's request, he had told Seth. "Rather a crusty choice for a liberal lion like Phil Desmond."

Desmond focused his sermon on the twelfth verse, setting it against the last words of the Psalm in verse 17: *"So teach us to number our days that we may apply our hearts unto wisdom.... And establish Thou the work of our hands upon us; yea, the work of our hands establish Thou it."*

Ludington judged the sermon a fine one, contrasting as it did the eternity of the divine with human temporality. Several times during the sermon, Seth had difficulty catching the preacher's words. He slurred them occasionally, and several times, his voice dropped to the edge of inaudibility. Desmond looked tired to Seth. The man concluded the sermon with a challenge to the congregation, exhorting the upturned faces to use the days given them for the doing of something that outlasts their lives—"the work of our hands," hopefully establishing some blessing in this aching world. The beadle clearly judged either the Gospel to have been proclaimed or the preacher to have exhausted himself as he unhesitatingly opened the door for Desmond as he slowly and carefully descended the short stairway back to earth, nearly stumbling at the last step. The attentive beadle grabbed a forearm to steady him. The ravages of the years, Ludington judged.

Chapter Four

June 17

"**A**uld Reekie has certainly not lived up to its sobriquet today."

The breadth of Harriet van der Berg's vocabulary had long since ceased to amaze Seth Ludington. He knew that she would have spent the months prior to their trip studying every stop on their itinerary and most of those in between. She would have learned that the city of Edinburgh, once choked with coal smoke, had been called "Auld Reeky." Her use of "sobriquet" did surprise him, however.

The day had indeed evoked repeated exclamations down the rows of the tour bus, gasps of delight at its warm and azure clarity. Blue days are somehow bluer in places where they are rarer. As they had left the Canongate Kirk following services and after-church tea to board their bus, Fiona had predictably named the day "lovely," to which her husband had replied with like predictability, "That's one." He counted the number of times she used the word each day. She was allowed five. Like many a Brit, Fiona overused her "lovelies."

But it really was quite a lovely day. The group had toured Edinburgh Castle, dramatically perched above the city on its Castle Rock. Lewis Ross, their driver, had opined that it was the "most oft-besieged fortress in Britain—twenty-six times in a millennium." Later in the afternoon, they wandered through the controversially contemporary and hugely over-budget Scottish Parliament Building. After this taste of the avant-garde, an excellent guide at the Palace of Holyroodhouse—a young woman with enough accent to be clearly a Scot, yet one comprehensible to Americans—had squired them through the ancient Edinburgh residence of the Monarch, set as it was just across the street. Venerable monarchy and fresh democracy facing each other across Horse Wynd.

Harriet offered an endorsement of the day over her starter at a late dinner—Anstruther crab with pickled cucumber and katsu curry mayonnaise. She, Seth, Fiona, and—awkwardly—Sarah Mrazek, were a foursome seated together at The Witchery, an Edinburgh culinary mainstay. The restaurant was set in a sixteenth-century house at the gates of the Castle, near the spot where the witches of Edinburgh had once been burned alive. Curious, Seth had thought, for a pricey restaurant to pay homage to such brutality. Harriet had suggested it after Seth had asked her to join him and Fiona for dinner after their day of touring. Seth had later included Sarah when it became apparent that she would otherwise be eating alone. The décor of the restaurant was either lavishly romantic or garishly over-the-top. Seth could not decide which, even though he had read that Andrew Lloyd Webber had declared it "the prettiest restaurant ever."

In the few days he had been with her, Seth had come to understand that Sarah Mrazek oscillated between loquaciousness and moody silence. As their dinner had unfolded from cocktails to starters to mains and desserts, the young woman—lubricated with Scotch, Italian wine, and politely attentive company—had edged her way into discomforting volubility. And the preferred subject of her many words was not the afternoon and its wonders, but the morning and its sermon, or more accurately, the preacher of the morning.

"The man is brilliant, just brilliant. I don't know what's going to happen to the seminary without him. He's made it what it is. He should never have retired. I don't know why he did. Yes, he's seventy-something, but he's incredibly young for his age. Age is only a number, you know."

She had finished her third glass of the Barolo that Seth had chosen to mate with the Scotch rib eyes that three of them had ordered. Fiona had picked away at her starter of compressed heritage tomato and decided against a main.

"The sermon was genius," Sarah continued, "Great words preached by a great soul. And, I mean, he's not just gorgeous on the inside, but on the outside, too."

This last declaration was met with silent discomfort around the table. Fiona knew what it was like to fall for a handsome guy in a collar, that enticing tension between desire and inaccessibility, but her handsome man had been unmarried and of her age. Harriet quite agreed with Sarah's appraisal of Philip Desmond, inside and out, even though her inclinations had never run toward male beauty.

Fiona broke the silence with a question, "How have you gotten to know him? Is Dr. Desmond your thesis advisor?"

"He's on the committee, but I'm Old Testament; he's church history. And it's a small school, so I see him all the time. He jogs, you know. I used to see him jogging all the time. Last fall anyway, but not since Christmas. He would do like ten loops around the seminary quad, sometimes twelve. You could see how incredibly fit he is in those little jogging shorts of his."

She nudged her wine glass toward Ludington for a refill. Fortunately, the bottle was empty. Harriet moved to redirect the conversation.

"Seth, I do believe it was wise of you to err on the side of caution and arrange for us to spend our nights in Orkney on the island of Hoy. It means making ferry trips each day, but we shall all feel quite secure."

Ludington was still jolted when his volunteer secretary and erstwhile investigatory sidekick addressed him by his first name. He was about to reply when Sarah interjected, loudly enough for diners at nearby tables to turn to look at her, "You gotta assume that any one of us could be a potential victim. A nut like that could go for any one of us. Crap, it's a small place, right? He could get word about some juicy Americans ready for the picking. And would this weirdo know the difference between ordained ministers and us mere unordained seminarian types?" She looked at Fiona and Harriet and said, "You're probably at as much risk as we are." Even in her winey haze, Sarah Mrazek sensed she had crossed several conversational lines. She excused herself for a trip to the loo, as she named it with a hiccup and a grin.

The three of them looked silently at each other across the table, Fiona finally saying, "I was watching her yesterday at the manse and today in church. She can't take her eyes off him. She follows him around, at a distance, mind you, but she always manages to be nearby. She's totally smitten."

"Like a stalker," said Harriet. "I have read about stalkers." Seth was surprised yet again at the range of the older woman's vocabulary.

Sarah returned from the women's room but did not take her chair. She thanked Seth for dinner and announced that she would walk back to the hotel. Harriet glanced at Seth, pushed her chair back to stand, and said, "I shall accompany you, my dear. I have consulted my map and determined the precise route to the Caledonian Hotel."

Sarah nodded a yes to the offer as she grabbed the back of her chair to steady herself to navigate the passage between the tables and out of the restaurant. Harriet took her by the arm, turned around to face Seth and Fiona, raised her eyebrows at them, and led the younger woman out of The Witchery and into an evening still light with the simmer dim.

"Oh my," was all Fiona had to say.

Seth said, "You know, she didn't sign up for the trip until after Phil and Penny did."

The dinner bill, promptly delivered by their waiter at the exit of Harriet and Sarah, elicited another "Oh my," this one from Seth.

"I should have checked the price of that Barolo."

"Seth, you are at a place in life where you really don't need to worry about the price of a bottle of wine. How many ministers can say that?"

"But we probably would have enjoyed wine a tenth the price nearly as much."

Fiona had long understood that her husband bore his wealth uneasily. It was not only the magnitude of it, but its ultimate source—one of those nineteenth-century lumbermen who had decimated the white pine forests of Michigan.

Fiona made the same observation she routinely offered when her husband embarked on one of his occasional descents into guilt, "Wealth is not a zero-sum game, Seth. You're being rich does not make the poor poorer." She had grown up in a clergy family that had struggled to stretch the stipend of a Church of Scotland minister to the end of every month. She did not share her husband's self-reproach over their money.

He said, "Those two bottles could have fed a family of five in Somalia for a month, probably six months."

"Perhaps, my dear, but they're in Somalia. Let's walk back through the Princes Street Gardens. There's still light."

Chapter Five

L ewis Ross had a wireless microphone attached to a headset, which allowed him to lecture about Scotland while simultaneously navigating its occasionally terrifying roadways. But he managed both with alacrity. As they approached Oban on the west coast, a three-hour run from Edinburgh, he held forth on the basics of Scottish islands, "To the west of Scotland, we have the great archipelago called the Hebrides. The Hebrides are divided into the Inner and the Outer Hebrides. Later today, you will visit one of the least of the Inner Hebrides, the small Island of Iona. The name "Hebrides" is derived from "Isles of St. Bride." She was a sixth-century nun from Kildare, a woman of great influence both there and here. I am sure Rev. Ludington will be able to explain to you how the Christian religion first arrived in Scotland—not from England as you might have assumed, but rather from Ireland, of all places."

Seth was unsure whether this comment was a dig at him or Ireland or perhaps a segue to Ross passing him the mic for a snippet of church history from the minister. Whichever it was, Ludington had no time to gather his thoughts before the man continued his geography lesson. "And then we have what are known as the Northern Isles. The Northern Isles consist of Orkney and Shetland, with little Fair Isle tucked between. That's where the sweaters come from. Later this week, your itinerary will include several days visiting the former island group, Orkney, the nearer of the two to the

Scottish mainland."

Ludington was again jarred by Lewis' effortless ascent into Oxbridge English, offered in measured tones with the barest hint of his native Scots. Happily, the man ceased his narrative as the bus began its winding descent into Oban. Lunch at the venerable distillery of the same name was followed with a tour of that font of finest single malt. They caught the ferry from Oban to Mull just in time. The bus took them across that island to yet another ferry, this one to Iona. Visiting motor vehicles were not permitted on the compact island, so they left Lewis to the comforts of Mull for the next day and a half.

Without Lewis, the group naturally turned to Ludington for tour narrative. He had done his homework, and on the ten-minute passage from Mull to Iona, he offered what he had prepared, "The island where we'll stay for two nights is of key importance to the history of Christianity in Scotland." As he launched into his lecture, Seth thought of those tour guides in New York who marched their charges around museums with umbrellas hoisted in the air. He winced at the thought and continued, "It was here that St. Columba arrived from Ireland in the sixth century. With twelve companions, he established what became a great monastery, one from which the faith was carried east to the pagan mainland. The abbey became a center for Celtic Christianity, a tradition distinct from the Latin Christianity of most of Europe. Columba was something of a utopian, one of the few whose dreams would long endure. He said he wanted to create "a perfect monastery, an image of the heavenly city." There was a scriptorium, of course, a place where monks copied books of all kinds, including—quite possibly—the famed Book of Kells. Iona Abby survived the horrors of raiding Vikings, but not the Reformation. It was ultimately abandoned, its buildings crumbling to ruins as monasticism fell from favor. But in 1938, a Church of Scotland minister named George MacLeod led a group that rebuilt the Abbey and founded an ecumenical movement called the "Iona Community." This Community, which will host us for a presentation and tour tomorrow, is still devoted to rediscovering the traditions of Celtic Christianity as well as offering visitors of all faiths a place for retreat and spiritual reflection. MacLeod famously said that Iona was "a thin place," one of those spots on earth where the scrim separating the temporal from the eternal was somehow more permeable." At that last word, their vessel bumped up against the impermeable reality of the Iona Ferry Terminal, saving Ludington from having to answer any questions about permeable scrims.

The three seminarians decamped to the more Spartan accommodations that the Community offered at the Abbey; the other eight of them were dispersed among the island's several B and Bs, the Desmonds and the Ludingtons drawing the five-star Ardoran. After settling in, the four of them relished a quiet dinner, a mutton stew graced with rosemary and new potatoes. Seth pleaded exhaustion after dessert, though it was largely anxiety about Fiona that motivated him to suggest they all turn in. She was looking wan and picking at her food again, though she spoke not a word of complaint. She seldom did. The two of them retreated well before the darkness fell and wiggled under a sumptuous duvet in a room facing east to Mull and, in a few precious hours of dim, the rising sun.

* * *

The second B of their Iona B and B was a breakfast piled hearty on their plates. Fiona finally ate, famished as she was. They sat again with the Desmonds and chatted about nothing but the weather, Penny and Fiona finally adjourning to the parlor for another cup of tea. As they left, Phil Desmond looked down at the grilled tomato he had chosen not to eat and said, "Seth, would you be willing to accompany me on a bit of a hike? Up to the top of "I Dun," as they call it, the not-very-high high point on the island. We're not due for the program at the Abbey till one. They say you'll need your hiking shoes, but it's not supposed to be that rigorous."

"Let's do it." Seth was rather flattered by the invitation and was pleased for the chance to be alone with Desmond. Even though the man knew nothing of what Ludington had suspected him of having done a half-century earlier, he felt that those erstwhile suspicions somehow still lay between them.

The day had risen both early and fair, and when they reached the peak, they could make out Tiree and Coll to the northwest. Phil had struggled with the hike, stumbling several times. Seth had finally taken his arm to help him the final yards. Seth also had to help him sit—rather uneasily—on a large stone so he might consider the cairn piled at the summit of I Dun. Desmond sat silently for a moment and then said, "St. Bride's well is just up here, you know. Tradition has it that she visited it once."

"St. Bride?"

"St. Brigit, they call her in Ireland," Desmond answered. Sixth-century Celtic nun, named after a Celtic pagan goddess. Founded a string of monasteries in Ireland, the great one at Kildare. Much venerated before the Reformation in both Ireland and Scotland, even though nobody knows whether she ever set foot in Scotland. Legend has it that when she was a girl, she gave away all the family butter and a jeweled sword to feed the poor. Gotta love her for that."

"Guess so," said wealthy Ludington with a twist of a smile.

"And legend has it she visited Iona and the well up here. At midnight on the summer solstice, they say it was. And she blessed it, blessed it so that it might bring renewal to those who washed in it, maybe even healing. The well of eternal youth, they call it. Pilgrims still trek up here and wash in its water. Of course, it was not only the water she blessed but the solstice as well. The date was—and still is—encrusted with the paganism." He nodded to where the well lay, not far from where he sat. "Not quite the solstice yet, but why not? Help me up, will you, Seth."

Seth offered him a hand, and the two men walked to the natural freshwater pool, a great rock to one side, a grassy berm on the other. They both knelt before the pool. Seth sank a skeptical hand into the frigid water and pulled it out quickly. Desmond plunged both of his beneath the surface, held them there, and then doused his face with the waters of St. Bride—not once, but three times. Then he looked at Seth and said, "You know that 'healed' is not the same thing as 'cured.'"

They sat for a moment, water dripping from the older man's face. Always the church historian and still the professor, Desmond went on, "Christianity took what it could from the old paganism and baptized it. The old heathen goddesses became Mary, or St. Bride, or St. Whoever. These days, some people want to revive it, the old paganism. But what they dabble with is usually a sanitized and romanticized version—communing with the earth, talking to the trees, vague spirits flitting about. The reality of it was harder, often cruel and brutal at its worst. For instance, it tended to glorify war, not always, but often. And there was ritual sacrifice, sometimes human. At its best," he went on, "the pagan world offered up an ethic of strength and courage and loyalty to family and clan. But it tended to despise compassion and often dismissed the weak as dispensable." The two men then worked their way down I Dun slowly and cautiously, Ludington often taking Desmond's forearm to steady the man.

The afternoon's program included a short presentation on the history and present work of the Iona Community that George MacLeod had founded eighty years earlier. The Community, they learned, has members not just on Iona, but dispersed about Scotland and the world. 'It's Christian," they were told, but "quite ecumenical, with core commitments to justice, peace, and the integrity of creation." They were squired through the Infirmary Museum, packed with stone reminders of the island's millennium and a half of history. It displayed sad remnants of the precious few of the island's 357 standing crosses, nearly all of which had been toppled by Reformation iconoclasm gone mad. Ludington led a brief prayer service in the Abbey, begging forgiveness, among other needful graces.

* * *

The group departed Iona early the next morning, so early as to arouse a few grumbles, especially from Hope and Ted. But the day's drive before them was longish and again included multiple ferries. It began with the little ferry from Iona to the Ross of Mull, where Lewis and his bus awaited them, then across Mull to the Oban ferry. The drive north skirted Loch Linnhe and brought them to Glencoe and a morning stop for some grim Scottish history. Lewis Ross rehearsed the tale of the massacre of Clan MacDonald in a slow and sober bass that suggested it had happened last week, not three centuries ago. He explained that in February of 1692, government troops eager to snuff out the last embers of another Jacobite rising had murdered "at least thirty MacDonalds, slaughtered them for their reluctance to swear fealty to the English monarchs, William and Mary." Ludington mused that Lewis had not noted that Scottish independence still remained contentious, though less murderously so. Nor did he happen to mention that the soldiers who carried out the massacre at Glencoe were Scots who had been ordered to do so by a Scot.

Back on the bus, Lewis drove them farther up the coast to Fort William and then turned east to course through the Grampian Mountains. These offered up vistas that elicited gasp upon gasp from the bus. Ludington was jolted to see how much timber was being harvested. He hoped the Scots were wiser stewards of the pines of the Grampians than his lumber baron ancestor had been of the pines of Michigan.

Fiona's father, as minister of the Canongate Kirk, was domestic chaplain to the Queen when she stayed at Holyroodhouse. He had contacted the minister of Crathie Kirk, who served as domestic chaplain to Her Majesty when she was in residence at the nearby Balmoral Castle. She was not, as her routine did not bring her north until late July. The minister of Crathie had managed to arrange for a private tour. That building, magnificent of course, was the pet project of Queen Victoria's German husband, Prince Albert. It was, as a result, precisely what one might expect—a Victorian-era German's notion of what a medieval castle really should have looked like. Historians suggested that the truer architectural inspiration for the castle was actually Sir Walter Scott's recently completed faux castle called Abbotsford. Whatever its inspiration, Harriet van der Berg was quite smitten with the place.

It was late afternoon when the bus backtracked a few miles to the village of Braemar and pulled up in front of the Fife Arms. It was as immodest as their B and Bs on Iona had been modest, a grand old pile that Ludington quipped to Fiona might be best described as "Highland Gothic." There were mounted stags—racks, heads, and whole, acres of varnished oak and kilts everywhere. The tour organizers had made it clear to him that the Fife Arms was not "within their customary tour budget price range." Ludington had decided to supplement that budget out of his pocket without mentioning it to anyone, though Fiona surmised he had done so. The village of Braemar was postcard-pretty, set as it was along the banks of the Dee with the Cairngorms towering to the north. But it was unapologetically touristy. The parade of shops seemed to specialize in ice cream and an endless variety of items fashioned from staghorn—everything from key fobs to corkscrews.

A long day of mountain roads had not served to settle Fiona's off-and-on descents into morning sickness, an illness that was now visiting her not just mornings, but many afternoons, evenings, and nights. She went directly to their room for a lie-down as Seth checked the group in. But by the time he joined her, she was insisting that she was up for a quick walk around the village and a bite of dinner in the hotel's Clunie Dining Room. "I don't want to miss that, Seth."

They had decided to eat dinner together, just the two of them. The room was not at all rustic, nor was the food, although venison was to be had. They lingered over their meals. Seth had devoured his grilled venison—fresh, perhaps taken from the hills about Braemar. At Seth's badgering, Fiona had eaten, though sparingly. She had dressed for dinner in her Davidson tartan, and as he watched her across to their table in the dimly lit room, Seth remembered how deeply he loved her. And not just loved her, but regarded her—that was the word that came to mind—regarded and respected her for her courage, for the awful and needful work she did for the U.N, for her reluctance to ever slip into complaint. As he watched her nibble in the candlelight, he hoped their daughters might grow into women like their mother. He did not only hope for it; he prayed for it daily.

But he could see that she was fighting off the nausea that stalked her, even this far into her pregnancy. They both decided to forgo dessert and coffee. "Seth, I am off to bed. It's to be another long day on the bus tomorrow."

"Fiona, I'm sure we could get you a car to Aberdeen in the morning and book you a flight to Edinburgh. You could rest up and relax with your parents. No more bus filled with auld yins."

"And no Orkney. I've come this far, Seth. I'll not miss it. And Ingrid is so looking forward to our visit. She's eighty-one, and I don't know how many more years she'll be spending her summers on Hoy. I'll be fine, Seth. Really, I will. Now, I know you'll be wanting to poke your nose into the Flying Stag. You go find it, and I'll just turn in."

The Flying Stag, the hotel's famed bar, featured exactly that—a whole mounted stag hanging from the ceiling, leaping over the bar. Ludington had read about the place online before they'd left New York and mentioned it to Fiona on the bus that afternoon. Deciding that a pint of Flying Stag ale would surely promote sound sleep, he kissed her goodnight and went in search of the bar. After taking in its dramatic namesake from the door, he ambled up to the bar itself, stood directly under the flying stag, and ordered a pint of the same.

As the bartender set the glass before him, he heard a familiar voice rise in anger behind him. He turned to see Phil Desmond and Al McNulty seated at a table in a nearby corner. Phil was facing toward him; Ed's back was to him. McNulty stood abruptly, almost tipping over his chair. He tossed his linen napkin on the table in front of Desmond and muttered, just loudly enough for Ludington to hear, "Improprieties. Hardly.... You got some cheek to even use that word." Ludington turned back to face the bar as McNulty strode past, red-faced, without noticing him.

Seth walked his pint of ale over to Desmond and sat in the chair McNulty had nearly upset.

"What was that about, Phil?"

"Nothing," he grimaced. "Nothing for you to worry about."

Chapter Six

June 20

After another painfully early breakfast, this one light and quick, Lewis Ross's bus wiggled them northwest from Braemar, over the Cairngorms and around Inverness, then farther and farther north—through Sutherland, through Caithness, those vast empty lowlands beyond the highlands, to the harbor at Scrabster on the Pentland Firth separating the Atlantic from the North Sea. Here, at the very end of Britain, a Northlink ferry would carry them even farther north to Orkney.

As they passed from the hills of Sutherland into the empty black-green flat of Caithness, Ludington rose from his seat and donned Lewis Ross's headphone-mounted microphone to do his duty. He had to stoop to keep his head off the roof of the bus. Pushing back the forelock of dark hair that was forever falling over his eyes and assuming what Fiona called his teacher's voice, he began, "We are, I believe, about to leave Sutherland, the second-most northerly county in the Scottish mainland. Its name means "land to the south," ironically enough. It was so named by its early Norse settlers for whom it was to the south. These same Scandinavians also settled both Shetland and Orkney. But they were hardly the first humans to live in Orkney. Indeed, as we will discover, these northerly islands were not marginal places in ancient times, but were actually centers of pre-historic civilization. Indeed, Orkney seems to have been home to humans for the last 8,800 years. In the course of our visit, we'll have the opportunity to visit several remarkable Stone Age archeological sites that date from the third millennium B.C.—Skara Brae, the Ring of Brodgar, Maeshowe, and the Ness of Brodgar. It's generally thought that the climate was warmer then; the summer days were long, of course, and the land and sea were both rich."

Ted Buskirk poked his hand in the air, "Reverend Ludington, so who were those guys, the ones who lived there before the Vikings? And what does Orkney mean?"

Nice student prompts, Ludington thought. "Nobody knows much about the ethnic identity of the pre-Norse Orcadians, but the people the Vikings found when they arrived were probably Picts. Nobody knows that much about them either, other than that they were a Celtic-speaking people. They didn't call themselves Picts; the Romans called them that. It meant "painted" or maybe "tattooed.""

Ted turned to Hope in the seat next to him and said, "Tattoos…. Awesome ancients. So, what does Orkney mean?"

The kid must be a pain in seminary classes, Ludington mused as he looked to his wife for help. He had prepped himself on Orkney, but not this bit of place-name etymology. She said, "'Islands of the Seals.' It's Norse."

Ted heard her; Ludington repeated the answer for the rest of the bus and rambled on. "The Norse began to settle Orkney in the eighth century, and the islands were essentially a part of Scandinavia for the next seven hundred years. The pagan Norse gradually converted to Christianity beginning in the tenth and eleventh centuries. It was then that the magnificent St. Magnus Cathedral was built, another site on our itinerary. St. Magnus—in Kirkwall—is the most northerly cathedral in Britain. In 1472, the islands passed to Scotland as part of a wedding dowry, oddly enough. Scots began to move to the islands, and the old Norse language called Norn was eventually replaced by a version of Scots, which is what many islanders speak today."

Lewis Ross had held his peace as long as he could. "And I myself can understand them. Mostly. But they'll clean it up for you, just like I do."

The Northlink ferry terminal in Scrabster was a glass-fronted, shiny, modern affair. The group had time for quick coffees and pastries before boarding the *MV Hamnavoe* for the ninety-minute passage to Stromness on the Orkney island, confusingly called Mainland.

They boarded and found their seats, Harriet sitting herself down opposite Seth and Fiona. The French twist she had assumed as her trademark coiffure a half-century earlier was as precisely in place as ever. "I must remark, this *Hamnavoe* is quite the beautiful vessel, is she not?"

Fiona smiled, "She is indeed. Did you know that Hamnavoe is the old Norse name for Stromness?"

"I did not. How very interesting." Such details really did interest Harriet, Seth thought to himself.

He was himself more relieved by the ship's size than by its fine fittings. The wind had risen, a stiff breeze out of the west, and the journey north, cross-wise to the rollers, looked like it could be an uneasy one. As a sailor, he noticed such things. He worried that ships, waves, and morning sickness would prove a discomforting formula. He took Fiona's hand.

Halfway through the passage, they sailed past the Old Man of Hoy laying off to starboard. The towering red sandstone stack rose from the sea on the west coast of the island. Seth and Fiona had gone on deck for some air and stood together at the *Hamnavoe's* rail on the lee side of the ship, out of the wind. Fiona's left hand lay on her husband's shoulder.

"It's the tallest in all Britain," Fiona said. "Become quite the tourist magnet, for birders especially. Grams says the locals worry it'll topple into the sea one day."

Fiona was not generally given to seasickness, but the ship's motion had quickened the morning sickness, just as Seth feared it might.

"Best we sit down," he said softly. Which they did. Fiona lay her head on her husband's shoulder for the rest of the passage. A right Stoic she is, he thought.

Stromness rose into view as the *Hamnavoe* slipped past Hoy toward Mainland. The village, grey-brown stone buildings clustered tight together with a few defiant trees hiding from the wind scattered among them, sat hard on the fine harbor at the base of low green and treeless hills. As Seth and Fiona disembarked and set foot on Orkney, she smiled in delight. He bit his lower lip with an edge of anxiety about bringing ten people and himself to islands haunted by a serial killer. "Nonsense," he whispered to himself, "You've taken precautions."

As they climbed back into Lewis' bus, Harry Mulholland said to him—not in complaint, but in wonder—"I did not think there was anywhere in Europe that was so much trouble to get to."

Lewis Ross took them a few miles east along the south coast of Mainland, the largest of the twenty-plus inhabited islands of Orkney, to a little place called Houton where they would board yet another ferry, the fourth boat in two days, this one to Longhope on Hoy. Seth stood at the front of the weaving bus, gripped the top of his seat, and offered yet another cautionary word, "Please go nowhere alone. Stay inside in the evenings and certainly at night. And no trotting off with locals, however friendly."

As they climbed aboard this last ferry, much more modest in size and accouterment than the *Hamnavoe*, Fiona said to Seth, "Ingrid once told me that Hoy means "the high island." Seth had marked the towering hills of Hoy as they had passed them on the *Hamnavoe*. In contrast, Mainland offered the merest undulating landscape. Seth mused and said, "these islands are as lonely as our island at home is not. They call Manhattan 'the island at the center of the world.' This is 'the island at the end of the world.' You know that ancient mapmakers speculated about a mysterious place that lay farthest to the north right before you sailed into oblivion. They called it Ultima Thule. Maybe we've found it."

Fiona smiled. Seth was a font of irrelevant trivia. It was one of the things she loved about her husband. "Grandma Ingrid was forever singing the wonders of the place to me, all my growing up—the geography, the old tales about the trows—the Orkney version of trolls—and quirky stories about the locals of today."

"So, the geography?" Seth asked.

"Well, Hoy is actually two islands, or almost two. The much larger portion—Hoy proper with its great un-orcadian hills—is to the north. That's where Grams has her place, in the Vale of Rackwick. The little island they call South Walls lies to the south of Hoy itself. It's flat and fertile like most of Orkney. The two parts of Hoy are connected, but barely, by a causeway, they call the Ayre. The village of Longhope is on the South Walls part, and so are most of the people, only a few hundred total. The water separating South Walls from the big part of Hoy is a bay they also called Long Hope. Confused yet?"

Actually, he was not. Ludington loved maps and knew most of what Fiona was telling him. But he was happy to listen to it from her. He could see her excitement rising, and not just at the prospect of seeing her grandmother. She had seen Ingrid in Edinburgh a few months earlier. It was Hoy that thrilled her more; a place that had so long lived only in her grandmother's tales was about to become incarnate.

As they stood in the bare passenger lounge, a tousle-headed young deckhand approached. "Your group bound for Longhope, eh? Stayin' at the Royal?"

"We are, we are," Seth answered. "But you'll be seeing us again. We'll be crossing to Mainland, most every day, to visit the sites, you know."

"What ilka group are ye? Like a school group, or a church group, or just all signed up for the same tour? All from one place in the States, are you?"

Seth's accent had obviously betrayed them. He waited a moment before answering. "We're from New York and Pennsylvania. A group of friends, friends, and family." He did not mention church, not hesitating to offer the slight prevarication.

"Well, welcome to peedie Orkney."

As he strode off, Seth turned to his wife, "Peedie?"

"Means 'little.' Classic Orkney. Grams always uses it."

The ferry set them down on South Walls in Longhope, the barest of villages, most of it stretched along the coastal road that led east and west. They did not even need to get back aboard the bus to reach the Royal Hotel. It was an easy walk from the pier. Lewis came along with his vehicle and the luggage. He helped Seth extract a dozen suitcases from the storage compartment, setting them in the parking area in front of the Royal for owners to retrieve. Luggage handling, Seth had been informed by the tour company, was one of his several duties.

Majestic the Royal Hotel was not, more like homey. It was a rambling two-story stucco-over-stone affair painted a light gray. Seth guessed it to be a large and expanded house that had been converted into a modest island hostelry. They were greeted with enthusiasm on the edge of excess by one of the couple who ran the place. He introduced himself as "Frode" and volunteered to help with the luggage, leading Seth through the larger of two entry doors that faced the street. Ludington assumed the pair lived in the hotel and that the other door led to their quarters. The main door opened into a small vestibule, rather too compact to be named a lobby. To the left was a Dutch door opening to what looked to be the hotel's small office. Ahead and to the right was a dining room with half a dozen tables. To the left was a compact lounge and service bar.

Ingrid Gunn, Fiona's grandmother, sat waiting in the snug lounge, cell phone in hand. She was a fit-looking and regal octogenarian. Her curly hair was cut short and dyed an age-appropriate gray-brown. He cheeks were rosy in the way of Brits who lived their lives in cold rooms. She was dressed in a tatty waxed Barbour jacket and was texting away on her phone as they entered the lounge. She sprang to her feet when she saw Fiona, who had rushed into the room ahead of Seth.

"Fiona, Fiona. How are you? I was just talking—well, not talking, texting—with your mother. The morning sickness, she says." Ingrid Gunn held her granddaughter by the shoulders at arm's length to judge for herself. You do look a peedie bit off, you do. I cannot tell you how happy I am that you're here."

They embraced in a rocking hug, at the conclusion of which she turned to Seth and offered a double-cheeked European kiss. "Welcome to Orkney, Seth. Welcome to Hoy. I'm glad you're here, too. Are you minding our girl?"

Unsure of which sense Ingrid was using the word "minding," he answered yes. He hoped that he was doing so in both senses.

After he had finished with luggage duties, Seth checked the group into the hotel, setting the tour vouchers as well as the passports he had collected on the bus on the little counter atop the bottom half of the Dutch door into the tiny office. The couple that ran the place were Norwegian, Vikings back for another raid, he thought to himself, but these were very friendly ones. Frode and Else Andresen were somewhere in their thirties, informal, transparent, and welcoming. She was tall and dark, with an easy smile. He was shorter than she, white-blond, with invisible eyelashes above wide-set light blue eyes on a face that reddened when he spoke. Else had already assigned rooms to the group. Seth asked her about keys and was informed that nobody locks doors on Hoy. She glanced at the vouchers and waved a dismissive hand at such bothersome paperwork. "No need for those. Actually, we don't even have keys to the rooms. You do not need to worry, Mr. Ludington, not on Hoy."

As Frode helped Seth with the luggage, the innkeeper said, "And everyone is free to use the car. We leave the keys in it." He pointed through the open door of the hotel to the dark gray Peugeot 405 parked next to the tour bus. "It's a manual shift, though. Americans have trouble working it sometimes. And dinner will be at 7:00."

With a few hours free, most of the group retreated to their rooms for a rest after a day of buses and boats. Fiona, who insisted she felt fine, was locked in conversation with her grandmother in the lounge. After concluding the arrival formalities, Seth sat down with them. Their conversation was about pregnancy and babies, of course. They turned to Seth when he said, an edge of worry in his voice, "No room keys. Seems nobody locks their doors here. Worries me."

"Oh, it's worse than that," Ingrid said. "They don't even knock, at least that's how it used to be, often still is. People just come in the house and call out 'hello' after they're in. It's considered rude to beat at someone's door and make them come let you in."

"Seth, some exciting news. Grams has got us all invited to a real Orkney wedding. Tomorrow night. An excursion into local culture, it'll be."

"It wasna' difficult to do," said Ingrid. "On the out islands, there's never been wedding invitation lists. Everybody's always invited. The bride's grandmother is an old friend. The family's from Lyness. Well, I did phone her up and happened to mention that you lot would be on Hoy the day of the wedding, only the eleven of you, and she insisted I bring you all along. The groom is German, I understand. They met at university in Aberdeen.

43

The bride's a sweet girl, though hardly a girl. She must be thirty-something. They do put off their marrying these days. The ceremony will be at the kirk, of course, St. Columba's just up the road. The reception will be at the Village Hall. Both an easy walk for you."

Dear Grams, Seth thought, knows everyone and everything that goes on in this little spot of earth. He thanked her and said he was sure the group would appreciate the opportunity.

"Local minister presiding, I assume?"

"Actually, no. They're importing one. The Pro-chancellor of the University in Aberdeen, the Rev. Doctor Iain Torrance, no less. They've gotten to know him there. She's a PhD candidate in something or other. Torrance is also a Chaplain to the Queen, you know. A Chaplain to the Queen come to our little island. Such an honor."

Ludington knew exactly who Iain Torrance was. In fact, he knew the man. Torrance had been the President of Princeton Seminary when Seth was a student there. "Small world," he thought to himself and mentioned that he knew the man a bit. He smiled at Fiona and saw that she was looking wan again. She offered no complaint as she made to rise, saying only, "Seth, I'm off to our room for a lie-down."

Ingrid rose with her, "And I'm off to Rackwick. You're touring all those brooding pagan sites tomorrow, I understand. I've seen them, so I'll pass. The wedding service at the kirk is at 7:00. See you there, then." Fiona had obviously minimized the morning sickness that was still plaguing her. Savvy as Ingrid was, she had not noticed how ill her granddaughter actually was. But Seth knew how adept Fiona was at covering it.

He said his farewells to Ingrid and went up to check on his wife. He met Hope Feely and Ted Buskirk as he headed up the stairway. The young seminarians were proudly hand-in-hand for the first time that Seth had noticed. They had checked out their separate rooms when they arrived, but having slept on both bus and ferry, they were in no need of rest.

Hope said, "Ted and I are off for a walk to see what there is to see. Frode gave us a little map."

"We'll stick together like glue," Ted said, "No worry. We'll be back in time for dinner. Else said it's at 7:00."

Seth discovered that Fiona was not taking the lie down she had planned, but was kneeling before the toilet in their tiny ensuite bathroom. She looked up at him, wiped her face with a damp wash cloth, and said, "Much better now." Seth helped her up, led her to the bed, and pulled back the duvet. He lay down beside her and said, "How about I rub your back?"

"That would be lovely."

Seth decided not to count that "lovely." It was, he knew, the third of the day. She slept fitfully, he not at all. He rubbed her back again at 7:05 to wake her. "You want to go down for dinner or not?"

"Yes to going down, no to dinner."

Hope and Ted were not back in time for dinner as they had promised. Seth watched the time as he and the group ate at three of the four tables in the Royal's little dining room. Fiona sipped an iceless Perrier. All were anxious, none more so than Seth. No one said anything until about 8:30 when Seth went to Harry Mulholland, who was seated with his wife Georgia, Sarah Mrazek, and Al McNulty. "Harry," he said, "I think we should go look for them, you and me. I've tried calling, but either their batteries are dead, or they left their phones. Knowing those two, probably the former. They never put them down; they obviously bought European travel plans for them."

Frode went along on the search as well, driving the old Peugeot. Seth sat next to him in the passenger seat, and Harry contorted himself into back. They drove east on South Walls along the narrow coastal road toward the old Martello Tower at Hackness, a logical destination for a hike. They passed St. Columba's Kirk on the land side of the road, a grim lump of gray stucco set in the middle of a field. The land around the kirk, indeed most all of South Walls, was open—verdant but treeless. They got out of the car when they reached the east end of the island and walked around the Martello tower. It had been built during the Napoleonic Wars to protect Scapa Flow from the French warships that all England feared. The French never came, at least not to Orkney. Seth prayed that his fears—worries about these two dumb kids, worries about his wife, worries about his little bus full of charges—would likewise come to nothing.

They worked their way along the back roads across the middle of South Walls until they came to the causeway that crossed from the smaller island to Hoy proper. As they drove over it, Frode told him that the locals called it "the Ayre." "Used to be there was only a sand spit connecting the two islands. Then they built the causeway over it." They drove slowly along the coastal road on Hoy, just opposite the village of Longhope that lay across the harbor of the same name. They turned back at North Ness, as far as they could imagine a walk taking the missing students. It was still light, of course. The sun would not set till well after ten o'clock, and even then, it did not really set. Orkney's summer nights fall into a dim gray twilight, waiting for the sun to rise sometime after four. They found no sign of the young seminarians, not on South Walls, not on Hoy, not anywhere. They returned to the hotel at midnight in hopes that they had perhaps returned. They had not.

Chapter Seven

June 20-21

After they got back from their search, Seth and Harry kept vigil in the hotel's lounge, Seth insisting that everyone else turn in. They sat side-by-side, silent and not facing each other. Their vigil was broken when the landline in the little office of the Royal finally rang—very loudly. It was 12:25. Seth had just looked at his watch—yet again. He had told Harry he was going to phone the local cops at 1:00, even though Frode had informed him that there were no local cops. The nearest police presence was in Stromness or Kirkwall on Mainland, a ferry ride away, and there were no ferries this time of night. Harry had told him that they would be unlikely to do much until more time passed anyway, twenty-four hours probably. At least, he had said, that's how it worked back home.

Frode poked his head out of the office as Seth rose from his chair. "Mr. Ludington. The telephone is for you."

It was a teary Hope Feely. "Reverend Ludington? It's Hope. I'm at this place called Melsetter House. I'm not sure exactly where it is, but the people let me in and said I could call. I didn't know your number, so the lady called the hotel. Ted's hurt."

"What happened, Hope? Is Ted alright?"

"Well, I think so, but not really. I had to leave him. I didn't want to. I know you told us to stay together, but he told me to go get help. He couldn't walk."

"Where is he, Hope?"

47

"Not too far from the road. He tried to get all the way down to the road, but after a while, he couldn't go any farther. He stepped into this hole in the ground by the creek and did something to his ankle. He can't put weight on it. We got as far as we could. I told him to sit there and wait, and I'd find somebody. So, I went on down the road and headed back toward the hotel, but no cars came. I mean none, not any. I couldn't call. Neither of us had any battery. So, I kept walking. All the houses were dark, but then I saw this really big house that had some lights on. It was, like, midnight by then, but I knocked anyway. They've been super nice."

"Stay there. What was the name of the place again?"

"The lady called it Melsetter House."

Seth asked Frode if he knew where Melsetter House was.

"Of course, of course. Just over the Ayre."

Frode drove Seth and Harry, first across the causeway, then a mile or so to a driveway that led up to a gray sandstone Victorian edifice, an immense house by Orkney standards, looming over the stunted trees around it. The front door opened before they reached it.

"I'm Amanda, Amanda Seater. Your young lady is in the kitchen. I gave her a spot of tea."

Hope Feely was no longer in the kitchen, but trailing right behind the lady of the house. When she saw Seth, she cried out, "We've got to go get him. He's waiting, alone. He can hardly walk."

After profuse words of appreciation to Amanda Seater, the four of them piled into the Peugeot, drove out the drive, turned left at Hope's direction, and continued farther down the coastal road. "Stop. He's up there." Hope pointed to the left and fairly shouted in Seth's ear. The four of them climbed out of the car, an anxious Hope Feely intent on leading the way up a shallow valley cut by a small stream toward a hill rising a few miles away. There were no houses in the valley. Not a light anywhere. For a moment, Seth thought to suggest that Harry stay in the car. He was fit enough for a man of sixty-something, but the path before them, such as it was, rose steeply over uneven ground. Seth quickly determined that he was not going to leave him alone. He was not ever going to leave anyone alone in Orkney.

The midsummer sun had set in the inconclusive manner of the far north, leaving everything in a gray solstice dim. Whispers of haar, as Scots name fog, were wafting in from the west, creeping over the hill and rolling down the little valley. Hope was clearly desperate to move fast, and as she scrambled up the path in what seemed a rising panic, she disappeared in and into the fog and out of Seth's vision. Her obvious anxiety was fueling his own. What had he been thinking, bringing his little flock, including a pregnant wife with a worrisome case of morning sickness, to this cusp of civilization, one with a loose killer, no less? He worked to stay between Hope ahead of himself and Frode and Harry fifty behind. He was desperate to keep all of them in his sight. Every once and again, Hope would stop and turn back to him. Then she would call out, "Ted," dragging out the single vowel of his name in a rising and falling pitch. No answer.

Finally, they heard a moan, muted by the fog, but audible. They found Ted Buskirk nearly a mile from the road up in the Glen of Barry. He was sitting along the banks of the burn in the dim. When he saw them coming, he offered up a few more telling moans and started rubbing his left ankle. He explained that he and Hope had set out to hike up the Glen, maybe to the little peak called "the Berry" that they had found on the map they had borrowed at the hotel. "It did not look to be as far as it was." One arm around Seth, the other around Frode, with Harry and Hope in the lead, Ted Buskirk limped dramatically down the Glen of the Berry to the road.

* * *

Very early the next morning, Else called the local Hoy nurse. Jilly Wilson arrived almost immediately and took a look at the left ankle of a now sheepish Ted Buskirk. She said they could have it X-rayed in Kirkwall if they liked, but she was confident it was not a break. "Believe me, I know a sprain when I see one." She wrapped it in an elastic bandage and offered the loan of a pair of old wooden crutches from the clinic. As Seth escorted her out, she raised an eyebrow and said, "Paracetamols every four hours. He's a bit of a drama queen, that one. It's barely swollen."

Ted's recovery was speedy enough to allow him to join the rest of the group for their day trip to Mainland. He was soon down to one crutch. On Seth's way to the bus to do a quick head count of his charges, Else pulled him aside and said in her Norwegian-inflected English, "The weather is saying a big storm to come, not today, but over the night and then during tomorrow morning. You'll be okay today, and okay for the wedding tonight, I think. But tomorrow…it may be, what would you call it…an-inside-the-house kind of day."

The ferry ride from Longhope to Houton was smooth, though the day was growing gray and brooding. The leaden water of Scapa Flow seemed to be waiting for something. Lewis chauffeured them to three of the Neolithic sights the tour had promised, all quite near each other on the island. Seth played tour guide, as Lewis seemed out of his depth in the Stone Age. The places they were going to see, Seth lectured, were among the oldest and best-preserved objects of human construction in all Europe, indeed all the world. They stopped first at the chambered cairn tomb called Maeshowe. It had once held death, now, its interior was soiled with Runic graffiti—some of it obscene—that had been carved in the dank interior chamber by later Viking vandals. But there was also a graceful, but tiny, incised dragon pierced with a lance. Next it was off to the Ring of Brodgar, a circle of standing stones, a slender and graceful sort of Stonehenge. Seth told them that historians seem to have no sure idea what purpose the ring might have served, though sacrificial rites and astronomical calculations were among the guesses. The ring was incomplete, some of the stones having been toppled by time. The remaining slender fingers of sandstone in the circle pointed—silently and purposeless—upward toward the low cloud that was now hiding the summer solstice's sun.

Lunch was at a roadside pub, pleasant enough, but talk among the group seemed to have grown subdued. After the lunch, they rambled around the Neolithic village of Skara Brae on the Bay of Skail, a few miles farther west on Mainland. It was a cluster of ten houses, impossibly ancient, constructed of piled flagstones backed by earthen damns on the outside. Inside each were stone hearths, beds, even little cupboards. They were once snug little homes for men who fished, women who baked, children who fussed and napped and played, all abandoned, abandoned for unknown reasons, and then buried in sand for the last four or five thousand years. Skara Brae, Seth told them, was unearthed not by archeologists but by a horrific storm in 1850. After they had climbed back on the bus, Ludington informed the group that another Orkney gale was in the offing for late that night. Storms seemed to be the chapter titles in the story of Orkney.

Both the little bus and the ferry back to Hoy were oddly quiet. Seth thought it was perhaps exhaustion, but then guessed it might be more. The approaching storm, maybe. But then it occurred to him that it was perhaps the contrast between the places they had just visited and those they had seen earlier in the trip. The sites that shaped the early leg of the tour had been so alive—the airy white and blue sanctuary of the Canongate Kirk filled with human voices belting out hymns, Iona, an island of faith that had been abandoned but was now resurrected and grown lively with a purpose. Even faux-medieval Balmoral was cheerful as old castles go. And people actually lived there. But the sites of this solstice day were not merely ancient; they seemed pulled down, drawn into the earth, dark and dead, and so proudly pagan. Such was the mood that lay over the little bus and then over the ferry back to Hoy, lay over them like a shroud.

Chapter Eight

June 21

All in all, it had proved a long day of grim old things. Seth noticed Harry and Georgia sleeping, heads bumping comfortably against each other on the little bus to Houton and then on the ferry back to Hoy. As they returned to Longhope, he hoped that a wedding with its promise of the new and happy was just the thing to counter the day. Or perhaps it would prove a clumsy contrast.

He put on a jacket and tie for the wedding. Not a blue blazer that Fiona called his "Presbyterian minister uniform," but a light gray flannel. He had not thought at first to bother with a necktie when he had packed, but at the last minute, had rolled up a black knit tie and stuffed it in a penny loafer. Ingrid had assured them that Orkney weddings were informal, but a jacket and tie would surely be appreciated.

He told Fiona that she looked lovely in her Davidson plaid. "That's my word," she smiled back without uttering it. He could tell she was not feeling well, though she said nothing. They went down the stairway to the hotel lobby single file, Fiona's hand on Seth's shoulder. It was a bit too narrow for arm-in-arm.

They found the Desmonds in the lounge, dressed for a wedding, he in a blue blazer and a clerical collar, she in a tweedy brown pantsuit. They were both enjoying Scotches, doubles it appeared, and not on the rocks. Ice, they had learned, was rationed at the Royal. They made a handsome couple,

Seth thought, though both seemed subdued. A demanding day of touring, perhaps. Seth said to Phil, "I'm rather looking forward to a wedding I don't have to officiate at." Desmond nodded in response, took another gulp of his Scotch, and grimaced, "Yes indeed. Love weddings I don't have to worry about."

The two couples walked to the kirk together, Ingrid Gunn leading the way. Phil Desmond had offered Fiona his arm as they left the Royal. Seth followed behind with Penny. When they entered the building, Fiona had dropped Desmond's arm and turned to her husband, "Seth, could we sit toward the back?" He did not have to ask why. It would permit an inconspicuous exit should she need to make one. They squeezed into St. Columba's rearmost pew, Seth and Ingrid on either side of Fiona.

St. Columba's interior was more welcoming than its exterior. An imposing raised pulpit was set on the long wall of its rectangle, towering over the modest communion table and lectern below. Preaching obviously held priority over sacrament. The pews on the main floor were tightly packed. There was a three-sided gallery of additional pews above on the second level, like those below, all focused on the pulpit. It was the interior's sea of light-colored wood paneling that spoke the welcome. Wood was precious in Orkney. Before they left the Royal, Ingrid had told him that the local story had it that some of the panels were from a Spanish ship wrecked on an Orkney beach during a storm when the Armada fled north after its 1588 debacle in the English Channel. She said that she thought it unlikely, however. Seth agreed to the unlikely, though he could not but wish it were true. It was the third mention of storms in a day.

Iain Torrance officiated, resplendent in the scarlet cassock and black gown of a Chaplain to the Queen. The service, straight out of the Church of Scotland's most recent iteration of its Book of Common Order, was delivered in Torrance's famously soft voice. In his brief sermon, he named marriage "a school for the soul." It is indeed just that, Seth thought to himself, actually graduate school for the soul. The wedding couple seemed at ease, not as anxious as some, and quite ready to be schooled. She was a pretty redhead; he was sharp-featured and blond, soon to go bald.

The smiling couple galloped out of the church and then processed behind a piper hired to lead the wedding party and guests to the reception at the Village Hall a few hundred yards down the road. Sitting in back and finding themselves at the end of the parade, Seth looked at his wife and asked, "You want to go back to the room? You're feeling lousy, I know you are."

Fiona sighed in resignation, "I think I'd better. I'm afraid of losing it. I mean my lunch, not that I ate any."

"I'll go back with you."

"No, you won't. I'll ask Grams. You'll need to say hello to Torrance. He spied you in the congregation. You can hardly disappear without a word, Seth."

Fiona found her grandmother chatting away with the bride's beaming mother and whispered into her ear. Ingrid cast a worried glance at Seth as she took her granddaughter by the arm and marched her out of the church. She was one take-charge matriarch.

The reception in the bare-bones village hall was as unlike a clubby New York wedding as Seth could imagine. No guest list. The only neckties were on the groom and himself. Half the island must have been there, more than a few of whom had not been at the kirk for the ceremony.

There was an open bar and a buffet table, though that was surely not the local word for the folding tables lined up and stacked with slices of Orkney beef and slabs of Orkney cheese, mountains of fresh crab meat, and peat-smoked fish, all local. The band had not cranked up yet, but they had arrived—two fiddlers and an accordion. It was to be feast first, then the dancing. Ingrid had warned them that weddings often went on till near morning, though the weather would probably dampen things this time. She had heard the forecast, too.

Seth found a place at a table with Harriet and the seminarians. He had decided to keep a close eye on the three of them. No sooner had he sat that Iain Torrance and his wife Morag came by, he back in his civvies, a garment bag draped over his arm. He said he had been jolted—his word—to see Seth in the congregation. Seth explained about the tour and his wife's Hoy connections. Torrance introduced Morag and then said that he had heard that Seth had married Graham Davidson's daughter. "I assume her to be that lovely woman seated with you in the back pew."

Ludington smiled proudly, "That's Fiona." He paused. "Actually, she's three months pregnant, and she's been plagued with bouts of really nasty morning sickness. It won't leave her alone. Seems to be getting worse. She really wanted to be here, but she wasn't feeling at all well. She and her grandmother went back to the hotel, I'm afraid."

Morag Torrance glanced at her husband and said in a kind voice nearly as gentle as his, "I'm so sorry. Remember that the Duchess of Cambridge had terrible morning sickness. But it passed. Not to worry."

Seth changed the focus of the conversation. "You know that Philip Desmond and his wife are on the tour. Another former seminary president."

"We do know each other, of course. Are they here tonight? I'd very much like to say hello to Phil." He looked at his watch "But we do need to catch the last ferry. We'd thought to stay the night on the island. The bride's family had made arrangements, but the weather…" His voice trailed off as he and his wife followed Ludington to the long table where Philip and Penny were seated silently, surrounded by locals who were not at all silent and clearly winding up for a memorable evening.

Desmond rose, less than confidently, to shake Torrance's hand, steadying himself on the back of his folding chair. Penny offered a wry and knowing smile that said "my naughty boy." Formalities accomplished, the Torrances set off for their ferry. Ludington was immediately on his cell phone to Ingrid, who said, "She's a tad better now. Was a bit sick in the loo when we got back, but that does seem to help. Seth, she wants you to take a peedie video of the wedding cog going 'round. She's all aflutter about missing it."

Earlier in the day, Ingrid had explained the wedding cog. A finely wrought wooden bucket with two upright handles, fashioned for the occasion, would be filled with spirits of any kind—whatever was at hand—and passed in a circle to every guest, young and old. "A sort of unholy communion," Ingrid had quipped. But Seth had thought there actually might be something very holy about it. Either way, Fiona had been determined to witness the cog, even if she would not commune herself.

He could see that the cog was not making the rounds yet, so he took out his phone and Googled "katemiddletonmorningsickness." A flood of hits introduced him to *hyperemesis gravidarum*. Five minutes of reading and Seth was suddenly sick himself—sick with worry. Every "katemiddletonmorn ingsickness" site—and there were plenty—was peppered with words like "severe nausea," "vomiting," "dehydration," "hospitalization," "serious," and "loss of pregnancy."

He looked around the room. Still no wedding cog. He went outside to stand in the evening light by the door of the Village Hall to make his call. Ingrid had given him the number for the island nurse, Jilly Wilson. She picked up on the first ring. Seth told her about Fiona, his worries, and Kate Middleton. She knew about *hyperemesis gravidarum*. She said that after the Duchess of Cambridge's pregnancies, everybody in Britain knew about it. Jilly Wilson told Seth she had actually planned to be at the wedding herself, but Doris Minton in Lyness was bad again and had called her in. She said she'd be at the Village Hall by 9:00 to take a look at Fiona.

Before he had a chance to tell her to go directly to the Royal rather than the Village Hall, she had hung up. Seth tried to call back, but it went to voice mail, and a message declaring that the mailbox was full. He phoned Ingrid to tell her he had called Jilly Wilson and that she'd be along to look at Fiona about 9:00. But she'd be coming to the Village Hall unless he could get to her. He'd keep trying to call and direct her to the hotel. If he didn't succeed, he'd have to wait at the Hall where he was and bring Nurse Wilson along to the Royal.

He went back inside and saw that the wedding cog was finally making its first pass around the room. He took the requested video, a video that included Phil Desmond taking the cog in his hands and raising it to his mouth, spilling a long steady dribble of its contents down the front of his clerical shirt. Penny had handed the cog to him, but she passed it on after he was finished, not drinking from it herself. The video also caught Sarah Mrazek watching them, grim-faced and intent. Seth went over to Harriet who was seated with the three students. He bent down and whispered in her ear, "Keep a close eye on Sarah and our two wandering lovebirds." He nodded to Ted, sitting opposite her, balancing his lone crutch; Hope was dancing in a circle with some local gents. He knew that Harriet was a night owl who seldom found her way to bed before midnight.

He returned outside to wait for the nurse. He could not keep his eyes off his watch. The nurse had said 9:00. It was 8:40 when Al McNulty passed him, headed back down the road to the Royal. He appeared disinterested and lonely. He offered Ludington no more than a curt nod. At 8:45, the Mulhollands left. Harry offered him a pat on the back, Georgia a faint smile, "Good night to you, Seth. Such a day. What is it they say here? Dour? But the wedding did brighten the mood. I liked the words of that service." She looked at Harry, "Especially the line about marriage being part of God's loving purpose. 'Loving purpose,' that brightened things up."

Sarah Mrazek left alone at 8:50. She did not even notice him standing at the door as she stamped passed him. At nine o'clock, the nurse had still not arrived. He walked fifty yards down the road to see if she needed to park at a distance. There were many more cars than parking places at the Hall. He turned back without seeing any headlights. He met Phil and Penny on the road, headed back to the hotel. Penny had her husband by the arm. She shook her head at Seth and offered a knowing smile, but spoke not a word. Phil's head was down, and he did not catch Seth's eye. He looked at his watch again. It was 9:10.

As he paced, he noticed that the wind was beginning to rise, the evening dim now darkened by low racing clouds. He had to put his hand to his head to keep his hair out of his eyes. A few sharp spits of rain left dark marks on the gray flannel of his jacket. It occurred to him that his vulnerably ill wife had been veritably alone at the Royal with no one to keep watch but a feisty old woman. He had seen the two Norwegian innkeepers at the reception and asked them if they had locked the front door of the hotel. They had not. In fact, they were not even sure there was a key. All this meant that after the ceremony and before some of the tour group had dribbled back to their rooms—a good hour—there was no one in the wide-open Royal Hotel but Fiona and Ingrid. What had he been thinking?

Chapter Nine

June 21-22

He found Fiona sitting up in bed when he returned to the hotel with the nurse, who had finally arrived at 9:30. They found Ingrid reading in a chair beside her granddaughter's bed. Fiona was indignant at Seth for having called in medical help without asking her. Ingrid soothed her granddaughter's stubborn pride as the nurse listened to the litany of symptoms that Seth had to coax out of her, all genuinely alarming, even as Fiona tried to minimize them.

After she had heard it all, the nurse offered a diagnosis. "Nasty morning sickness that needs plenty of fluids, maybe some anti-nausea meds. It asks for a close eye, it does, especially at three months. Late for such morning sickness. Dehydration is the main worry, but not the only one. Could move into your *hyperemesis gravidarum*." She pressed her point on Seth, "Not there yet, but you'd best keep a close eye, Mr. Ludington."

Two of the antihistamine tablets from the bottle she had left behind, and Fiona did manage to fall asleep. Seth had watched her as he struggled to sleep himself. He finally did, if fitfully. Not only was he worried about Fiona, but the wind kept waking him. As he had lay listening, it struck him that the sound of wind he was accustomed to was mostly the sound of wind moving through trees. In a land without trees, the sound of wind was foreign, hauntingly so, mostly whistles through the old sash. Wind alone—just moving air—was silent. There had been some rain against the window as well, horizontal rain, but not much. Mostly, it had been the unrelenting and ferocious wind.

* * *

Seth lay in bed early the next morning, watching through the leaded window pane of his room as the solstice dim inched toward something like daylight. Another hour's sleep was going to elude him, so he rose, stumbled to the bathroom, and splashed frigid water on his face. He looked at himself in the mirror and sighed at the face that stared back. The last two days had bequeathed dark circles under his eyes and a few fresh worry lines on his forehead. His visage perfectly reflected his mood. Who takes a busload of trusting congregants, naïve students, and an aging seminary president and his wife to the ends of the earth, knowing that particular end of the earth was home to a serial clergy killer? Even worse, what husband would drag his pregnant wife to such a place? Fiona, he had come to understand, was life to him. The babies she carried were life to him.

He heard her stir in the bed.

He was toweling his face when a knock came to the door, soft but insistent. He threw the towel on the bed and saw that the knock had roused Fiona as well. He called out to the door, "Coming, coming," and pulled on a pair of jeans. He opened it to see Penny Desmond, knuckles in the air about to knock again, dressed in one of the Royal's white terrycloth bathrobes, a little "R" embroidered on the pocket.

"Penny? Come in, come in." She did so without hesitation, but stopped just inside the door. Even at seventy-four, fresh from sleep and without her usual attention to makeup and hair, Penny Desmond was a handsome woman—medium height, classic features, once-blond hair now colored to an age-appropriate blondish-gray.

"Seth, Phil's off somewhere. I woke up, and he wasn't there. I mean not in bed. We like to go for morning walks, but we almost always go together. He wakes me up to go."

She was clearly concerned.

"I'm sure he's fine, Penny. New place, change of habit perhaps. Maybe he didn't want to wake you. When did you see him last?" Such were his words, but not his thoughts.

She hesitated, "Well, last night, actually. We left the wedding reception and walked back toward the hotel. He said he wanted to walk down to the pier to get some air. He'd had a few drinks, and I assumed he simply wanted to clear his head. I was exhausted. I told him so and went up to our room. I fell straight asleep."

"He came back to your room last night, didn't he?"

"Well, to be honest, Seth, I can't say for sure. I mean, I assume so, but I really don't know. It's a small bed, and I couldn't tell if he'd been in it or not. Seth, he'd actually had more than a few drinks. I guess that's why I'm worried. The pier, I mean."

Ludington told her to go get dressed and that he'd go look for her husband. As she turned to leave, he thought to ask, "Penny, did you check to see what clothes he was wearing? I mean, what of his clothes are gone—last night's or something he would have put on this morning?" She said that she had not looked but she would. She walked quickly down the hall toward her room as he shut the door. He turned to see that Fiona was now sitting up in bed. She had heard the conversation.

"Harry and I'll borrow the hotel's car." "Again," he thought to himself. "Yet another search for a wandering sheep. Three in two days. I can't believe she let him wander off alone." He sat on the bed next to Fiona and gave her a peck on the cheek, "He's probably just off for a morning stroll. Could you sit with Penny? If you're feeling up to it, I mean. Or maybe Harriet could. Those two seem to be getting on again."

He picked up his cell phone from the bedside table and called Harry. He then dressed without shaving or taking his morning shower and phoned Harriet and told her about Penny's visit, "Harry and I'll get the car and look for Phil. Could you sit with Penny? Fiona said she would as well."

Ludington found Frode in the little office, up early and poking away at his laptop. This time, Seth asked about using the car. "Keys are on the dash," he said. "No need to ask, Mr. Ludington. You look like you have some worries in your mind."

Of course, the man knew about the clergy murders the two prior years. But he did not know that the guests at his little hotel included two ministers and three seminarians. Ludington saw no reason to tell him. Frode obviously did not feel he needed to accompany him on this second search. Harry came down the stairs and rolled his eyes at the prospect of another hunt for a missing member of their tour group. They walked out the front door to the parking area and found the hotel's car. Harry said, "You drive, Seth," but walked to the right side of the Peugeot, opened the door, and saw the steering wheel. He mumbled, "Forgot," and circled around the car to the passenger door.

They drove to the pier first, parked, and walked its length. The wind made walking along it, even standing on it, a challenge. Harry was holding his Harris tweed jacket closed, tight to his chest. Seth leaned into the wind to keep himself upright. Neither went anywhere near the edge. Even in the sheltered harbor called Long Hope, the waves were running two feet. Short rollers crashing against the west side of the pier sent salt spray ten feet in the air and into their faces. Seth could only imagine what the more open waters of Scapa Flow—or the Atlantic Ocean, for that matter—must be like. The two men looked at the angry water, then at each other, and hurried back down the pier and to shelter of the car. They drove the length of South Walls, all three miles of it, back through the center of the island, then across the Ayre as they had done the day before. The car rocked in the wind as they crossed the narrow causeway. They drove along Hoy's main road, almost to Lyness, before they turned around. Not only was there no sign of Phil Desmond, there was no sign of anyone. The storm had every soul tucked away in the scattered stone houses of Hoy.

They returned to find Penny with Harriet and Fiona, the three of them downing serial cups of tea in the Royal's lounge. Seth shook his head to say, "no luck," as he and Harry approached the women.

"Didn't see him, but we could have missed him. Penny, two things. Did you figure out what Phil would be wearing? Did you check his clothes? And I can't believe I didn't ask you this…. Does Phil have his phone? I assume you would have tried calling him?"

"His jacket and clerical shirt are not in the closet. That's what he had on last night. I guess he must be wearing them. And his phone's not on his charger. I tried to call him at least a dozen times, again just now. It goes right through to voicemail."

"Could be out of battery. If he's in his dog collar, we have to guess that he went off somewhere last night. I wish I knew if he had his phone. Penny, do you think you could check your room for the phone again? Look in pockets. Or call it and listen for the ring. I'm always leaving mine in a pocket. Maybe Harriet can go with you." Seth cast the woman a pleading look. He wanted to give them both something to do. Penny and Harriet walked out of the lounge toward the stairway up to the hotel's guestrooms. Seth sat down with his wife as Harry left in search of Georgia and breakfast.

"How are you feeling?" he asked his wife, "Sleep help?"

"Meds help. Haven't boked since last night."

"Seth, while you were gone, Penny opened up a bit. She's frantic. She's worried sick inside of that outward composure. But it's a lie, it is. Calm's been bred into her. She talked to Harriet. They go way back. You know that, of course, back to when Phil and Penny were at Old Stone. The two of them have picked up over the last few days as if thirty years haven't gone by. They kept talking about Phil. They both adore the man. In their different ways, of course. All the Phil talk was starting to feel pretty awkward, I mean, with him off somewhere and you out looking for him. Like he was past tense. Penny asked Harriet if she thought she should phone their daughters. Harriet said not yet, but that turned the conversation to children. They've got the three girls, you know. Penny started talking about them instead of talking about Phil. She's one ferocious mother. And I think she's an equally ferocious wife, all hidden away behind that New England Puritan reserve. She told me that you'll find yourself doing everything and anything to protect them, to keep them safe and happy. I like her, Seth. She's all rugged love beneath the smooth."

"Oh, and Grams called. She's driving back down from Rackwick for lunch. I told her about Phil gone off somewhere, told her to keep an eye out."

Chapter Ten

June 22

It was going on nine o'clock when, after a quick cup of the Royal's mediocre coffee and assurances from his wife that she really was feeling decent, Ludington wiggled his long legs into the hotel's Peugeot yet again. He drove around South Walls, winding his way through unpaved side roads that he and Harry had bypassed on their earlier search. His anxiety rose with each empty lane that he wiggled down, many of them coming to dead ends at the sea. His cell phone rang as he bumped along the two-track leading to the two crofts at Snelsetter near the south coast of the island.

"It's Fiona. Grams just called. Seth, they found a body way up in Rackwick. It's inside the Dwarfie Stane. A couple of birders staying at the hostel hiked out there early this morning. They went back to the hostel and told the manager. She called the police in Kirkwall, and then she called Grams. The two of them are fast friends, go back forever. I guess the woman is pretty upset. They don't know who it is, I mean the body, but they said it's an older man."

Seth closed his eyes and prayed. He prayed two prayers. One that it wasn't Philip Desmond. He questioned that prayer as soon as he had offered it. If it wasn't Phil, then it was somebody else's husband or son or father lying dead in an ancient tomb. His second and cleaner prayer was that Penny and her girls would find the strength of soul they were going to need if it was Phil. He turned the car around at Snelsetter and headed back down the two track to the main road faster than he should have. With every pothole, the Peugeot bottomed out, and Ludington's head hit the car's roof liner.

He found his wife in the lounge, still sitting with Penny and Harriet, half-empty cups of cold tea on the table in front of them. Fiona stood, came to Seth, and said softly, "I haven't said anything. No reason to until we know for sure."

"Sit with them, would you? I'll go outside and call Ingrid if you could text me her number."

"It'll be her landline. Not much mobile service up there she says, at least not usually."

Seth stepped out the front door of the Royal and walked to the lee side of the building and out of the wind. It was beginning to lay down, but the breeze was still stiff enough to make phone conversation difficult. He found Fiona's text with Ingrid's number and jabbed it into his cell. She picked up on the first ring. Ingrid seemed to know who would be calling. "Seth, is that you?"

"It is. Fiona told me about the…Dwarfie Stane." He was loath to say the word "body."

"Yes, yes," she said. "Tillie's here with me at my cottage. She's quite upset. The hostel is just across the lane from me. She called, and I promised tea. The pair that found the body out in the Stane, they're here too."

"You've called the police, Fiona said."

"Of course. Not me; Tillie called. First thing, she said. But Seth, the ferries are nae running, because of the hushle you know—the storm. The police will nae be able to cross from The Mainland for a bit yet. Seas are still running too high. They said to leave everything as it is. Not to touch a thing."

Seth hesitated before asking the second of the two questions that lay on both their minds. The first, of course, was whose body lay in the Dwarfie Stane. But Ingrid would hardly know that, at least not for certain. So, he asked the other question, "Did the police say anything about the murders—the Sod Stuffer murders—when Tillie called."

The matter of the Orkney murders had not been broached with Ingrid, not by him, and as far as he knew, nor by Fiona or Harriet. "Ingrid, you know, the two murders, last year and the year before. We read about them in Edinburgh. I mean, the same time of year and...well, Neolithic sites...." He thought about what he had just asked and said—as much to himself as to Ingrid, "No, of course they didn't mention it. They wouldn't say anything, but it's got to be what they're thinking." With a tincture of relief, he added, "But nobody knows about our visit, I mean about some clergy types being here on Hoy."

His self-comforting observation was met with a long silence. "Ingrid? Are you still there?"

"Seth, people actually do know about you. I phoned Tim at *The Orcadian* last week, before you got here. I thought Fiona's visit might be of interest to the paper. You know, a human interest story, as they call it. A granddaughter of a Hoy native come for a visit with her husband and people from his church, come all the way from America. Tim interviewed me, he did. On the phone. And I emailed them a photo of Fiona. They ran a peedie story in this week's issue. It comes out Thursdays. I haven't seen it yet, but Tim called to tell me they ran it and to watch for it. It even mentioned Brigit's wedding and that you had all been invited to come along. He said they included the photo of Fiona." She paused, considering the implications of what she had told Seth, and said slowly, "I'm sorry. I'm sorry if I've done something wrong."

Seth realized that it had just come clear to the woman how costly her phone call to Tim at *The Orcadian* may well have been. It would do no good to point it out to her. He could hardly scold the woman, so proud that her granddaughter, the U.N. lawyer, had come to visit. It had never occurred to her that a newspaper story would tell all Orkney—serial murderer included—that American clergy were visiting Hoy the third week of June.

Seth merely said, "You mentioned that the two birders who went to the Dwarfie Stane—the ones who found the body—were there with you. Do you think I might speak with them?"

"I'll put on the girl. Julia's her name. She's the better one to talk to. The boyfriend is still shaking like a leaf. They had quite the fleg out there at the Stane."

"Hello? This is Julia." It was a confident voice, but questioning.

Seth explained who he was and why he was asking about what they'd found in the Dwarfie Stane. He said, "A friend is unaccounted for and we're concerned." Then he asked, "Are you sure the person you found in the tomb was dead, not merely unconscious?"

"Oh, dead he was," answered Julia in an even voice. "I gave him a good poke. And, well, he had all that grass and dirt, or maybe it was peat, stuffed into his mouth. I don't see how he could even breathe."

"Can you describe him, Julia?'

"It's pretty dark in there, inside the tomb, I mean. And Jim and I didn't think to bring a torch along. But I could tell that it was an older gent. Grayish hair. And he was wearing a sport coat and a dark shirt. Maybe it was black. He was lying on his back with his knees bent up. We dashed back to get help, back to the hostel. Lousy mobile service out there. It's a mile, probably two, from here. And the Dwarfie Stane is set back off the road in the middle of some moorland tucked under the Dwarfie Hamars as they call 'em. That line of tall cliffs to the south. Spooky place."

Seth winced. He had dared to hope against hope, as the Apostle had put it, that some stranger lay in the Dwarfie Stane, perhaps even one not dead, maybe only dead drunk. But Julia's news veritably confirmed Seth Ludington's fears. Philip Desmond—retired president of Philadelphia Theological Seminary, prominent church historian, former pastor of the congregation he himself now served, a man for whose safety he was personally responsible—was almost surely lying dead in a rock-cut tomb on a windswept Scottish island with earth stuffed down his throat. He found the grace to thank Julia and pressed the little red icon on his iPhone. He should have asked about a clerical collar. Odd that Julia had not mentioned it. He prayed again the second of the prayers he had offered an hour earlier. He was quite sure that the first was not to be answered as he had prayed it.

Chapter Eleven

L udington poked his head into the hotel's lounge, where his wife sat in a circle with Harriet van der Berg and Penny Desmond. He caught Fiona's eye and gave her a quick sideways nod. Their ten-year marriage had reached the point where wordless communication had become dependable. Nods, raised eyebrows, subtle smiles, even grimaces, offered in specific contexts, were mutually comprehensible language. Fiona excused herself, rose, and went to the Royal's front door to join her husband. He took her hand, and they went outside together. The wind, loaded again with sharp spits of occasional rain, tossed Fiona's red-blond curls into her face. She swept them back with her hand and held the hair out of her eyes.

"Fiona, I'm going up to Rackwick. I think it is Phil, probably. I mean, it's gotta be. The ferries aren't running and the cops are stuck on Mainland. I have to make sure before I tell Penny anything. Could you hold the fort here, you and Harriet? I should be back in an hour or so."

"Oh my God," was all she said.

"Oh my God indeed." He spoke the words as a prayer as much as an exclamation of horror. Neither of them routinely trespassed the Third Commandment.

On his way to the car, he grabbed a tourist brochure with a map of Hoy from the little stack on the table just inside the front door of the hotel. It was probably the same brochure that had piqued Desmond's interest in the

Dwarfie Stane the day before. A map was hardly needed to navigate the roads of the island, however. There was really only one main road.

He drove the borrowed Peugeot west across South Walls to the Ayre and crossed to Hoy proper. The wind may have laid down a bit—it was hard to tell—but the car still shook as he crossed. The squeaks the windshield wipers insisted on making annoyed him. The road took him along the east coast of Hoy, winding its way north, the roiling white-capped water of Scapa Flow rising and falling into and out of view to his right. The map told him that just before the road ended at Quoy at the northern tip of the island, he would need to turn left on Hoy's only other road of any length, a trail that wound its way through a long valley to the Vale of Rackwick on the west side of the island. Halfway to Rackwick, in the proverbial middle of nowhere, a little arrow on the map pointed to the location of the Dwarfie Stane.

The drive took just over thirty minutes. The left turn off the main road toward Rackwick had been marked, as was the small parking area at the bottom of the path that led up to the Dwarfie Stane through the heathery valley labeled on the map as the "Trowieglen." The brochure said that the name meant "valley of the trolls." It also noted that the Stane was a "rock-cut chambered tomb carved some five thousand years ago into a huge block of sandstone deposited in the valley by an ancient glacier." He parked the Peugeot and set out for the tomb—a tomb five millennia old had been put to use again, perhaps only for the second time in its history. At first, and then in dryer stretches, the path was over sand and gravel; farther along it was covered with wood planks laid over wet peaty ground.

The rockface cliffs that Julia had named the Dwarfie Hamars rose in front of him as he walked. Ward Hill, the highest peak in Orkney, towered behind him. To his right, the Trowieglen sloped seaward to the Vale of Rackwick. The walk took him nearly fifteen minutes, even with the gale at his back. When he came to the Stane, it seemed to Ludington that it was lounging in the heather as if resting after a long night. It was a flat and forbidding block of gray sandstone, maybe thirty feet long and fifteen feet wide. A low door had been carved by unknown ancients into one of the long sides. A smaller stone that had obviously once covered the door lay a few yards from the square black mouth that offered entrance into the tomb. The Dwarfie Stane was a natural thing that had been made unnatural five thousand years ago. It now seemed that it had been made unnatural once again.

Ludington hesitated before peering into the darkness. The door and the tomb it opened into were far too low for him to enter unless he dropped to his knees. He did so, and prayed again, this time for himself. He waited another moment for his eyes to adjust to the dark mouth of the tomb and crawled inside on all fours. The interior had been laboriously carved out of the stone to form a small chamber that extended right and left to either side of the entrance. To the right was a pair of niches, forming what looked like a raised twin box bed chiseled into the stone. It was nearly as wide as it was long, but not nearly long enough for a modern human. In the farther of the two niches lay the Rev. Dr. Philip Desmond, his knees bent up tight so that he might fit into the too-short stone bed. His jacket was buttoned, his eyes were closed. He looked peaceful, save for the peaty mess erupting from his open mouth. Ludington sat back on his haunches and looked long at Desmond's body. His clerical collar was missing.

He sighed, then he prayed, "Almighty God, from whom we come, unto whom we return, in whom we live and move and have our being, acknowledge a sheep of your own fold, a lamb of your own flock, a sinner of your own redeeming. Receive him into the arms of your mercy.... And with your great love, comfort those who are about to mourn... " Those were the words that came to him, old rote words. But no tears came, not because he was unmoved, but because tears seldom came to Seth Ludington.

As he walked back to the car, the west wind was against him and still largely untamed. Needles of wet stabbed at Ludington's face as he walked directly into it. The hike back was slower going. After he finally climbed into the car, he had to figure out how to work the heater. The French do everything a bit differently. Late June and he needed the heater, he complained to himself. He debated whether to drive the mile on down the road to Rackwick to talk to the two birders and fetch Ingrid or head directly back to Longhope. Once there, he would have to tell Penny that her husband of 50 years was dead. He dreaded the doing of it, but after a bare moment's consideration, he turned the Peugeot around and headed back to the hotel. Interviewing witnesses was the cops' job after all, and Ingrid, independent as she was, could get herself to Longhope in her old Land Rover.

It was almost 10:30 when he returned to the Royal. He found the three women still seated in their circle of waiting. He pulled up a fourth chair between Fiona and Harriet, opposite Penny. He sat and looked at the woman.

"It's not good, is it, Seth?"

"No, Penny, it's not." He had been in hospital rooms and nursing home chapels when such news was delivered, usually by a doctor, but the duty of bearing the news of death had never before fallen to him. He looked to his wife, then back to Penny, "Some hikers found Phil early this morning, up in Rackwick, or almost. He's dead, Penny."

He dreaded telling her the details of his death almost as much as the fact of it.

She reached to her right and took Harriet's hand, held it tightly, and asked, "What happened?"

He told her about Phil laying in the Dwarfie Stane, but did not mention the sod stuffed in his mouth. She would know that soon enough. He used the word "peaceful" in describing him. True enough, but not quite the whole truth. Tears came to Penny Desmond, silent tears. She spoke none of the common protests that it could not be true. And she offered up nothing like wailing, not even quiet weeping, only silent tears washing down her cheeks. No mascara to darken them; they were perfectly clear tears. Harriet handed her a lace handkerchief. She took it, ran it across her face, and said, "I want to see him. I want to go to Phil. Now."

Seth explained that the police had been called and would arrive as soon as the ferries were running, but that they had been instructed nothing be touched at the site. He also told her that the Dwarfie Stane was at the other end of Hoy. "Better to wait, Penny."

"I don't care. He's my husband, and I want to go to him. I'm going. I can find it." She stood and turned to Ludington with a defiant look perfected over a lifetime of privilege, and headed toward the door. "You can take me, or I'll go on my own." She looked to Harriet for support. Harriet glanced at Seth and raised her eyebrows. Seth did not move.

Penny marched out of the hotel like a woman accustomed to being obeyed. Ludington rose and followed her out of the hotel to the parking area. She went to the passenger's side door of the Peugeot, realized her error, and walked around to the U.K. driver's side. She yanked the door open, got in, and turned the key. The car lurched forward, killing the engine. It was in gear. She stared at the manual shift lever to her left, lay her head on the steering wheel, and wept, now audibly. Seth heard her mutter loudly enough for him to hear "Stupid stick shift, never learned to drive one."

She finally climbed out of the car and glared at Seth. "Okay, so I'll walk. You can't stop me." She turned from him and strode east toward the causeway.

"Penny, okay, okay, come back. Get in the car. I'll drive you. But you'll need to get a jacket and better shoes." She was wearing a pair of beige leather flats, almost ballet slippers.

She agreed, and went back into the hotel to change. He followed behind her to find Fiona and Harriet still in the tiny entrance lobby. He explained that he was going to drive Penny up to Rackwick and then said to both of them. "Probably best to tell the rest of the group. And tell them that nobody—I mean nobody—is to leave this hotel." It was now the day after the solstice, that favored day of the killer, but Seth Ludington was hardly wont to allow any more risk.

He found Frode and told him what had happened. This time he asked to use the car. He then went up to his room and found the pair of hiking boots he had brought along. The loafers that had made the first trip to the Dwarfie Stane were muddied and wet.

When he came back down to the lobby, Al McNulty was in wait. "Due diligence, Mr. Ludington. That's what we call it in my line of work. You brought us to these islands knowing that a serial killer was on the loose. That's not due diligence. Now look what's happened." He turned away without waiting for a response and strutted into the Royal's dining room and its little self-service bar.

Seth drove, Penny sat silently at his side. He drove slowly, hoping to stall their arrival at the Dwarfie Stane so that the police might be there before them. The rain had stopped; the wind was less persistent. The car was steady as they crossed the causeway from South Walls to Hoy.

Though Seth Ludington was relatively new to parish ministry, he had witnessed grief often enough. Penny's insistence on going to her husband was grief—grief and the utterly normal irrationality that so often rides with it. At least, that was how Seth Ludington reasoned as he drove north along the banks of Scapa Flow. He looked to the right and saw a few white horses born of the storm breaking sideways on Hoy's beaches. He knew that somewhere in those frigid waters lay the battleship *Royal Oak*, sunk by a German U-boat in 1939. If he recalled correctly, more than 800 British men and boys went down with her. Today's grief multiplied by 800.

There were no police cars in the car park at the bottom of the trail to the Dwarfie Stane when they arrived. He pulled in, slipped the gear shift into neutral, and left the engine running. He said to Penny, "Let's wait a bit. I'm sure the police will be along." In fact, he was not at all sure that was true, even though it was now almost noon. When they had left Longhope, Frode had told him that he had called about the ferries and been told that they were about to resume service. Seth told Penny as much, adding that it would be best to wait for the authorities, but she was not to be dissuaded. "I want to go to Phil immediately." She opened her door, got out, pulled her jacket tight about her, looked at the path, and then back at Seth in the car. Without speaking a word, she was saying, "You can come with me or not."

Of course, he was going with her. They walked side-by-side most of the way, over sand and gravel at first, then single file on the wooden walkway. When the Dwarfie Stane finally rose into view, Penny stopped, turned to Seth, and strode on. She stopped only when they arrived at the tomb.

"Penny, you don't have to do this."

"Well, I do."

She knelt in the jeans she had changed into and crawled into the tomb. Ludington was on his knees behind her. She turned to her right, sat back, and looked at her husband lying in his stone niche—so properly dressed, reclining easily, hands crossed as if he'd been laid out in a casket. But his knees were raised awkwardly high... and what looked to be sod was stuffed into his mouth. She wept again, softly, but did not turn to Ludington for comfort. She went to her husband and kissed him on the forehead, sat back, and whispered, "Can I say he's at peace? I know that's what people say."

"Let's go, Penny. The police will be along soon. She nodded and turned to crawl out of the tomb, Seth about to follow her. As they did so, they both saw the whiskey bottle lying on its side in the small open space opposite the niches. It appeared to be nearly empty. Seth noticed that it was Highland Park, the more famous of the two local Orkney single malts. Penny reached for it.

"Leave it be, Penny. We're not supposed to touch anything."

She looked back at him, "But what will people think?"

She reached for it again. Ludington grabbed her wrist to stop her.

Chapter Twelve

June 22

They walked without words from the Dwarfie Stane back to the car park. Seth saw the police car approaching at a distance, its blue light flashing silently, winding its way west along the ribbon of road from Quoy to Rackwick. The wind had at last exhausted itself; Scapa Flow had laid down enough for the ferries to run.

He didn't need to point out the car to Penny; she saw it as well. When they got to the parking area, they stood waiting on either side of the Peugeot, Penny's back on the closed door of the car, leaning against its side, her head turned away from Seth. She was watching the light flashing rhythmically, drawing nearer. No siren ripped the calm of Trowieglen. Now, the air was barely moving. The sun was daring intermittent appearances. It was not quite warm, though it might be by the end of the day.

"Penny, last night Phil was wearing his collar. It's not there now. Did he take it off? After you left the wedding, I mean?"

She jerked her head around to look at Seth, "I don't know. He often did take it off after some event where he wore it. Said it scratched his neck."

The Ford Focus Estate pulled up behind the Peugeot. Seth saw that it was marked "Police," but only in English and not bi-lingually in English and Gaelic as was usually the case in Scotland. Odd the things you notice at times like this, he thought to himself. Unlike most of the country, Scots Gaelic had never been spoken in Orkney.

The light ceased its pulse as the two uniformed officers emerged from the vehicle. The older, a wiry man in his late fifties with disobedient sandy hair and a sea of freckles approached Ludington, who had moved around the car to stand at Penny's side.

"I'm Chief Inspector Magnus Isbister." Turning to his companion, a round young woman with jet-black hair cut short, he said, "This is Constable Abby Munro. Might I ask who ye are?"

"I'm Seth Ludington." Before he could introduce Penny, she said, "I'm Penelope Desmond. It's my husband. In that Dwarfie Stane place." She turned her head in its direction in case they didn't know where it was.

Constable Munro glanced sideways at her superior, both of them clearly alarmed. He asked the obvious question that was troubling them, "You've already gone up to the Stane then, have you?"

Aware that they had deliberately trespassed a crime scene before the police had arrived, Penny said, "I had to know. I had to see him. He's my husband."

"We touched nothing, of course," Seth said. Not quite true. Penny had kissed the body.

Ludington explained—as cogently as he could manage—that he was the leader of a small American tour group, that one of their number had gone missing either the night before or early that morning, that his own wife's grandmother lived in Rackwick and had phoned about the discovery in the Dwarfie Stane. As the ferries were down and because they had no idea when the police might be able to get to Hoy, Reverend Desmond's wife had insisted that she go to the place to determine if it was her husband who had died. He offered this narrative defensively, not mentioning his preliminary solo visit to the Stane.

Ludington was cut short when Isbister fairly barked, "Reverend? A minister is he?"

"Yes." Ludington knew that both of them were thinking the same thing. They exchanged a knowing glance. He sighed, "Beuy beuy," then looked at Penny Desmond and then Ludington. He translated, "Oh my, that is to say. I do so wish ye hadna' gone to the Stane. But what's done is done." And then to Penny, I'm awfie sorry for your loss, Ma'am."

After that word of condolence, the man took charge, sending Penny with Constable Munro on to Rackwick, telling them to wait there, as he wished to interview both her and the young people who had made the discovery that morning. He would be along shortly. He then turned to Ludington, "The deceased seems to have been identified, but I would like you to confirm it in my presence, if you would."

Constable Munro put an arm on the flat of Penny's back, ushered her gently toward the police car and opened the door for her. Before she climbed in, Penny turned to Ludington and mouthed, "Thank you."

Ludington and Isbister set off, walking briskly up the path to the Dwarfie Stane. It would be Seth's third visit to the tomb that day. He hoped it would be his last—forever.

Isbister said, "Tell me of your group, Mr. Ludington, and tell me what you know of the Rev. Desmond."

Ludington told him the tour had been organized for the small congregation he served as minister in New York, but had come to include several participants from Princeton and Philadelphia Theological Seminaries. This included Desmond, the latter institution's retired president, three seminary students, and a member of that seminary's board of trustees, a layman. He noted that Philip Desmond was a highly respected American churchman and that he had once been pastor of the congregation which he himself now served. He again made the Orkney connection between his wife and her grandmother, Ingrid Gunn, the woman who had called them at Longhope with the news of the discovery that morning.

"When did he go missing, Rev. Ludington? And where are ye biding?"

"We're at the Royal in Longhope."

"Aye, I know it."

"The when is not so clear," Seth said. "Penny will tell you what she knows, but she seems unsure about exactly when he might have gone off. They parted last evening, she said, after a wedding we all attended in Longhope. Dr. Desmond went on for a walk, for a bit of air, Mrs. Desmond said. She went straight to bed and fell asleep before he returned. She slept through the night. He was not there when she awoke." He related the events of the morning—the 7:30 knock on his door, his searches, Ingrid's call. He now felt obliged to tell Isbister about his first visit to the Dwarfie Stane, "I felt I had to drive up here and see if it could be Phil. I mean, before I said anything to his wife. I saw that it was, touched nothing, and went straight back to break the news to Penny. I tried to convince her to wait, wait until the authorities—I mean you—arrived, but she was insistent on seeing him. She said she had to. I guess I can understand that." Seth found himself defending her.

The two men walked easily up the gentle slope toward the Dwarfie Stane. Ludington was impressed with the older man's vigor. And he was unusually loquacious for an Orcadian. "I assume you are aware that two clergymen have been found murdered in Orkney these last two years. Both in June, on the 21st. Both were found at Neolithic sites on The Mainland." He did not note the fourth commonality—that both had earth stuffed in their mouths.

Isbister said, "They were local, both of them. Actually, the second was an incomer. English, he was. But he had lived in Kirkwall for several years."

Ludington nodded, "We read about the deaths in the newspaper last week when we arrived in Edinburgh. It worried me, of course. I thought to cancel the Orkney leg of our trip, but that seemed an overreaction. We did alter our itinerary so that we would spend all our nights on Hoy. So remote. I figured it to be safe." Self-recrimination, an emotion that often surfaced in Seth Ludington, had been rising in him for the last several hours.

Isbister said, "Well, we're havin' all the ferries leaving Hoy monitored, now that they're running again. Checking IDs of everybody gettin' off, not that there are many. We'll have a record of every person leavin' the island after service went down last evening. The last ferry ran at 8:30. From Longhope to Houton. No runs at all since then, not until the one we took to get here."

He stopped and turned to Seth, "Mr. Ludington, these kinds of things don't happen in Orkney. Other than these two…" He hesitated and added, "or three maybe. Save for this business, there have been but two murders in all Orkney in the last half century. Two murders in fifty years, both of them solved by the way. It's a safe place. Safest in all Britain, they say."

The irony weighing that last statement seemed to have escaped Isbister.

"Of course, there was worry as the date came 'round," he said. "We put watches on every clergyman or clergywoman in Orkney, all 19 of them. Warned them as well, not that they needed much warning. And we posted watch on a dozen Neolithic sites. That's not all of them of course. Had to import help from Thurso and Wick to cover even those. Myself, I was up all last night at the Ness of Brodgar. We didn't even consider Hoy or the Dwarfie Stane. It's a minor site, and so remote. And the minister to the few peedie kirks on Hoy actually bides on The Mainland. We didna' know of your visit, of course. If it's what this might prove to be, I am sorry, Mr. Ludington. For all Orkney, I am sorry. Was he a friend, this Philip Desmond?"

Ludington summarized the nature of their relationship, again including the fact that Desmond had once led the congregation he now served. But he did not mention the matter of the bones in the ash pit, the event that had introduced him to Desmond a few months earlier. He summarized, "I respected the man enormously. I would have been proud to count him a friend."

Isbister crawled into the Dwarfie Stane first, Ludington behind him. The cop sat back on his haunches, saw the wad of peat exploding from the mouth of the corpse in the niche, and whispered, "Another one." Then he turned to Ludington and said, "Can you confirm the identity of this man, sir?"

"The Reverend Doctor Philip Davis Desmond."

"Are you certain?"

"Yes, and so is his wife."

Isbister reached his hand out to gently touch the nearer elbow of the body. Desmond's hands were touching each other, folded over his abdomen and his neatly buttoned blue sport coat. It looked almost as though the man had been at prayer when he died. Or perhaps his hands had been placed that way, in the manner of undertakers laying out a body in a casket. Isbister pushed the elbow, then pulled it, and said, as much to himself as to Ludington, *"Rigor mortis* has set in. It's cool in here, so it might have taken longer than the usual two or three hours, but it's still in place. He died either vera late last evening or sometime during the night."

Ludington nodded and said, "I saw him in Longhope last night, just after nine. And those two kids said they found him early this morning. It fits."

Isbister looked at Ludington, rather surprised at the man's foray into deduction. They walked back to the car park more slowly than they had walked out to the Stane. Both men were pensive and silent until Ludington spoke again. "Chief Inspector, it was publicly known that our group was visiting Orkney, and that it included clergy." He told Isbister about Ingrid's call to Tim at *The Orcadian* and the story the newspaper had run in the past week's edition.

"Comes out Thursdays." Isbister said, "Usually gets to our place Friday or Saturday—today. He winced. "Hadn't gotten to it yet. Damn it all."

Seth sensed that Magnus Isbister seemed to feel comfortable in his presence. The man had dared to hint at his own regret.

"I'm about to retire. Mr. Ludington. End of the year, six months. I'll get this bastard before I go. I promise you. I'm a church goer, myself. St. Magnus in Kirkwall. In fact, they've asked me to serve as Session Clark when I retire. So, this is a bit personal, you might say."

Seth dared to ask the obvious question, "Any suspects?"

He hesitated in answering, "Not really. One theory, not mine though. You'll soon meet Chief Superintendent Alastair McCormick. He'll be arriving by helicopter later this afternoon." An edge came into Isbister's voice. "He'll be lead investigator… again. Sent along by the Procurator Fiscal, Scots version of your American prosecutor. McCormick was on the last two murders as well. From Inverness, he is. And he'll bring along the scene of crime types from the Major Investigation Team—forensics, footprints and fingerprints, you know. And an autopsy, of course. All of which got us close to nowhere the last two times. Isbister looked at Ludington, gave him a wry smile, and said, "These murders are too big for the likes of an island cop like me."

"He has this theory, McCormick does. I should warn ye, because he might press it with you and with Mrs. Desmond. Obviously, the killer hates clergy. But why? McCormick's theory is pedophilia, that the guy was molested by some pedo in a clerical collar and is out for a lifetime of revenge."

"Any basis to McCormick's thinking?" As Ludington asked the question, he could not but think of the endless abuse scandals plaguing the Roman Catholic Church. Such a stain on all the church, one that a cop might imagine bleeding into other denominations.

"Well, there were rumors about the second of the two victims, the incomer. Nothing proven, no charges ever brought, but Orkney's a small place. And it's a delicate subject. Delicate everywhere, I suppose, but especially here. You see, there was a spate of accusations on South Ronaldsay, thirty years ago now. Tore the community apart. Tales of a pedo ring, Satanism, the whole horror show. Proved to be hysteria, all snirled up. I was not on the force then, but I doubt anything ever happened."

"So, you don't buy McCormick's idea?" Ludington was taken aback by the man's candor, surprised that they were even having this conversation.

"Well, I'm not sold. But who am I?" Just the native who knows these islands like the back of his hand.

Chapter Thirteen

L udington and Isbister had driven but a mile from the Dwarfie Stane car park when the Vale of Rackwick exploded into view before them. The sun had burned away much of the day's gray; fresh light broken by cloud shadows fell across the valley. Seth thought he had never seen a more beautiful place on God's earth. To see such a splendor on such a day as this was painfully incongruous.

At his side, Magnus Isbister played guide. The place coming into view was a happier topic than the reason of their visit to it. "The great hill to the right they call Moor Fea, and to the left, that cliff, is Mel Fea. Fea is an old Norse word. Means a hill. The valley between, leaning down to that arc of beach, that's Rackwick. Crofters and fishermen settled the place, the land is a bit richer than most of Hoy. Cut peat to keep warm, they did. Peat-smoked fish was the local specialty. Now incomers have turned the peedie old crofts to summer places. Good to see somebody here, though. Sir Peter Maxwell Davies, the composer, he had a place here. The school closed in the '50s. Turned it into a hostel for tourists, bird watchers mostly, like the two that hiked out to the Dwarfie Stane this morning."

Isbister pointed to his right, "The path to the Old Man of Hoy starts about there."

They parked the Peugeot next to Isbister's police car in the unpaved lane that wiggled up toward Moor Fea and the old school, now repurposed as the basic accommodations of a youth hostel. As they climbed out of the car, Constable Munro emerged from the tidy stone house across from the hostel. "We're over here, Chief Inspector. Mrs. Desmond is here, and the pair who found the body."

This is Ingrid's home, thought Ludington. It was a summer place now, but she had lived here year around as a child. She had gone to school in the building across the way before her parents left Hoy for Mainland as had so many out-islanders. Her house was well-kept, but had not been enlarged. Fiona had told Seth that Grams had modernized it, added "mod cons" as the Brits say—decadent luxuries like heat, electricity, and plumbing.

They entered through the low door of the house, Isbister first, Ludington behind him, to find Penny sitting next to Ingrid at a rough wooden table in the kitchen, cups of untouched tea before them. Constable Munro was standing with them. She said, "The pair what found the body are in the main room." She tilted her head toward a larger sitting room to her left."

Isbister went into that room, sat himself down with the two young birders and introduced himself. Munro stood to his side and prepared to jot notes in a tiny spiral notebook—not that there would be many notes to jot. Names and addresses came first. Seth could hear every word clearly from the kitchen of the small house. Penny and Ingrid listened as well. Both of them said that they were from Perth. At Isbister's bidding, they offered what he called their statement, the tale of their morning hike and what they discovered. Julia did most of the talking. Jim still looked shaky. Julia said they had left the hostel early, well before eight, and driven to the trailhead as she named the car park where the path to the Dwarfie Stane began. Then they hiked up to the Stane. She guessed they had gotten there at about 8:10 maybe 8:20, but could not be sure of the exact time. No, she assured Isbister, they had touched nothing, save to give the guy a poke to see if he were maybe only asleep.

Isbister asked them if they had noticed anything else inside. They shook their heads. Then he asked about the whiskey bottle. Ludington realized that Isbister had seen it but had said nothing to him. No, Julia insisted, "All we saw was the dead guy with dirt in his mouth. We left pronto, right after I poked him, that is. Didn't see a whiskey bottle. It was pretty dark in there." She looked to Jim for confirmation. He shook his head, eyes still trained on his muddy hiking boots, and mumbled, "Didn't see anything but him." Then Isbister asked the question he had saved for last, "Did you see anyone—anyone—either up at the Stane or coming or going? Any cars on the road?" Jim lifted his head and spoke for the first time, "Not a soul. I mean nobody. God-forsaken place. Quite unnerving."

Isbister thanked them and told them they were free to go, but asked that they stay on the island for a day. They would need to give their statement again, and then sign written versions when a "higher-up," as he named McCormick, arrived from Inverness.

Isbister rose and came into the kitchen. "Mrs. Desmond, I regret having to put questions to you at a time like this, but it will be helpful in resolving the matter of your husband's death." Ludington realized that no one had yet used the word "murder."

Looking from Penny to Ingrid, Isbister said, "It would be best if we spoke privately."

Ingrid Gunn understood and rose from her chair. "I'll just go across the way and check in on Tillie. I'll bring the young ones along with me so you can talk here."

Seth was unsure whether he was included as a "young one" and should follow Ingrid to the hostel or go sit in the car to leave Isbister alone with Penny Desmond. The question was answered when Penny spoke, "I would like Seth to be with me, please. I consider him to be my pastor." Ludington was taken aback by her declaration.

"If you wish," Mrs. Desmond. I cannot require Mr. Ludington to leave."

Isbister pulled a chair from the kitchen table, its legs screeching across the stone floor. He sat opposite Penny, the silent Constable Munro, notebook in hand, took the chair beside him. Isbister nodded to Seth, who sat himself next to Penny as Ingrid and the birders left the cottage for the hostel. Before Ingrid closed the door behind them, she turned back to Seth and offered up a sad smile.

Penny Desmond's narration of the events of the evening before and her waking to find that her husband was not beside her in bed was related precisely as she had offered it to Ludington earlier that morning. The sequence of events, indeed the very words she used, were almost exactly the same. If anything had changed, it was the woman's demeanor. A few hours ago, she had been a bundle of nervous yet controlled energy. Now she was calm in a way that suggested she had eased into an emotional disconnection from events. As he listened to her speak, interrupted only occasionally by questions from Isbister, Seth thought about how much culture prescribes a person's emotional affect. He had grown up in much the same world as Penny Desmond—privileged, sophisticated, urbane..., and studiously controlled. Public display of emotion was *déclassé*, though that word would never have been used to describe it. Such a judgement would have been *déclassé* itself. The several funerals of assorted Ludington relatives that he had attended in his youth had been studies in such reserve. So, he understood Penny Desmond, though he believed a flood of tears would probably come soon enough and that it would do the woman a world of good. Hopefully, she could weep in her daughters' arms in a few days' time.

Isbister was methodical in his questioning, but nothing surfaced that Seth did not already know—the wedding reception, when the Desmonds had left it, their walk back to the hotel, Phil's decision to go on a bit farther to the pier, Penny going to the Royal and to bed, sleeping the night through and waking to find herself alone.

Isbister then asked, "Did Rev. Desmond know of the Dwarfie Stane?"

"Yes, she answered. "Phil was interested in it. He was a historian, you know. Fascinated by old things. The older, the better."

"How did he know about it, Mrs. Desmond?"

"He picked up a little brochure about places to visit on Hoy. At the hotel, I assume. There was a bit about the Dwarfie Stane, a picture, and a map as well. He showed it to me on the bus yesterday. Actually, he may have even mentioned it earlier, back when we first made plans for the trip."

It seemed obvious to Ludington that Isbister knew McCormick would be interviewing Penny himself yet again, and that she would be asked to make and sign a written statement. From what the local cop had hinted about the man, McCormick would do it with a heavier hand. Isbister thanked Penny, and again offered condolences, personally and on behalf of all Orkney. His words impressed Ludington as heartfelt.

Penny asked if she was free to return to the hotel. Isbister said she was, and Ingrid had offered to drive her. As she rose from the table, Penny said, "Chief Inspector, you must understand that I have some telephone calls to make. Can you tell me when my husband's body will be released? I obviously have to make plans." As he listened to her take control, Ludington was again struck by the woman's courage, and for want of a better word, deliberateness. He could imagine her being a major force on the assorted Philadelphia not-for-profit boards she doubtless served on.

Penny allowed Seth to embrace her after he walked her to Ingrid's old Land Rover. He held her for a moment, drew back, and saw a single tear roll down her cheek. As the two women drove off, Isbister approached him and said, "Walk down to the beach with me, Reverend Ludington?"

Isbister was silent as they made their way down the half-mile of rutted road to the wide concave beach that lay at the foot of the Vale of Rackwick. Though the wind had finally stilled, rollers were still washing several yards up onto the shingle. They sat side-by-side on a large rock and looked out over the roiling Atlantic.

Isbister told Ludington that he had phoned the Procurator Fiscal in Inverness early that morning and told her of another body discovered in another Neolithic site. "'Yes,' I said when she asked, 'with sod stuffed in the mouth.'" I gave her the coordinates of the Dwarfie Stane. I knew she'd call McCormick, and I knew that she'd assign him to lead the investigation... again."

Ludington nodded and spoke more loudly than he would have liked in order to be heard over the surf, "You should know that Phil was drinking last night. Penny probably won't say it, but you need to know."

"Heavily?"

"Honestly, yes, both at the hotel before the wedding and then at the party after. And he was wearing his clerical collar last night at the wedding and the reception. It's not there now, only the black shirt. There was a crowd around last night, inside and outside the hall. I obviously didn't know anyone beyond our little group. Locals mostly, I suppose, I mean people from Hoy. But others, perhaps."

Isbister cast a stone into the oncoming waves, "What are you thinking, Mr. Ludington?"

"Well, I don't know, maybe he bumped into somebody, somebody with a car, and he got on to how he wanted to see the Dwarfie Stane. Like I said, Penny and Phil passed me as they left the village hall. Cars parked everywhere. People hanging around. Having a smoke or a pee most of them. It was just after nine, I'm sure of the time. It was still quite light, of course. The storm hadn't blown in yet...."

Ludington's speculations were drowned out by the roar of helicopter blades as a chopper raced north over the beach and up the Vale of Rackwick toward the sleeping Dwarfie Stane. Isbister grimaced and muttered, "Himself has arrived." He looked away from the chopper and down to the stone they were sitting on. He said with a guffaw, "Well, guess I'm between a rock and a hard place." It was the first hint to Ludington of the man's affection for wordplay. He guessed that the rock was the one they were sitting on and the hard place was riding in the helicopter.

Chapter Fourteen

June 22

Isbister turned to Ludington, "Might as well follow me to the hard place. He'll want a word with you. They'll be putting down at the Dwarfie Stane car park. They won't want to get that machine anywhere close to the crime scene. Blow all the evidence about, if there is any, this time. You'll have the great pleasure of meeting Detective Chief Superintendent McCormack."

Isbister and Ludington walked back up the hill to their vehicles parked at the hostel. Constable Munro was waiting by the door of the Ford Focus Estate, drumming her fingers impatiently on its roof. Isbister and Munro climbed into the marked car, drove down the trail and turned onto the road toward the Dwarfie Stane parking area. Seth followed Isbister in his borrowed Peugeot. Isbister seemed to be driving more slowly than needful. No siren, not even the roof light was flashing now.

The helicopter's long, sagging blade was still rotating slowly when they arrived. Four men, one in a Police Scotland uniform, the other three in matching blue windbreakers, were emerging from the machine. All crouched low as people do in proximity to helicopters, even though the blade is yards over their heads. The one in uniform was attempting to have a conversation with the others. The chopper was less thunderous than it had been, but still painfully loud in the Trowieglen, which was beginning to fall back into its eerie tranquility.

The man in uniform glanced away from his conversation as Isbister walked toward him. "Where the hell have you been, Isbister?" The speaker, who Ludington assumed to be Chief Superintendent Alistair McCormick, dragged out the two S's in Isbister's name as he spoke it, snake-like. He looked to be in his early forties, perhaps fifteen years Isbister's junior. His dark hair was shaved close in a buzz cut. He was big and jowly, almost bear-like. "Bear or snake? Which one?" Ludington thought to himself. McCormick did not move to shake Isbister's hand. He completely ignored Munro. It was as if she were not there. He looked at Ludington and said, "So, who's this?"

Isbister finally spoke. "This is the Reverend Seth Ludington."

"Reverend?" McCormick whispered, "Suppose the body is a reverend as well. Shite. "

Isbister answered with a soft, "yes," explained that Ludington was the leader of an American tour group, and that he had identified the body as that of another minister traveling with his group. "Constable Munro and I have already taken statements from the victim's widow and the young couple who discovered the body this morning."

"McCormick waved an arm vaguely in the direction of the three men who had climbed out of the chopper with him and said, "Scene of the crime squad, for what they're worth. So, where's this dwarf stone of yours?"

Isbister did not correct the man's pronunciation, "I'll show you. It's a peedie hike, it is." He then walked a few steps away from the Inverness cop and the forensics crew. He drew close to Ludington, and said softly so only he could hear, "We'll be at the Royal in a few hours. He'll want to talk to the birders here first, get their statements. Then he nodded toward McCormick, raised an eyebrow, and said, "Ye might want to give Mrs. Desmond a heads up."

McCormick turned to face Ludington as the forensics team began to extract cases containing their equipment from the helicopter, "I'll be wanting to talk to you, padre. Where can I find you?"

It was the first time Seth had been addressed as "padre." It was, he knew, a World War II word for military chaplains. "We're staying at the Royal Hotel in South Walls. I'll be there, as will Mrs. Desmond and all of our group. Chief Inspector Isbister knows where it is."

McCormick grunted a response and turned to the forensics team at the helicopter, "Be quick about it boys." Then he said to Ludington, "Well, stay there, you and your lot—all of you—stay there."

As Ludington worked through the gears of the Peugeot on the drive back to the hotel, his thoughts turned to Penny Desmond and what lay ahead of her in the next few days, over the following weeks, and then in the life before her. He imagined the phone calls she would have to make to her daughters and the flight back to the States with a casket in the plane's cargo hold—assuming the body would be released in a timely manner. He thought of the funeral back in Philadelphia. It would surely be held in the seminary chapel. It was a small sanctuary; the place would be packed. Would Penny move to be near a daughter? He had no idea where the three girls lived. He thought of Penny alone when the rush of the funeral was over, and the waves of sympathy had passed, alone after a fifty-year marriage. He had the impression that it had been not only a long one, but a very happy one.

He thought of that day a couple of weeks before the previous Easter when he had found himself in Phil Desmond's office at the seminary just prior to the man's retirement. In addition to the portraits of former presidents of the institution that adorned the room—a gallery of sober, mostly Victorian-era gentlemen in black—there was a small color photograph of younger iterations of Phil and Penny Desmond. It was not hung on a wall, but sat perched on the corner of Desmond's massive desk, turned so that someone in the visitor's chair might see it. Mr. and Mrs. Desmond were smiling broadly in the photo, sunglasses pushed up on their heads, sitting in a vintage sports car—a two-seater convertible, dark green.

Desmond had noticed Ludington looking at the photograph. "Penny's fiftieth," he said. "The car was her birthday present from me. 1960 MGA in BRG—British racing green. Her dream car since college. She was very particular about the color. We still have it." Desmond had then picked up the photo to look at it more closely. He had smiled at it and handed it to Ludington. To smile at a photograph that you saw every day of your life said something.

Just before he reached Lyness, a small white van with an STV logo plastered on its side flew past him, headed north. The media was onto the murder. A private event was about to go shamelessly public. The cops would be guarded in what they said to reporters, at least for now. So would Ingrid Gunn. He was less confident that the two young birders would be circumspect when confronted with the chance for a flash of on-camera fame.

When he arrived at the hotel, Ludington found Penny sitting with Harriet and Fiona in the lounge. He told them that the local Orkney police and a detective from Inverness, plus an investigatory team, had arrived, the latter by helicopter. The investigation was to be headed by a Detective Chief Superintendent named Alistair McCormick. He told the three women that McCormick seemed to be "a pretty aggressive cop, one with strong opinions." He did not mention the man's theories about pedophilia—an abused victim seeking serial revenge against clergymen. He also named the two local cops, Magnus Isbister and Abby Munro, but did not note that McCormick and Isbister clearly disliked each other, nor did he say that he liked Isbister.

Harriet rose, pulled Seth aside, and whispered, "We have telephoned the girls. I mean to say, Penny did. I sat with her as she placed the calls. They are absolutely devastated, as you might imagine. They want to fly over, but I believe Penny successfully dissuaded them from doing so, at least for the moment."

* * *

McCormick, Isbister, and Munro arrived at the Royal just after four o'clock. The Inverness cop strode through the front door, the other two trailing at his heels. They had driven down together in Isbister's patrol car. The whole of Hoy had surely heard the siren wailing the entire way. The chopper and the forensics team were obviously still up at the Dwarfie Stane doing their methodical work. McCormick and the two local cops found Ludington sitting in the lounge holding his wife's hand. Harriet van der Berg and Penny Desmond completed the silent circle of mourners. Else had set out tea. No one was drinking it.

McCormick entered, put his thumbs in his belt, looked at the three older women, "I'd like to talk to Mrs. Desmond first, privately." He did not know which of them was Penny Desmond.

Penny looked up at him, her face a mask, "I'm Penny Desmond. When can I bring Phil home?"

McCormick did not sit, even though there was an empty chair in front of the low table in the lounge. "The forensics team will finish up at the site later today. Your husband's body will then be flown to Inverness. For an autopsy." He seemed to utter the word with some pleasure.

Penny looked surprised at this news. "Is that really necessary?"

"I'm afraid it is. Is there somewhere we can talk, Mrs. Desmond? You and me and DCI Isbister here." He poked a thumb in Magnus' direction.

"I insist that Rev. Ludington be with me. I need him with me."

McCormick rolled his eyes at the ceiling, "As long as he keeps his mouth shut."

As Ludington listened to McCormick's conversation with Penny in a far and quiet corner of the Royal's dining room, it was unclear who was interviewing whom. Alastair McCormick had met his match in Penny Desmond.

She said, "You will apprehend whoever did this to my husband, will you not?"

McCormick assured her that they would, that they had a theory about the motivation behind what he called "these murders up here in no man's land." "No resource will be spared; I can promise you that, Mrs. Desmond."

Ludington guessed that the resource not being spared was largely himself, Detective Chief Superintendent Alastair McCormick. McCormick asked Penny to review the events of the night before, turned to Isbister seated next to him, and barked, "Take notes of names and times, Isbister. So, tell me about your husband's movements last night. I understand you went to a wedding. "

Penny did not answer his question. Rather, she asked her own, again, "Mr. McCormick, when will my husband's body be released."

"I cannot make promises. It will be flown south tonight after the SOC team is finished. In the chopper. The coroner says he plans to do the autopsy tomorrow, probably in the morning. Then maybe."

"You can understand my need to know, can you not? There are plans to be made, Mr. McCormick."

Penny Desmond was in control again, though an insistent DCS McCormick ultimately cornered her into rehearsing the chronology of the events of the prior evening yet again. Nothing about the narrative had changed. It was precisely as she had offered it to Ludington early that morning and then to Isbister a few hours ago.

After a curt thank you to Penny Desmond and speaking the needful condolences, McCormick and Isbister moved on to interview and take written statements from all the members of the tour. After the group, they took statements from Frode, Else, and even Lewis Ross, the bus driver. Though masking it as best he could, Ross was obviously enjoying the excitement. Seth overheard him say to himself as he left the interview corner of the Royal's dining room, "Seen a lot in my tours, I have, but never got one murdered."

Chapter Fifteen

June 22

Ludington was the last member of the tour group to be asked for his formal statement. As he went to the interview corner of the dining room, he noticed Frode rummaging through the modest stock of liquor in the service bar. Frode looked up at him, "The detective from Scotland, the big one, asked if we were missing a bottle of Highland Park. I'm not sure, but I think it is so. I thought we had three."

As his interview unfolded, Seth surmised from the close attention he was receiving, the detailed follow-up questions, and the furious note-taking accompanying his answers that the information he had to offer was especially valuable. He assumed it to be so because he had so closely noted the exact times when people had left the wedding reception the night before when he had been waiting anxiously at the door of the village hall for Jilly Wilson, the tardy nurse, glancing at his watch every five eternal minutes.

After jotting down all the names and the times in his little spiral notebook, doubtless borrowed from Constable Munro, Isbister asked him how Phil Desmond had seemed the night before. Ludington told them that the man appeared to have been having an enjoyable time at the reception.

"Had he been drinking, then?" Isbister asked, though he already knew the answer to the question. He was asking it so McCormick would know without his having to disclose that Ludington had opened up to him about it earlier. That could further cloud their already overcast relationship.

"Yes." Seth answered, looking at Isbister and raising his eyebrows to say, "I know what you're doing,"

"Heavily?" asked McCormick.

"Well, I cannot be certain, but perhaps."

"Anything else of importance, Reverend Ludington?"

"Well, maybe. When Phil and Penny left the village hall last night, he was wearing his clerical collar. You know that it wasn't on him in the Dwarfie Stane. It's probably not important, but you should know." He explained without being asked, "They snap on and off the clerical shirt. Held in place with old-fashioned collar buttons. They can be a bit uncomfortable."

Isbister took in this detail and said, "He could have lost it anywhere."

McCormick grunted disagreement, "Serial killers like their souvenirs."

He then asked Ludington the routine homicide cop question, "Do you know any reason why someone would have wanted to murder Philip Desmond? Any enemies you know of?"

Ludington demurred, saying that he did not really know the man that well. In fact, had only met Philip Desmond twice before this trip to Scotland. He did not go into the events of a few months earlier, events that had occasioned those two meetings with Desmond, irrelevant as they were. Nor did he think it the right time to mention the quarrel he had witnessed between Desmond and McNulty in Braemar. And he chose not to bring up Sarah Mrazek and her curious fixation with the man. It was horrifically obvious to all of them what had happened to Phil Desmond. He was a random clergyman in exactly the wrong place at precisely the right time. It was also clear that neither McCormick nor Isbister, nor any of the weight and wisdom of Police Scotland, had any idea who the Sod Stuffer (as the media would surely still insist on naming him) might be. Nor did they know where he was, or if he might kill again—tomorrow, or as was more likely, come the next summer solstice.

It was nearly seven o'clock by the time McCormick had interviewed everyone at the Royal. Frode found Seth and Fiona in the lounge. "The story was on the ITV news program at six. They did not say who he was, I mean Mr. Desmond, but the girl they interviewed, she talked about the

94

sod business. This is too much sadness, and bad for Orkney. Come, Else has some light dinner ready. You must eat."

Harriet had taken Penny to her room, insisting that she needed rest. The rest of the group had gone for a group walk after their serial grillings. Seth had gotten clearance from McCormick for them to leave the hotel if they promised to stay together. Harry said he would make sure they did so and that he would have them back by seven.

Before he left, Ludington heard McCormick order Isbister to remain on Hoy at the Royal, "Watch them close. Don't let any of them wander off alone, especially the clergy types. And book me a room in Kirkwall. At the Highland Park House." He then told Constable Munro to drive him to the Houton ferry.

Isbister sat with Ludington at dinner, the hour of which had been delayed by the events of the day. Fiona had nibbled on soda crackers and Orkney cheese during the afternoon and insisted she was not hungry. Seth guessed that she was afraid to eat much, for fear of seeing it again. The meds the nurse had given her were taking off the edge, but only the edge, of her morning sickness.

Harriet arranged for sandwiches to be brought to Penny's room for the two of them, though Penny protested that she was anything but hungry. "You must eat, my dear," Seth heard her say to Penny. True, but Harriet van der Berg, mistress of propriety that she was, could not imagine dining in public when your husband had just been murdered.

Dinner was an Orkney take on the ubiquitous U.K. pub fare, the plowman's lunch—cold cuts, cheese, and fresh bread. Isbister ate heartily, Ludington sparingly. Isbister slathered butter on a thick slice of bread. "Mr. Ludington, it seems your guess could be right."

"Call me Seth. Please."

"Seth? Humm." Isbister leaned back in thought, "The third son of Adam and Eve, the one who was neither the victim nor the murderer. Cain and Abel, you know. Well, I suppose you would know that. Guess that must have made Seth the first cop in history." He smirked and said, "Savvy sleuth Seth."

Seth smiled at Isbister's verbal playfulness, smiled for the first time that day, "Actually, I think God was the cop. Cop, judge and jury. So, what do you think happened, Chief Inspector""

"Call me Magnus, Magnie actually. Please."

"Magnie, what do you think happened? To Phil Desmond, I mean."

"About what you guessed—probably. McCormick surmises—and I think he's getting close here, in spite of himself—that the killer saw the write-up in *The Orcadian* about your tour group and that it included several clergy. He saw that you were bidin' on Hoy and that you were invited to a wedding. He knows the scene will be a bit chaotic, as Orkney weddings tend to be. He also guesses that local clergy are being watched come the twenty-first of June, and Neolithic sites as well. Right about that he was. So, he got himself to the party at the Village Hall—several hundred people dancing and drinking and hanging about outside around the cars. He picked out Desmond as clergy. He was wearing a clerical collar. He and Mrs. Desmond left at 9:10. You clocked it. Mrs. Desmond then leaves her husband to walk on to the pier alone, dressed in his clerics and well lubricated. The fellow sidles up to Desmond. Makes himself out to be a friendly local. Asks Desmond if he's enjoying his visit to Orkney. Desmond says something about wanting to see the Dwarfie Stane. Or maybe the guy mentions it first, like a tour guide, and asks Desmond if he's seen it. Then he offers to show it to him. It's maybe half-nine at this point, still vera light. Off they go, either in the guy's car or maybe the hotel's loaner. More booze on the way and yet more when they get there. You know about the empty whiskey bottle inside the Stane. Then he drugs him, or maybe already had. Laced the whiskey with something. Then a jab in the arm. We're expecting the autopsy to find fentanyl, like the last two. Fatal dose of the stuff. He would have just gone to sleep, Seth. Never knew what was happening."

"But why, Magnie? Why? Is McCormick still stuck on his pedophilia theory?"

"Yes, but he's altering it a bit. Still thinking the guy was abused by some cleric when he was a kid. But his victims aren't necessarily pedophiles but they're ministers like his abuser. I mean, he could hardly have thought

Desmond a pedophile. And even if he were, how could he have known? So, now McCormick is thinking that the guy has generalized his hate, or anger, or whatever it is, generalized it to all clergy. Makes a bit more sense, I have to say."

"So, Magnie, who is it? And where is he?"

"I have absolutely no idea, neither about the who nor the where. And neither does McCormick. But Seth, whoever he is, here's the question— how did he get himself off Hoy? If he did, we ought to have his name on a passenger list. We've been checking every last soul who took a ferry from Hoy to The Mainland since they started up running again today. We're still monitoring them and we'll keep it up for the next week. The list of passengers is not that long. And so far, nobody on it looks in the least likely. Mostly women, bairns and old gents. And a few tourists—all couples or little flocks of visiting birders with binoculars about their necks."

Seth took in this news, "Or he could still be on Hoy. Magnie, maybe he lives here. Or maybe he'll stay on the island as long as he needs to."

Chapter Sixteen

June 23

The next morning at breakfast, Seth took a sip of the Royal's coffee. He had thought Scandinavians were supposed to be good at coffee. He looked at Isbister across the table, "Magnie, another thought, maybe it's God he hates. Not clergy, but hates God himself... or herself."

DCI Magnus Isbister had decided he needed to pass the night with an eye on the front door of the Royal. The faux leather chair he had pulled from the lounge to the entrance hall had proved less than conducive to sleep. He was tired and hungry. He was presently doing something about the latter problem as he attacked the very full Scottish breakfast Frode set before him. Seth and Fiona were both seated with him.

"And men of God are as close as he can get to God, eh? And why, Reverend Ludington, would a man, or a woman, hate God?"

"I can imagine any number of reasons. But he only needs one."

"I suppose. So, McCormick called last night when he got to Kirkwall. He asked me—actually told me—to ask Mrs. Desmond if she knew the password for her husband's mobile. They found it on him, in his jacket pocket. I was loath to disturb her so late, but McCormick was insistent. Anyway, they got into the phone last night. Didn't find much. Not that many recent emails, I mean real ones, not adverts. And no texts. No texts asking him if he'd like to visit the Dwarfie Stane."

Seth nodded, "I've heard that retirement comes with a blessed retreat in the flood of daily emails."

Magnus nodded, "There was one interesting email, though. He got it yesterday. Sent from the U.S. early in the afternoon. He would have received it about six our time. Marked 'URGENT'...in caps." Isbister opened his phone and scrolled through his emails. "McCormick forwarded it to me. He wants me to ask if you know the bloke who sent it. Named Barkman, Henry Barkman. Looks to be some business with Desmond's seminary. Any idea who he is?"

"Henry Barkman's the President of the Board of Trustees at Philadelphia Theological. Can't say I really know him. I only met him briefly, at Desmond's retirement fete a few months ago."

Seth recalled how Barkman had found him standing alone in the giant tent set up on the seminary commons. He had introduced himself by noting the Old Stone connection between Ludington and Desmond. Barkman had then smoothly pivoted to the fund-raising effort underway at the seminary "to support scholarships for students from urban churches like yours." Seth had judged it was a well-executed maneuver, though white-collar Old Stone was not quite the kind of urban congregation whose students the new fund would be aimed to help. Barkman had followed up with a phone call a week later. Seth had made a sizable contribution "in honor of President Philip Desmond," to whom he felt he owed a debt, in that he had suspected the man of infanticide.

Isbister handed Ludington his iPhone 6. "Have a look at his email. Any idea what it's about."

The email in question was open. The sender was noted as "Henry Barkman." Seth read it, *"Dear Phil, Hope this finds you well. You need to take a look at the attached. Looks like you may have been right. Call me ASAP. HB."*

Isbister did not reach to take his phone back, so Seth opened the first of the three PDF's attached to the email. He guessed the cop actually wanted him to have a look at the attachments. It was a prospectus from an investment firm called "Plowshares for a Better Future." The second was a prospectus from another, this one called "Invest for Tomorrow." The third was a prospectus from "The Giving Back Fund." "Well, good for the board of Philadelphia Theological Seminary, and good for Phil Desmond, he thought."

"What do you think it is, Seth?" Isbister reached out his hand for his phone.

Ludington knew that the seminary's endowment was considerable, north of 500 million. Like most theological schools, he assumed that Philadelphia Theological Seminary's budget was endowment-driven. The students didn't have the money for steep tuition. The alums, most of them ministers, had little more in their pockets, and were often buried in school debt themselves. Endowment income paid the bills at most seminaries. To invest some of an endowment in socially responsible investment instruments was an act of courage. They often earned less and sometimes bore more risk. Students were often the ones pressing the issue. He'd have to ask Ted and Hope if they knew anything about advocating for socially responsible endowment investments. They were both at Princeton, not Philadelphia, but students at the two nearby institutions were often in communication. And the pair impressed Seth as the types who would push on social justice issues, even if it broke the seminary. God bless them.

He told Isbister as much and said "I'll call Barkman and see what's so urgent."

DCI Isbister rose from his decimated breakfast, "And I need to phone Himself and let him know you all survived the night. He'll be back among us this afternoon."

As the man walked out the Royal's front door to make his call, Fiona turned to her husband. "I see it in your eyes, Seth Ludington. The waking curiosity. The overweening sense of responsibility. Maybe a shadow of the old guilt. Remember you're a preacher, not a detective."

Seth looked back at her. "Flip side of the same coin, I'm discovering. Figuring people out, you know. Their hopes, their fears. Their passions— the sweet ones and the not-so-sweet ones. Why they do what they do."

Fiona said nothing at first. She let the silence sit between them and raised a skeptical eyebrow, "Lovely."

"They count even when uttered ironically. That's one."

"I need some air, Seth. I'll be right out front. And I won't talk to strangers."

Ludington picked up his phone and dialed the number he had for Henry Barkman. It was in his log from the call he'd gotten from the man about the scholarship fund a few months earlier. As he punched it in, he recognized the old Philadelphia area code—215. The call went to an answering machine on the sixth ring. The recorded voice was a woman's, "You've reached the Barkman's. Leave a message after you hear Oatmeal bark." After Oatmeal barked, Ludington explained who he was and asked Barkman to call back. He avoided the word urgent. He did say, "It's important, Henry." He did not mention Desmond's death. It's not the kind of news you leave in a phone message. The number was obviously the Barkman's home land line. Some people still had them. He then opened the Notes app on his phone and keyed in the names of the three funds whose prospectuses Barkman had sent to Desmond. Something to check out.

Isbister walked in just as Seth was headed out the door to check on Fiona. He knew she was still feeling "peaked" as his mother would have said. But covering as usual.

"Seth, do you have a moment?" Ludington assumed Isbister wanted to know if he had gotten through to Henry Barkman. "Sit with me, if you would, and put on your theologian hat."

He could see Fiona through the window, arms crossed, looking out at the waters of Long Hope from where they sat in the same quiet corner McCormick had used for his serial interviews the day before. "Seth, you said you could imagine a person hating God. I can imagine people ignoring God, or simply not believing in God, but hating God, actually hating God? Why?"

Seth looked at his hands laid across each other in his lap, "Sometimes people imagine God sitting up in God's heaven, wherever that may be, and wiggling a finger to decide who gets in a car crash today, or who's going to be diagnosed with Parkinson's, or who gets to die of cancer. Personally, I don't believe it's that simple, but if you do think it's that simple, you just might hate God if it's your wife who dies in the car wreck or you get Parkinson's or your child has leukemia. It's sometimes called the "high view of providence." It's close to what Augustine believed, and Calvin as well, more or less. It rubs rough with modern ideas about freedom of will and the reality of evil—evil like car accidents, Parkinson's and cancer. Is God the author of evil? I don't think we can know that much. Know that much about God, I mean."

Isbister sucked in his breath. "So then, a man who did see things this way could be so enraged by something that happened to him, or something that happened to somebody he cared about, that he wants to get back at God? So maybe killing some men of God would accomplish that?"

"Maybe. But that's not the only reason you might hate God. Example... Nietzsche hated God in his own way, but not because of any suffering he'd experienced or because of the evil roaming the world. Nietzsche actually thought some suffering might do you good."

"Who are we talking about?"

"German philosopher. Late nineteenth century. Friedrich Nietzsche. He decided that God was dead, so I guess you can't say that he exactly hated God. But then, maybe you can hate the dead. He really despised the Christian notion of God. I mean a God of compassion, a God who loves the weak, a God who loves everybody. Love and grace and mercy made him want to puke. Nietzsche thought that if God were dead, there's really no right or wrong, no ultimate truth. Actually, he might have been right about that. He decided that everything's about a quest for wealth and strength and power. Pretty pagan, actually. So, you might say that he hated the Christian God—dead or alive."

"Well, this Nietzsche of yours is dead and gone."

"Oh yes. Died a madman. But he has his disciples, though most probably can't spell his name. In fact, most of them have never even heard of him."

Chapter Seventeen

June 23

Seth left Isbister to reflect on hating God and went to find Fiona, now sitting on one of the two stone benches on the north side of the Royal, gazing across the waters of Long Hope, now gone at last to gray glass. He sat beside her. She draped an arm around his shoulder.

"I really am feeling better, Seth. Maybe it's passing. That or meds or the gallons of tea Harriet and Grams keep pouring down me. In fact, I'd like a walk. Such a sweet day it is. Grams and Harriet are locked in conversation in the dining room."

"I saw."

"They've hit it off. Two feisty old dames who've conquered life in spite of it all. Gramps died about the same time as Harriet's Margaret. Both devastated, both alone, both plowing on."

He nodded in agreement. "Frode was talking about this Lifeboat Museum. It's just across the Ayre. Two miles, maybe three. You up for it?"

"Am I not my grandmother's granddaughter?" She stood and nodded her head in the direction of the Ayre. "So, what are we waiting for, Seth Ludington?"

They strolled hand-in-hand to the Ayre, across its causeway, then left down the barest of roads toward the tiny cluster of crofts named Brims. The Museum, they discovered, was the old Long Hope Lifeboat Station, now disused, a basic shed set hard on the water of Aith Hope on a spit of land called Brims Ness that poked its head bravely into the Pentland Firth separating Orkney from Scotland. The old runway that had launched lifeboats from the building into the water was still in place. The place was open, but unattended. Inside, the long narrow room was dominated by a decommissioned motorized lifeboat named the *Thomas McCann*, but they soon discovered that the emotional heart of the museum was the tragedy that took the lives of eight men, the entire crew of another vessel, *Lifeboat TGB*, on the night of March 17, 1969. In a Force 9 gale with waves to sixty feet, they had set out in response to an SOS from a Liberian-registered freighter, the *MV Irene*.

Fiona read the names of the lost men aloud. Three were named Johnston, three were named Kirkpatrick, all from tiny Brims. Two faded telegrams of condolence were tacked up behind glass, one from the Queen, the other from the Queen Mother. Another note quoted one of the crew, who had said their work called them to do "only what any human being would do."

"Do you think that's true, Seth? Is risking your life for strangers really what any human being would do?"

"*Any* human being? I rather doubt it. Those men didn't know a soul on that Liberian freighter. It begs the old question, it does. Is that kind of a love natural, I mean a love wider than kith and kin, one willing to sacrifice for other human beings simply because they're human beings? Or do we have to learn it? Or maybe it's a gift? I lean against the first possibility, that it's natural."

"Calvinist that you are."

"I would guess the man never would have thought self-sacrifice to be natural. Maybe I am a Calvinist. If so, it's barely, just barely."

They returned to the hotel to find Ingrid Gunn and Harriet van der Berg rising from their breakfast table, even though it was nearly two o'clock in the afternoon. Ingrid corralled her granddaughter, sitting her down and pressing yet more tea on her, tea accompanied by the cookies she had made, though she named them biscuits. Harriet, who had already eaten several of Ingrid's biscuits, made straight for Ludington.

"Seth, I need to speak with you. Ingrid has outlined several observations that could well be of crucial import in our case. Observations that the authorities have perhaps overlooked."

"Our case?"

"Well, that is to say, my confidence in Mr. McCormick is not supreme. Obdurate man. I do rather like Mr. Isbister. However, one must note that in two years' time they have gotten nowhere in their investigations. Perhaps we can be... well, supportive, you and I. We do have some experience in such matters, of course. Sit with me."

Somehow Ludington knew this was coming—the call to play the reluctant sleuth. Actually, not all that reluctant, he had to admit. They retreated outdoors to the same stone bench where he had found Fiona earlier. The bench and the day had since grown almost warm. The sky was cloudless and—rare in Orkney—nothing so much as a breeze troubled the water of Long Hope, now morphing from gray to blue under the gaze of the long midsummer sun.

Harriet had organized her thoughts, as she did every corner of her life. "Ingrid very precisely pointed out several cogent facts over our breakfast this morning. She has lived much of her life on these islands. They are rich in lore, both factual history and fanciful myth. Ingrid knows Orkney, Hoy especially, knows it all quite thoroughly. I like her, Dominie, I mean Seth."

He smiled at her correction. Part of him missed van der Berg's erstwhile habit of addressing him in the manner of her upbringing in the old Dutch world of the Hudson Valley. He had encouraged her to stop it, though. After all, the word meant "Lord," and it irritated his egalitarian instincts. But he had to confess that part of him appreciated it for the anachronism it was. The world was being stripped of too many of its antique curiosities.

She pressed on, "Ingrid outlined several potentially relevant veracities to me. She did not note their possible connections to Reverend Desmond's death, but I think she recognizes them. You will surely see the possible relationships, as did I. First, Ingrid pointed out the obvious, that the date of all three of these horrific murders is June 21, the summer solstice of course, at least most years. From what Mr. Isbister said to you, the police have recognized the consistency of the solstice date. But have they noted the theological implications of the summer solstice? You would surely know much more about such matters than I."

Harriet van der Berg was a mistress of subtle flattery. Her years as an executive assistant to powerful men had taught her the skill. She always knew just how far she could go without falling into fawning. Ludington smiled at her coaching compliment.

"I am a bit out of my depth with paganism, he said, "but I understand that both equinoxes and solstices figured prominently in many ancient religious systems. This appears to be true of whoever it was who built many of these Orkney sites. When erstwhile pagans converted to Christianity, the church often adopted and adapted the old dates and repurposed them. The winter solstice morphed into Christmas. Nobody really knows the date of Jesus' birth, but the winter solstice was the perfect day to mark it—the day the nights grow shorter and the days longer—the day light begins to overcome the darkness."

"Precisely as John's Gospel says, am I correct? And what did we do with the summer solstice, Seth?"

"Made it the Feast Day of John the Baptist. Actually, John's day is the 24th of June, and of course Christmas actually falls a few days after the actual winter solstice. The old calendars were off by a few days."

"So, do you think that the police—I mean Mr. McCormick and Mr. Isbister—have noted such theological considerations? Frankly, I think not. Seth, you must know that Ingrid is experiencing great remorse over this tragedy and what she imagines to be her role in it. She's guilt-laden about encouraging Fiona and our little group to visit Orkney in the first place. And she is filled with self-reproach over her telephone call to the newspaper and the subsequent story they printed, that article betraying the presence of clergy on Hoy. Now she is eager to assist in the resolution of the tragedy. At any rate, she pointed out to me that some of the Neolithic sites on these islands are religious, pagan of course, but not all of them. Some are secular, as it were. She observed that the three victims were not left at just any Neolithic archeological sites; they were all placed at Neolithic sites with religious associations. Two were placed in tombs, and the one in that Ring

106

of Brodgar. Her point was that these are not random Neolithic sites. All three are connected to the old religion. Frankly, one would have thought that the police might have noted this."

"Perhaps they have, but it's gotten them nowhere. Isbister seems savvy."

"Maybe. Seth, you are consistently generous in your appraisals of fellow human beings. Appropriate for your calling, I suppose." She smiled coyly at Ludington and continued, "Ingrid mentioned one additional matter. She was a bit reluctant to disclose this, but she did so when I asked her what she was suggesting by her observation that both the solstice and the sites of the murders had a connection with the old pagan religion."

Harriet paused for effect, which she tended to do only when she was about to speak something of great weight.

"Seth," she said slowly, "It seems that not all of Orkney's pagans sleep in history."

"What are you saying, Harriet?"

"Ingrid has a friend, a local woman about her age named Dee Ritch. Dee has a granddaughter, a young girl in her teens. The girl is just out of high school and working as a waitress in Kirkwall. Dee has told Ingrid—and told her more than once—how very worried she is about this granddaughter. Some time ago, she came to suspect that the girl had fallen in with a bad crowd in Kirkwall. The girl had chopped all her hair off, dyed it coal black and installed a ring that pierces her left nostril. Ingrid said a tear came to Dee's eye when she mentioned how she had once braided the girl's long red hair. Typical teenaged behavior perhaps, but then Ingrid said that Dee found some very troubling literature that the girl had left behind after an overnight visit. Literature about what is called "Neo-paganism."

Van der Berg raised a judgmental eyebrow and proceeded to unfold the details of the story.

"Dee's no church-goer, but I guess she still manages grace before the evening meal, at least when she has guests. Well, when the girl last visited, the child pointedly refused to join in table grace. Dee confronted her about it, and according to Ingrid, they had quite the scene. The girl had once been very close to her grandmother, but it seems she was now rather enjoying the effect her defiance had on poor Dee. Teenagers can be quite cruel, I understand. Anyway, in her anger, the girl blurted out that she is now a pagan, a Neo-pagan to be precise. She said that she had joined a group on Mainland and they call their group a 'hearth.' They meet weekly. Dee pressed her, and she told her that some in her hearth are a bit older and that a few of them are quite antagonistic toward Christianity, though her granddaughter says she is not herself. She claims it's all the same, different religions she means. Just different words and names. The girl—who seems to be a bit of a naïf—repeated to Dee some frightful things ostensibly said at these hearth meetings, venomous things about the church and Christian clergy. My guess is that the girl repeated it to poor Dee for its shock value. Really quite nasty, Seth. Ingrid relayed some of it to me. I would hesitate to articulate it to you."

"Don't hesitate to articulate, Harriet."

Van der Berg looked out the window and then back at Ludington. "Well, if you must. Right after refusing to participate in table grace, the girl told her grandmother that one of this group says the islands would do well to rid themselves of both the kirk and its lying ministers, all of whom he called... I can't say the word, Seth. It's perhaps familiar to you. It starts with a "b" and suggests a person of illegitimate parentage. That, of course, is the literal meaning. His use of the term was doubtless metaphorical."

"Doubtless," answered Seth, his irony lost on Harriet.

"Well," Seth added, "Isbister needs to know this. And McCormick. He's supposed to be back on Hoy any time. I'll talk to them, Harriet. They'll surely want to talk to Ingrid's friend. What was her name?"

"Dee Ritch. She lives here on Hoy, in a place called Lyness."

Ten minutes later, Ludington spotted the marked Police Scotland Ford Focus Estate approaching from the ferry dock. Constable Munro was at the wheel, Alastair McCormick in the passenger seat. The car pulled into the Royal's parking area next to the tour bus. McCormick extricated himself from the car with a grunt. Isbister was at the door of the Royal, indulgently awaiting his superior.

Ludington rose from the stone bench and rounded the hotel to intercept the two policemen. He caught them as they met without words of greeting or handshake. He said to both of them, " Do you have a moment?" Some connections have come to light that might be helpful to you."

Isbister said, "Of course." McCormick merely nodded, but followed Seth into the hotel. The three men sat in the corner of the dining room, the two cops on one side of the bare table, Ludington across from them.

"So, what is it?" McCormick asked.

"A couple of connections that might be helpful, and then a bit of news, something you may or may not be aware of."

Isbister nodded interest and asked, "Connections?" McCormick looked out the window and said nothing.

"Might be nothing, but, well… the murders all occurred on June 21, the summer solstice, of course. And the three of them, all Christian clergy, were found in Neolithic sites. Not just any such sites, but ones with religious associations—pagan, of course, the old religion. Point is, both the sites and the summer solstice were of significance in the old paganism. It may be important. You would probably know better than I, but it strikes me as curious."

McCormick snorted incredulity. Isbister furrowed his brow.

Then he told them about the existence of a group of Neo-pagans in Orkney. As he related this last bit, he acknowledged that it was fifth-hand information, passed mouth to ear too many times, Dee's granddaughter to Dee, Dee to Ingrid, Ingrid to Harriet, Harriet to himself, and from him to the cops. Such telephone game information was often the bane of accuracy.

When Ludington finished, Isbister said to both men, "I can talk to Dee Ritch. I don't really know her, but I know where she lives." He looked to his superior and said, "I can pop by and get the name of her granddaughter. This could be a lead, sir. Unlikely, but maybe."

"Ach, Isbister, it's just more of your typical Orkney nonsense. What? Druids and pagan priests and human sacrifices? We know the second victim was a pedo. I've seen this stuff before. Bet the first one was as well, no matter what you think. Whatever, our killer finally runs out of pedos and decides to take it out on any bloke in a collar who's handy."

Ludington decided to push the point.

"With all due respect, Mr. McCormick, perhaps he's motivated by a hatred of clergy for other reasons. What I mean to say is that maybe his animus has nothing to do with having been a victim of sexual abuse. Perhaps he hates clergy simply because he hates what they stand for."

As Ludington offered this challenge he was only too aware that any speech that begins "with all due respect" is a gauntlet thrown down.

Isbister bravely joined him in the challenge.

"Mr. McCormick, I know we've been over this a thousand times. But it's all surmise, the past sexual abuse as motivation, I mean. Let me talk to Dee Ritch and her granddaughter. What do we have to lose, sir?"

Ludington could only imagine what it took for Isbister to address his younger superior as "sir" and twice in one conversation.

Chapter Eighteen

June 23

"Reverend Ludington, have you seen Sarah? Hope and me haven't seen her anywhere, not today or yesterday."

Ted Buskirk had found Ludington in the Royal's lounge as he was slipping his phone into his shirt pocket. After his awkward conversation with McCormick and Isbister, he had again called the only number he had for Henry Barkman, chair of the board of Philadelphia Theological Seminary, about his email marked "urgent" on Desmond's phone. He had again gotten voicemail and had left another message, this one a tad more urgent, again after Oatmeal had barked. It was four in the afternoon on Orkney, eleven in the morning on the American East Coast. The man was retired and ought to be at home. Maybe he was out of town. He'd have to call the seminary in the morning. They would have a work or cell number for him. He turned to face Ted Buskirk, who had a vaguely urgent look on his face.

"Reverend Ludington, we haven't seen Sarah, haven't seen her at meals or anywhere. It's got me and Hope sorta worried. She never misses breakfast, but she didn't show up yesterday, not this morning either. We usually eat with her. And she's been kinda emotional the whole trip. Weird."

"Have you tried her room, knocked on her door?"

"Yep. Nada. No answer."

Seth thanked Ted for his concern and went to find his wife who was sitting with her grandmother in the lounge pouring over photos on Fiona's phone.

Shots of the unfolding gut-renovations of their brownstone on 84th Street in New York, more recent people pictures taken days earlier in Edinburgh, Iona, and Balmoral, and a fuzzy sonogram of the twins taken just before they left New York a week earlier, both clearly—at least to trained eyes—girls.

"Fiona, would you come with me to check on Sarah? Ted says they haven't seen her since the night of the wedding. Better to have the two of us check together. Don't really want to barge into her room, a man alone."

Fiona nodded her assent and led her husband up the stairs to Sarah's room. Seth knocked on the door. The rooms at the Royal were not numbered, but named after smaller islands that lay around Hoy. Sarah's was labeled *"Flotta."* There was no answer. He knocked more loudly and called out her name, then again, almost shouting the second time. Still no response.

He looked to his side at Fiona. She whispered, "We'd best go in and check, Seth."

Ludington turned the knob and pushed at the door. Like all the rooms at the Royal, there was no lock. Nevertheless, the door resisted. Something was blocking it. He pushed harder. The door finally gave away and he tumbled into the room, almost falling to his knees. He saw that a chair had been wedged under the doorknob. He also saw that Sarah Mrazek's bed was occupied. The bedclothes were a tangled mess. He turned to his wife, and they both moved to the side of the bed.

"Sarah?" he said, as a question.

He lay his hand on her shoulder and shook her ample body, "Sarah? Are you okay?"

A moan, then a barely audible croak, "Go away."

Fiona pulled the chair that had been used to block the door over to the bedside and sat in it. Seth stood behind her, resting both hands on his wife's shoulders. Better to explore the depths of this woman-to-woman, he thought, whatever this was.

Her face was turned from them, buried in a pillow. "Sarah, it's Fiona. Would you like to talk? We're worried about you."

Sarah Mrazek sat up in her rumpled bed and turned a blotchy face to Fiona and Seth. Her eyes were swollen from weeping. "He's dead. There's nothing to talk about. I can't believe he's dead."

This declaration was accompanied with silent tears. Seth could see that the pillow was wet with those that had come before. He thought it a wonder there were any left in her to weep.

Fiona turned to look up at her husband and said, "Let me sit with her." Seth assumed his wife was hoping her silent presence might coax the woman into speaking of her too-extravagant sorrow.

He said, "Wise. Thank you, Fiona. I really need to talk to Harry about something."

Ludington left his wife at Sarah's bedside and found Harry and Georgia Mulholland bent over a card table in the dining room working a jigsaw puzzle. They looked to be about a third of the way through it, one of the pile of puzzles stacked in a corner of the lounge. The tour group's forced sequestration had come to this, Seth thought to himself. The puzzle's box cover was propped up on the table with a drinking glass. It read, "1,000 Pieces," and displayed a photograph of the present Queen and the Duke of Edinburgh riding in an elaborate gilded carriage. The puzzle looked to be formidable. Seth heard Georgia say to her husband, "I'm stacking horse pieces over here. And Harry, do refrain from tapping them every time you fit one. Unbecoming little declaration of triumph."

Seth did not take the empty chair at the table. He cleared his throat and said, "Harry, do you have a minute? I need to talk to you about something."

Mulholland looked at his wife, who said, "You go ahead. I'll work on Prince Philip."

Harry Mulholland was the Clerk of Session of Old Stone Church, the highest office to which a layman might be elected in a Presbyterian congregation. The Clerk was a person with whom the pastor obviously had to work closely. The two of them had done so dutifully but awkwardly in the couple of weeks immediately following the unhappy events of the prior Lent. But after Harry's revelation and prayer at the May Session meeting, the two men had rediscovered the deeply appreciative, even affectionate, relationship they had previously enjoyed. Sometimes forgiveness requires not only truth and grace, but hard bluntness and softening time.

The two men walked outdoors and around the Royal to the stone benches facing across Long Hope. The day had warmed enough that Harry took off his Harris tweed jacket, this one loden green with brown leather elbow patches. They sat side-by-side, looking not at each other, but at the gray water before them.

"Harry, there's something off with Sarah Mrazek. It's some of the things she's said to me and Fiona, especially when she's been drinking. And she was the last person to sign up for this trip. She didn't apply to go until after Phil and Penny came on board. She hadn't expressed any interest before that. Both Fiona and I have watched her since we left New York. Harry, she was utterly fixated on Phil Desmond. She talked about him all the time. And she really knew a bit too much about him. Now the woman's absolutely distraught, grief way out of proportion. She's locked herself in her room since yesterday. Pushed a chair against the door. We had to break in. Fiona's sitting with her now. Harry, she seems to be one very fragile young woman."

Ludington knew that Harry Mulholland's work in the NYPD had included not only homicide, but that in earlier years he had worked several stalking cases. He had told his new pastor as much when they had first met nearly two years earlier. To lubricate that first conversation in which he had told Ludington he was retired, Seth had asked the stock follow-up question put to retirees, "What kind of work did you do." He had been mildly surprised when Mulholland said he'd been a policeman. Ludington's second question had been, "NYPD detective, fascinating... Did you specialize in anything particular?" He had answered, his bluntness intended to jolt, "Before murder it was stalking."

Harry now smoothed the coarse fabric of the tweed jacket he had laid across his knees, "Seth, it reminds me of some of the cases I worked mid-career, stalking cases, one of them high profile. The last one became a homicide, not the high profile one, though."

"You think Sarah could have been stalking Phil Desmond?"

"Could be, Seth. Stalkers tend to be needy types, socially awkward, problems with intimacy. There are different kinds. I went to a seminar on stalking after my first case. Down in DC. They said it takes a variety of forms, all neurotic of course, sometimes even psychotic, they told us. Back in the '90's some shrinks in Australia came up with a sort of stalking typology. It helped me understand what I was up against with these guys. They're more often men, you know. Some want to find intimacy with a person they've zeroed in on. Sometimes they think their love is actually reciprocated; sometimes they know it's not. And there was one type they labeled predator. Real psychos. No interest in a relationship. Just want power and control. They can be a real threat. But most stalkers are simply sad and lonely, not usually dangerous. A major bother if you're the one getting stalked, often a very scary major bother. Sarah may have been fixated on Desmond, maybe even stalking him, but I don't think she's the predator type. Not from what I've seen."

That's helpful, Harry. Whatever is going on with her, Sarah needs to get help."

"I know they do therapy on them. Probably better than locking them up. I could never quite figure out what they really wanted, I mean my stalkers. Did they really want intimacy with the person they were after? I always kinda wondered what would happen if the person they were stalking responded, you know, positively. I used to have a collie dog that loved to chase Canada geese in the park. Never caught one of course. Geese can fly, dogs can't. But I always wondered what would happen if she'd caught one. Not sure she knew."

Seth looked at his Clerk of Session and added a parallel memory. "I had to take a psych course in college, undergrad at Michigan. Required, even of a history major. Taught by a young teaching assistant. My expectations were low. I was wrong. I remember a lot of it, especially a lecture she gave on intimacy. Don't recall the words so much as a gesture she made to demonstrate how we often feel about love and intimacy. She put down her notes and came around the lectern. With one hand, she made the come close gesture – palm horizontal, upturned, fingers wiggling, beckoning us to come closer. With the other hand, she made the stay away gesture, the stop gesture—palm vertical, raised toward us and fingers up, stiff and spread. Then she smiled gently and said, "Most of us do something like this, at least sometimes."

Seth then offered the twin gestures, not toward Harry, but at the flat water of Long Hope before them, and said, "To love and be loved can be terrifying—wonderful and fearsome at the same time."

"Seth, if Sarah was stalking Phil, my guess is Penny would know."

"Probably, probably. No reason to ask her now, though. She's got more than enough to deal with."

Chapter Nineteen

The two policemen, one stubbornly Scottish and stubborn in general, the other insistently Orcadian, had spent an unhappy night in one of the two rooms still available at the Royal Hotel. It was a tiny attic space bereft of the luxury of an *en suite* bath and furnished with a pair of camp beds set uncomfortably but necessarily close to each other. Constable Abby Munro had been blessed with the other open room, named "*Swona,*" on the second floor and with facilities attached.

Magnus Isbister was no complainer, but he grumbled out these details to Seth Ludington over a breakfast he had barely touched, there being no one else handy to whom he might explain the dark circles under his eyes.

He pushed the slab of black pudding to the edge of his plate and said, "He snores. He'll surely soon get himself back to the comforts of the Highland Park House, one way or another. His night in our room—which is aptly named "*Muckle Skerry*" by the way—seems to have greatly displeased him."

The unhappy detective from Inverness was sitting alone at a table under a window overlooking Long Hope, eating as heartily as Isbister wasn't. The two men watched as McCormick pulled his phone from his jacket pocket after it had launched into an impressively loud ring. As McCormick listened to the call, he pulled a small notebook from his jacket pocket and jotted down some lines.

After McCormick finished the call, he pushed away his empty plate as if

117

in displeasure, rose and strode over to Isbister and Ludington. "Autopsy report is back. Mrs. Desmond has a right to hear it. Might as well go over it just the once, simple as it is. You'll want to hear it as well, Isbister. Where is she?"

Isbister looked questioningly at Ludington, who answered, "She's been walking a lot. Not alone, of course. With Harriet or my wife. I think she's probably with Miss van der Berg."

As he spoke, Penny Desmond and Harriet van der Berg came through the Royal's front door and entered the dining room, arm in arm but unsmiling. Ludington judged it happily providential that van der Berg was present when Penny Desmond had come to this unmarked and tragic intersection in time. The two women had known each other – though off and on – for half a century.

McCormick turned to them, "Mrs. Desmond, may Chief Inspector Isbister and I have a word."

"Of course, but I'd like Reverend Ludington to be present again... I insist."

The two policemen, Penny Desmond and Seth Ludington retreated to the now familiar far corner of the dining room. Isbister pulled the table as deep into that corner as he could and arranged four chairs so that none faced into the room. It was as private a space as the Royal offered without retreating to a bedroom.

McCormick opened his notebook, "Mrs. Desmond, your husband died as a result of an overdose of a drug called zolpidem. Looking at his notes, he named the drug class in disjointed syllables, "Non-benzo-dia-zep-ines. Commonly known under the brand name Ambien. "

A startled look washed over Isbister's face at this news. He started to speak, but checked himself.

"He also had a high—very high—blood alcohol level. Can't get an exact number that long after death, but it was high."

Penny Desmond looked down at the table, then out the window at the water of Long Hope. She was wearing no mascara that might have blackened the lone tear that trailed down her cheek. She said nothing for a moment, then asked, "Would it have been peaceful?'

"Ambien is a sleep drug. I assume so. But it reacts with alcohol. Can induce coma, they said." McCormick paused and added, "Sometimes death, if there's enough of both."

The Scottish cop looked back at his notes, "Just a few other things." He read what he had jotted down from the phone call he had gotten a few minutes earlier, "'No evidence of soil, grass, or peat materials in the bronchial tubes or lungs.' Means he didn't suffocate, Mrs. Desmond. He was asleep, probably already dead when the stuff was put in his mouth. He wouldn't have even known."

As McCormick relayed these details to the widow, Ludington was pleased to see that even this rough-edged cop could deliver such news with a tincture of mercy.

"Three other things," McCormick said, reading again, "'No evidence of cancer, heart disease, or other morbidities. Significant muscular atrophy as might be expected in a very sedentary seventy-six year old,' it says."

McCormick suddenly pinched his notebook closed, without mentioning the third "other thing" in the autopsy report.

Guessing that the gathering in the corner of the dining room may have borne discomforting news to Penny Desmond, Harriet van der Berg walked over to the table and put a hand on the woman's shoulder. Penny looked up at her and said, "Could we have another walk, Harriet? Walking helps."

After the two of them had left, Isbister dared the hanging question, what he guessed to be the third "other thing." In a voice inflected with inquiry, the Orkney cop said, "Injection site?"

McCormick answered with a black look and shook his head.

The awkwardness was broken by Isbister's phone ringing, classic doorbell, but soft. He took the call without leaving the table. The caller on the other end was speaking loudly enough for all of them to hear. It was an eager young male voice with the thickest of Orcadian accents. "Mr. Isbister, it's Andrew here. The note's arrived, it has. In the post this mornin'. Exactly as the other two—letters cut out of magazines and pasted on a piece of cardboard, nine-by-eleven, unfolded, just like ransom notes in films. Reads the same as the second – 'ANOTHER APOSTLE OF LIES SILENCED.'

119

Postmarked Stromness on Saturday, day before yesterday."

"Thank you, Andy. You're handling it with the gloves, of course."

"Yes sir. I guessed what it might be before I opened it. Addressed to the Kirkwall station, it was, to nobody in particular, like before. I sealed it up in a plastic evidence bag, the envelope it came in as well."

"Well done, Andy, well done. I'm thinking Mr. McCormick will be along on the next ferry to Houton, or maybe Stromness. The Houton ferry arrives at noon, I think, but I'll check on both. You may need to meet him at the one or the other. I'll let you know."

He rang off and said to McCormick, "That was Constable Harris in Kirkwall, he said…"

McCormick broke in, "We heard. We all heard, Isbister. Well, seems our Sod Stuffer's a day late with his correspondence this time 'round."

He rose and said, "We're both off to your big island, Isbister, you and me. It's him again of course. Now it's completely obvious. I'll want you to get onto that list of ferry passengers leaving Hoy. I'll focus on this note. Munro'll stay here to keep an eye on this lot."

Isbister nodded and said, "What about talking to Dee Ritch before we go? It could be something. I mean her granddaughter, the solstice, and Christian-hating Neo-pagans flitting about Orkney."

"The note and the passenger names are what matter, Isbister. They're solid, not speculation. I want us focused on them. And now I'll want a quick shower. Tell Munro I need to use the one in her room. And get us on one of your damn ferries off this rock." He stood and left for his morning shower in the room named *"Swona."*

Isbister phoned Constable Munro who was standing guard outside the hotel's front door keeping track of Americans. He warned her about the impending shower to be taken in her room and told her that he and McCormick might need a ride to the ferry. "You'll stay here, Abby, keep an eye on everybody. Don't let them wander about on their own."

As Isbister finished the call, Ludington said softly, "Injection site?"

"You might as well know, Seth. The other two victims had been injected with fentanyl, deadly dose. Synthetic opiate, easy enough to get on the street, even here. And their autopsies showed that both had also ingested a drug called Rohypnol, prior to the fentanyl injection, or so we assume. Popularly called a 'roofie,' both here and in the States. Date rape drug. No Ambien in them, either time. Serial killers do change their M.O. sometimes. Just surprised me, it did." He looked at Ludington, "Was I that obvious?"

Ludington nodded and asked another question, "A day late? The note I mean."

"Perhaps. The first two were stuck in a post box either the night of the murder or very early the next morning. We received the first the morning of the 23rd, the second arrived the day after the murder, afternoon of the 22nd. Desmond was killed the night of the 21st and the ferries back to The Mainland didna' take up again till the afternoon of the 22nd. We know the note was mailed from Stromness, which is on The Mainland of course, the next day, Saturday the 22nd—surely late on the 22nd. Point is, he posted it rather later than the other two. We've got the names of every soul on both ferries from Hoy to The Mainland since they started running again. There werena' that many, and none of them likely – women and children mostly. A few men, and I know most of them. How did we miss him?"

Seth nodded at Isbister's chronology and its implications. He said, "Well, it means he's got to be on Mainland now, not here. A bit of a relief, I guess. Got himself off this island somehow. I mean to mail the note from Stromness."

"So it would seem."

Isbister paused and added, "Reverend Ludington, perhaps Dee Ritch's granddaughter could use a peedie pastoral visit from you. Talk some theology with the lass, ye ken."

Isbister did not throw Ludington a wink—the matter was too grave for such a gesture—but he might as well have.

Chapter Twenty

After picking at his breakfast, Ludington found Harriet van der Berg staring uneasily at the one-thousand puzzle pieces she had carefully spread out on a card table in the Royal's lounge. She had turned them all face up and was presently sorting them by color. The box that had held them sat on the chair next to her, prognosticating the final product of her efforts—a photograph entitled *Skara Brae by Moonlight.* It was an earie and arty shot of yet another of Orkney's Neolithic sites, this one a clustered village of stone houses that had been unearthed and awakened from its Brigadoon slumber by a wild storm—yet another storm—in 1850. It was a secular, not sacred, site—as if the ancients made much of a distinction. And no bodies had shown up at Skara Brae, either in 1850 or more recently.

Nodding at the puzzle pieces, Harriet said, "Do I dare hope that you have come to save me from this, Seth Ludington?"

"Perhaps." He sat, picked up one of the puzzle pieces, looked at it and said, "I think this one's a bit of heathery turf. It'll go near the bottom somewhere." He set it back down. "There really are a lot of puzzles in this world."

"Not all of them solvable, but most of them more important to work out than this one, to be sure." She nodded at the sea of tiny pieces of *Skara Brae by Moonlight* spread across the card table.

"Isbister as much as told me to have a talk with Dee Ritch's granddaughter. McCormick has him busy checking out the list of ferry passengers—

everybody who left Hoy on both ferries after Desmond was killed. Their assumption is that the guy got himself back to Mainland on one of them. Isbister told me he has sent a note like the last two times. Anonymous of course. Letters cut out of magazines, would you believe? It was postmarked from Stromness. Mailed on Saturday, so he's got to be there now."

"Seth, there are other ways to leave this island. A private vessel perhaps."

"Possible. But Scapa Flow was still churned up from the storm. It would have been iffy for a small boat, but it might have been possible. I think Isbister understands that. He's not keen on the list of ferry passengers. He's looked it through, he said. It's not very long, and he just doesn't think it promising, but McCormick insists."

Ludington leaned back in his chair. "Harriet, you mentioned Ingrid's self-reproach about the newspaper article. I understand it completely. In fact, I identify with it. I took on the leadership of this tour group. I brought them to these islands knowing two clergymen had been murdered on them exactly the time of the year we'd be here. Point is, I guess I simply have to do something. I can't sit here and pray that they find whoever it was who took Phil's life, a life for which I was responsible."

"Prayer usually ends up inviting some kind of action, doesn't it? I believe you have occasionally preached as much."''

"Harriet, would you talk to Ingrid and fish for the name of Dee's Ritch's granddaughter? And see if you can find out the name of the restaurant where she works in Kirkwall. If I ask her about it, she's going to get suspicious and say something to Fiona. Just see if you can work it out of her. Curiosity, idle chatter you know."

"Are you suggesting that women chatter idly, more so than men?"

"Of course not. Never. But it does seem that you and Ingrid have become friendly enough for you to wiggle it out of her. It's less suspect than if the question were to come from me. You are good at this, Harriet."

"Flattery is my métier, Seth. You wear it less comfortably."

Ludington smiled at her rebuke. "Fiona says her grandmother is driving down from Rackwick for a late lunch."

"I know. I was asked to join them."

Two hours later, Harriet found her pastor entering the Royal as he returned from a visit he had decided to make to St. Columba's Kirk down the road.

"I had to have another look at those wooden panels they like to think washed up from the Spanish Armada. Good story—unlikely story—but they are rather extravagant to have been the work of Scottish Presbyterians."

"Another mystery to whet your insistent curiosity, I suppose. Humm. We had a chatty brunch, Ingrid and Fiona and myself. Dee Ritch's granddaughter is named Shelly Waterson, her daughter's daughter, obviously. She waits tables five days a week at an establishment called The Harborside Fry in Kirkwall. Near the water, again obviously. Dee's mentioned to Ingrid that the girl works only weekdays, so she's likely to be on shift today, lunch and dinner both. She spends the week on Mainland and comes back to Hoy weekends. She has what Ingrid calls a 'bedsit' in Kirkwall. A studio apartment, I assume."

Seth nodded his appreciation and went to find Else or Frode to see if he might take the Peugeot on the two-thirty ferry to Houton. He found Else, and though she was always eager to please her guests, she agreed on the loan of their only vehicle if Ludington would do the bit of food shopping she had planned to undertake herself in Kirkwall later that day. She apologized for the request in Norwegian-warped English, "I am hating to ask such a favorite of a guest, Mr. Ludington. I hope you do not find it a problem. Keep a total of your costs for back payment."

Her shopping list proved to be brief. Ludington thanked her for the loan of the car, assured her that a "favorite" was no problem, and promised to return the car that evening.

He caught the Houton ferry just in time and rolled the car neatly onboard, remembering the last time he'd driven onto a car ferry, one that ran from Charlevoix to Beaver Island in Lake Michigan. His parents had decided to celebrate his mother's 60th birthday at a resort on the island, avoiding having to host overnight guests at their own place in Pentwater, a hundred miles to the south on the Lake. Even though what they called "the cottage" was certainly large enough for any birthday house party.

He had asked his mother, "Why Beaver Island?" "Never been there," was her answer. Quite a good answer, he had thought to himself.

He got out of the car on the Orkney ferry, noting that the vessel was not making its scheduled stop at the island of Flotta. Nobody to get off or on, he surmised. He stood at the rail and watched as the boat slipped by the unsightly North Sea oil terminal on the northwest side of that island and then moved beyond it and out into Scapa Flow, still rolling a bit from the storm. He went to the other side of the ferry to get a better look at the little uninhabited isle named Cava resting flat and silent off their forward port quarter. He thought to himself that he was doing precisely what both the police and he himself had forbidden him and his group to do. He was setting off alone, a clergyman headed to the very island that was apparently home to a clergy killer.

Even more dicey, he was going in search of a contrary teenager who'd gotten herself into paganism and was going to try to ferret information out of her about a little cluster of fellow pagans—pagans he vaguely suspected might—just might—know something about the circumstances that led to the murder of three Christian clergymen. Ever since Isbister had hinted about his having a talk with the girl, he had been imagining how he might approach Shelly Waterson. He was not a cop with authority to ask questions and demand answers. He could play reporter or writer, but that might raise her defenses. He could simply be an American curious about the old religion of Orkney, but doubted that would be quite enough. He knew he had one resource he could make use of, one way to encourage a young woman to open up to him. The very thought of doing it made him uneasy, needful as it might be. Though the sun was blazing and there was the barest breeze, he pulled the collar of his windbreaker tight around his neck. Looming guilt chilled him to the bone.

After landing in Houton, he Googled directions to the Tesco in Kirkwall so he could take care of Else's shopping list. He was surprised to find asparagus on it, and even more surprised to find piles of it in the Tesco. How extraordinary to be able to buy asparagus in this Ultima Thule of a place. She wanted five pounds. Frode would obviously be serving asparagus in the next day or two. With Hollandaise, or perhaps with only olive oil, sea salt and fresh pepper. Frode was a fine chef.

He loaded the groceries into the Peugeot's trunk and Googled The Harborside Fry. The Google voice—still the chipper American woman whom he and Fiona called Monica—wove him through the narrow and labyrinthine lanes of gray stone Kirkwall. It looked much like many a Scottish town, but it was especially tidy and had a Nordic accent. Most buildings were low and tight to the street with doors often brightly painted. The red sandstone tower of St. Magnus Cathedral rose proudly several streets to his right. The restaurant was indeed near the harbor, but not on the water. He drove past it to find a precious parking space in the Harbour Car Park.

The Harborside Fry, oddly spelled without the "u" on the quaint carved wooden sign above the entrance, was more pub than restaurant. Dee Ritch had said Shelly was a waitress in a restaurant. She was doubtless happier to imagine her granddaughter as a restaurant waitress than as a pub barmaid. The place was smallish and dark, but looked clean enough. The oily odor that greeted Ludington as he entered betrayed the featured fare to be the predictable fish and chips. He found a small table near the lone window and sat, wondering what the odds were of being served by Shelly Waterston. The odds proved very good, as it soon became apparent that the girl comprised the entire wait staff of The Harborside Fry at four o'clock on a Monday afternoon.

She approached his table with a smile and without a menu. She was attractive in an elfin way, hair chopped short and dyed as coal black as Dee Ritch had lamented. A row of piercings—tiny gold rings—descended down her right earlobe. And the one in her nostril.

"What can I get for ye, sir?"

Ludington asked for a half pint of whatever local stout she might recommend. She suggested Orkney Skull Splitter. "Dark and complex," she added.

"Skull Splitter?" Ludington asked her, offering a vaguely flirtatious raised eyebrow. "Sounds dangerous."

"It's not your skull it'll split. Named after a Viking Earl of Orkney back when, dude named Thorfinn Skull Splitter."

"How can I resist?"

Skull Splitter was as dark and complex as promised. Ludington nursed it while he played with his phone. When his glass was nearly empty, he brought up the Neo-pagan website he had poked around that morning, the home page of the SPC—the Scottish Pagan Community. When Shelly came by to ask about a second Skull Splitter, he was careful to lay the phone down on the table where she would see it—open to the SPC's home page.

She looked at the phone and then at Ludington, "Are you into the old religion, then?"

"Curious, just curious. And yes to another Skull Splitter." He ordered it though he had no intention of drinking it. One had begun to take its toll.

He looked up at the girl and held her eyes a bit too long. He felt guilty flirting with a teenager twenty years his junior, even if it was for a cause. Seth Ludington perhaps looked a decade younger than his near forty years and he was joltingly handsome. His two-year college girlfriend, almost fiancé, and Fiona's immediate predecessor, had once told him that he was one of the few beautiful men she had ever known who had not been morally corrupted by his looks. Her beauty, he came to understand, had corrupted her, a reality that had finally soured their relationship. He brushed his long dark hair out of his eyes, knowing as he did so that he was using his appearance to work the poor girl. She blushed in response and went off to fetch a second Skull Splitter. When she returned with it she sat herself in the chair across the table from him.

She looked at Ludington and said, "You're an American I'm guessing. We get a few in Orkney. Not many."

"I'm from New York City." He hesitated a moment and said, "I'm James." Not quite a lie. It was his middle name.

"Beuy, New York City. Never met a buddy from New York City. I'm Shelly." She smiled, but slightly. "So, I've been gettin' into the old religion myself. We've a peedie group of us gets together to talk about it, you know. Meet Monday nights, we do. Tonight, that is… I'm off work at eight."

Chapter Twenty-One

June 24

Seth Ludington answered her subtle invitation—not with a word, but with a wry smile and a bare nod that embarrassed him even as he offered them. The awkwardness of the moment was broken by a noisy gaggle of men in blue boiler suits bursting through the door. They were talking loudly for Orcadians, a soft-spoken tribe if ever there was one. They were obviously after-work regulars, as they greeted Shelly by name. She rolled her eyes, rose from the table and said, "Gotta go."

As she got to her feet Ludington spoke her name, "Shelly…" She looked back at him. He smiled and said, "Any chance I could get some of your fish and chips?"

"You bet," she answered with an Americanism. Ludington guessed that she, like most of the world, watched too much American television.

The fish and chips came in a single faux newspaper cone laid on a heavy china plate. Real newspaper probably bled ink into the fish. Shelly even brought him a knife and fork wrapped in a cloth napkin. The fish and the chips were fresh from the fryer and so hot Ludington had to let them cool. Hot and fresh was the secret that made the Brit classic not merely palatable, but delectable.

He left the restaurant at about six o'clock. The place had filled by then and Shelly was busy, but not so busy that she failed to catch his eye as he turned to find her on his way out the door. Both waved cautiously. A sly see-you-later wave.

Ludington had a couple of hours to kill, so he wove himself through the tangle of Kirkwall's streets toward the looming tower of St. Magnus. The Cathedral had been on the tour group's itinerary, but he was unsure whether they would now get to see it. Ludington very much wanted to. He had read that it was one of the best preserved Medieval cathedrals in Britain. It was said to be small as cathedrals went, but its perfect proportions disguised its modest size. As he approached the church, he saw that the walls were built of alternating layers of yellow and red sandstone, lending the building a merry, almost playful, face. It was open but empty late on a Monday afternoon. He picked up an informational brochure at the front door. It included a floor plan that led him down the center aisle to a side pier in the choir where rested the relics of St. Magnus himself. The church had been built to house them in the middle of the twelfth century. It was this resting place of old bones that he especially wanted to see.

As a Protestant, Ludington did not believe that relics—even those of the saintly—held any special power, but the Medieval Roman Catholics who built the cathedral did. Like most every corner of Scotland and nearly all of its kirks, St. Magnus Cathedral had been Protestant for most of the last 500 of its years. Protestant though it was, they had kept the bones nevertheless. Out of regard for both history and the man, Ludington assumed.

Magnus Erlendsson, one of the two earls of Orkney in 1115, had been a murder victim. He had been killed on the order of a jealous nephew and rival for power. The story, woven into the *Orkneyinga Saga*, had it that it was the nephew's cook who had struck the blow, and had done so as Magnus knelt in prayer. Orkney had been ostensibly Christianized by then, but much of life and most of politics had yet to be converted from Viking manners. Indeed, Orkney would be half pagan for centuries, even after everyone had been baptized. Maybe it still was. Maybe we all still are. After all, both Magnus' ambitious nephew and the cook with the axe were Christians, officially at least.

Seth Ludington had always been suspicious of precipitous changes and quick conversions, whether historical or personal. He recalled an acquaintance in seminary who said he had been saved five times. The man relished telling the stories of five emotion-charged conversion experiences. But in Seth Ludington's own experience, real change almost always took time. The world does change, people actually do change... sometimes, but usually with time.

If anyone understood that, it was he. For twenty years—until Easter Day a few months earlier—he had hidden the secret of the death of a young girl with whom he had toyed the summer after his sophomore year of college. He had not caused her death, but he was sleeping off a drunk in the cockpit of his father's yacht as she drowned trying to swim for the shore. His parents' money had hushed it up for twenty years, successfully veiling both his complicity and the fact that the girl had been pregnant with his child. For twenty years the truth of it had slept restlessly in him—silent and corrosive—until he finally had to own it—own it to his wife, own it to his church, own it to himself. His wife had forgiven him, and so had the church, mostly anyway. He was still in the process of forgiving himself. He understood enough about the Seth Ludington he had become to realize that what he was presently doing—this insistent sleuthing—and what he had done over the last Lent in New York—two quests to out the truth—were probably a curious sort of penance, atonement undertaken to set something right because he had once set something so wrong.

He reached out and touched the pillar that held Magnus Erlendsson's bones. He did so out of respect for Magnus and for every victim of wrongful death. As he rested his hand on the cool stone he could not but think of Philip Desmond. He could not but think of the infant bones that had rested for fifty years in the ash pit of his home in New York. He could not but remember Sara, who had drowned that summer night, drowned with his child in her womb.

He pulled his hand from the stone which suddenly felt so cold it burned. He turned and sat in a nearby pew facing into the chancel where a cross— a smallish and delicately carved wooden cross—was set atop the reredos. Another murder victim.

Seth Ludington knew that he was hardly totally converted himself. He had never had anything like a conversion experience, but he did know that he had changed over the years, over many years. Change had first seeded itself in him his senior year at Michigan when he had begun to suspect that life might be more or less without meaning, or at least without any meaning beyond a pursuit of pleasant things. At age twenty-two he had all the pleasant things any human being might want, but he was empty. This ache for something like transcendence, a something-beyond-himself around which to shape a life, was what had led him to seminary. He hoped they might know the answers there. They did purport to have them—in their books and the lectures. But for him, the answers had not come so much in words as they had come in people, people who accepted him as he was, people he met who lived lives beyond themselves. Very slowly, something like an answer had wormed its way to him.

He thought of the day more than a decade ago when a long-haired, left-over Jesus freak working the crowds in Times Square had strode up to him and asked him if he were saved. Ludington had been startled by the question and answered, "I think so." The kid had then asked him, "When?" He had answered, "I don't know." But later, he realized he did know. He had been saved over time, a long time, starting two-thousand years ago.

Seth Ludington knew that his life had been an easy ride, a downhill coast propelled by privilege, nudged along by the fact that he was white and male. And wealthy. And handsome. He felt guilty about all these things that were not his doing. But in time and over time, this guilt embedded in him because of who he was, as well as the guilt occasioned by what he had done and not done, was translated into a longing to do something that made some sort of a difference to the world. He disliked that phrase. "Making a difference" was such a tired cliché, but like some clichés, it held fragments of truth in its weary hands. Helping to find a murderer would perhaps be a way to make a difference. Precluding yet more death would surely be a way to make a difference.

He looked down at the stone floor and thought about the evening that lay before him – an assignation with a teenager in black lipstick and multiple piercings, then attending a Neo-pagan hearth in some dark Orcadian pub.

He decided it would be a good idea to pray.

Chapter Twenty-Two

June 24

The front steps of the Cathedral faced west and were well warmed by a slant evening sun that was nowhere near setting. Seth Ludington sat on the hard stone, pulled out his cell phone and called Harriet van der Berg.

"Harriet, I've met your Shelly Waterston."

"She's not mine, Seth."

"Well, she's invited me along to her hearth. They meet Monday evenings as it happens. Lucky for us."

"Providence, Seth, not luck. We've had this conversation before."

"I simply wanted you to know. No need to say anything about it to Fiona. I'll catch the late ferry back to Hoy. Just tell her I should be there by eleven or so. How is she feeling?"

"I assume you mean the morning sickness. I think the worst of it has perhaps past. I certainly hope it has. She ate a hearty dinner. One must assume that nurse Wilson's medication has had a salubrious effect."

He slipped his phone back into the pocket of the suede blazer Fiona had given him for his birthday a few years ago. It was the kind of indulgence he would have never bought for himself, but enjoyed when it came as a gift. He rose and headed toward the harbor to meet Shelly Waterston, walking slowly along the narrow road in front of St. Magnus ironically named Broad Street. He arrived a few minutes before eight and waited in a shadowed niche across Bridge Street from The Harborside Fry. Shelly emerged at eight sharp, dressed in black jeans and Doc Martens, dragging a leather motorcycle jacket in her right hand. She lifted it and slipped it on. Then she scanned the street. Ludington stepped out of the niche into the light. She saw him, smiled, and crossed Bridge Street toward him.

"We meet at the Viking Bothy, only a few blocks," she said. "I phoned Ronald and told him I was bringin' along an American friend."

"Who's Ronald?"

"One of the hearth. Great guy, really smart."

The Viking Bothy was just up the hill from the harbor. The place was only a few inches more than a hole in the wall. It served no food beyond crisps and peanuts—free with drinks. Inside, it was not as dim as Ludington had imagined. Shelly led him to the nearest thing the pub offered to a dark corner—a three-sided booth with seats upholstered in faux leather. It had been repaired in several places with duct tape of a color nearly matching the vinyl. There were four people in the booth—two men and two women. All were young, at least they were younger than Ludington.

Shelly smiled shyly at the group as she introduced Ludington, "This is James. He's from New York, New York City. He's interested in the old religion."

They were welcoming. As Seth and Shelly slipped into the booth, hands were extended and names offered—"Sheila," "Henry," "Helena," "Shane."

Henry smiled a broad and transparent grin. "Come all the way from America, have ye?"

"I have. Always wanted to visit Orkney."

"Well, welcome to Kirkwall." He pronounced the town's name in local dialect—"Keerkwaa".

Ludington said, "A lot of people say it that way. So, why's it spelled "wall" at the end?"

Henry was pleased James had noticed. It offered him the opportunity for him to explain. "'Keerkwaa' is closer to the old Norse. We like it that way. Goin' back to our history, you know. Even though it means 'church bay.' Too bad about the 'church' part."

Shelly leaned back and said, "Aw Henry. Don't be raggin' on the Christians again. It's all much the same—old religion, new religion. All boils down to the same thing in the end."

A waitress appeared and three pitchers of stout were ordered. As the beer arrived and conversation was heading back in the direction Ludington had hoped, two more people approached the booth, a man and a woman. Both appeared older than Shelly and the other four. Ludington judged them to be mid, maybe late thirties.

Shelly called out a greeting. "Donna, Ronald. Hoped you'd make it. Ronald, this is my American friend, the one I told you about, James from New York."

Ludington realized that even here, New York City bore cache. Donna sat down next to Shelly. She was darkly attractive in skin tight jeans ripped at the knees and a blue blazer over a beige blouse.

Ronald, still standing, extended a hand to Ludington, looked down at him and said, "Welcome to Orkney, James." I'm Ronald—Ronald Linklater."

He sat down in the booth, now tightly packed, opposite Ludington. Ronald was pleasant looking enough—medium height, thinning sandy hair. The freckles that had probably plagued his youth were fading. He was dressed in pressed khakis and a green and brown pull-over woven with figures Ludington recognized as Nordic runes. He saw Ludington examining the sweater and said, "They spell 'Orkney' in the old runes."

As stout flowed from the pitchers into plastic cups, conversation began to circle back to the earlier question—"Do all religions boil down to the same thing?" This question seemed a contentious matter for the group, one they had regularly argued over.

Shelly said, "Odin or Thor, Moses or Jesus. They're just God symbols; they all point at the same thing, the big old mystery. We pagans, we're people what like to go back to the originals, at least the originals here on these islands."

Shane countered with male loftiness, "Shelly, my dear. Thor and Jesus were not exactly on the same wave length, ethically speaking. Thor is power, strength, courage. Jesus…, he was all weepy compassion. 'Help the weak' stuff. All the 'blessed are the meek' crap."

Ludington noticed Ronald Linklater smiling in what seemed agreement. Sheila, a loquacious red-headed sprite next to Henry, deflected the emerging edge in the conversation, "It's like that story of those blind men and their elephant. What you imagine an elephant to be when you can't see it depends on which part of it you touch. Touch a tail and elephants are skinny like snakes. Get ahold of a foot and they're like trees."

As this dubious image sunk in around the booth, Shelly altered the direction of the table talk and said, "So, I was back on Hoy over the weekend. There's been another murder. On Hoy this time. They found him in the Dwarfie Stane up by Rackwick. Not many details on the telly or the radio, but the copper on the telly as much as said it was another minister killed. Must have been the Sod Stuffer, you think?"

They had all heard the news already and nodded acknowledgement. Ludington assumed that the police were withholding Desmond's name and nationality until they were confident that all family had been notified.

Shane said, "It's bad for Orkney, it is. Stuff like that doesn't happen here."

Shelly, assuming authority because she was a Hoy native, said, "He was murdered on the twenty-first, the solstice, just like before. Funny we didn't get together for a summer solstice ritual this year. We had the meeting on the winter solstice, right before Christmas."

The faces around the booth turned to Linklater, as if for explanation. He said nothing.

Sheila wrinkled her nose at the memory of the day, "And it totally creeped me out. Dead pig with its throat slit up on the moor, dark as Hades it was. Blood all over everything. But I liked the toasting-the-gods part well enough." She giggled and said, "Got myself blootered for Odin."

With that memory evoked, plastic glasses were raised and touched, and stout was gulped in honor of Odin. The old god's name was spoken softly in this public place and the plastic glasses made an unsatisfactory sound as they came in contact. Not the sharp clink of true glass.

Ronald Linklater spoke for the first time. He did so in measured tones, professorially, "Sheila, you might want to visit a slaughterhouse for contrast. Sacrifice was absolutely central to the old religion. It was often a part of funeral rites. Sometimes it was done in preparation for an important undertaking. It was animals usually. Sometimes more than animals, but rarely. Of course, the Christians ended it with their once-and-for-all sacrifice nonsense."

This silenced the booth. His young disciples may have been Neo-pagans wending their way back to the Pre-Christian past, but they were as latitudinarian as most of the young are, indeed insistently tolerant, even of Christians.

Linklater looked at his watch and then at Donna, "I'm off to work." He stood to leave. The rest of the booth were not quite ready to end the meeting, such as it was.

Her voice gone chipper, Shelly said, "One more round, what do you say?" She left for the bar to fetch refills for two of the pitchers.

Linklater was a few steps behind her, but as she approached the bar, he turned toward the door leading to the street. Ludington said, "Back in a sec" and rose. He followed Linklater out of the Viking Bothy and into the evening, still half-light in the strange way of evenings in the far north.

The man was standing outside the pub as if he were waiting. Ludington approached him, looked to his side and then directly at him and said, "You probably guessed that I'm not here in Orkney for the beaches and the birds. I've gotten interested in the old religion. I came to Orkney because it's closer to the surface here. As luck would have it, I happened on Shelly today. She says it's something you know a lot about, the old religion I mean."

Linklater said nothing in response. Ludington filled the silence, "Maybe we could get together and talk—talk theology, you know. Have a drink or two. I've got a ferry to catch tonight, so maybe tomorrow if you're free."

Linklater said, "So you're not bidin' here on The Mainland?"

Ludington did not answer the man's question. He dared not mention Hoy, as he feared it might connect him to its American visitors that had been reported in *The Orcadian,* and that one of their number found dead in a pagan tomb.

So, he made a strategic decision. He said, "You should know that I was actually once ordained as a minister. Years ago." This was literally true, but a misdirection in the way he said it. It suggested that he no longer honored that ordination. Then he added, "But a person is always growing, changing, reevaluating, you know." Equally true, and equally misleading.

Ludington could not discern whether or not this revelation surprised Ronald Linklater. The man's affect was consummately opaque, but he smiled and said, softly, "I can hardly wait to talk. Let's meet here, at the Bothy. Eight o'clock tomorrow. You have a phone number?" The invitation was not spoken as a suggestion or question. It was clearly an instruction.

Ludington gave him his cell number and said, "I am eager to learn. Oh, and the country code is 1."

Linklater nodded in response, said, "1. Yes, how nice for you Americans." He walked away, up the slight hill and away from the harbor.

Ludington went back into the Viking Bothy and joined the remaining members of the hearth. They were downing glasses of stout and chatting away with a fresh animation, fueled perhaps by beer, or maybe by Linklater's absence, perhaps by both. Shelly was happy to see him back, and said, "Ronald's our scholar, he is. Reads up on pagan ways. He fancies himself our guru, but there's a peedie helping of anger in him. Rubs the rest of us wrong, sometimes. Kinda disses Christianity. Us? We don't bother with Christianity. Each to his own. Anyway, it's dyin' out."

As he excused himself and rose to leave, Ludington could see disappointment in Shelly's eyes. He did not want to string the girl along, nor did he want to close the door to Orkney's Neo-pagans that she had cracked open. He smiled at her in as avuncular a manner as he could manage and said something vague about maybe stopping in at the Harbor Fry for another Skull Splitter before he left Orkney.

He left the pub and headed toward the car park where he had left the Peugeot. As he walked Kirkwall's dim lanes, he thought to check the ferry schedule on his phone and discovered to his alarm that the last boat from Houton to Hoy was departing in fifteen minutes. There was no way he could make it. He'd have to spend the night on Mainland. When he had left the car earlier in the day, he had noticed a small hotel opposite the car park. There was no alternative. He found it; was relieved that they had a room—*"en suite,"* the young girl at the reception desk declared proudly.

He went to the second floor room, glancing over his shoulder down the stairs behind him as he climbed. He unlocked the room's door with its old-style key. Card keys had not yet found their way to the Kirkwall Arms. He bolted the door and flipped the swing lock closed as well. He sat on the bed and made two phone calls.

Magnus Isbister picked up on the third ring, answering with a clipped and questioning, "Hello."

"Magnie, it's Seth. I've met Dee Ritch's granddaughter, Shelly Waterson. At the pub in Kirkwall where she works at. I fished a bit, and got myself invited to a meeting of her group. Six of them, plus her, at a place called the Viking Bothy."

"Aye, I know it." If he was pleased that Ludington had taken action on his veiled suggestion, his voice did not betray it.

"Magnie, They're a bunch of kids, innocent enough. Except for one guy. He's older. In my business you get pretty good at reading people. This guy looks like a loner, seems aloof. Sees himself above the rest. They respect his knowledge about paganism, but I think he frightens them a bit. There's an antipathy toward Christianity in him. You do have to wonder about a man in his thirties hanging with a bunch of kids ten or twenty years younger. He seems to be nudging them into dark territory. Maybe he's recruiting, maybe grooming. And get this, they didn't gather for the summer solstice last week like they had for the winter solstice last December. And I got the impression they think that Linklater should have organized it, but didn't. Point is, he was not with them that night. Yes, I was only with the guy for an hour. What do I know? But I thought I should call on it."

"Did you get his name?"

"Linklater, Ronald Linklater."

"Good Orkney name, Linklater. But not all that common. Ronald Linklater… Rings a bell in my head, though. Seth, where are you?"

"I've got a room at the Kirkwall Arms. Missed the last ferry."

"You're still on The Mainland? Alone?" Ludington could hear anxiety spilling into anger in Isbister's voice. "Here is what you do. You lock the door. You do not answer if anyone knocks. You do not go out. I will be in the lobby at eight o'clock tomorrow morning. I will call up to your room and wait for you to come down. Only then do you leave the room. Then we talk. Do you understand me? Meeting a teen-ager into Neo-paganism is one thing. Attending a pagan hearth meeting in the Viking Bothy is another."

"I got it, boss." He said nothing about a second meeting planned with Ronald Linklater.

His next call was to Fiona. Her voice betrayed the fact that she had not been asleep. She said, "I'm sitting here in the lounge with a ginger ale and Harriet. She's drinking Dubonnet and gin. Frode says it's what the Queen Mother drank. How he would know that I cannot imagine. When will you be here? I know Isbister wanted to speak with you again. And Harriet rather hinted that you two were doing some sleuthing yourselves. Seth, please be careful. Our babes need a father."

He explained the missed ferry and getting a room at the Kirkland Arms, but he said nothing about Shelly and his meeting with the hearth nor about Ronald Linklater, much less Isbister's concern. "Get your sleep, Fiona. I'll be back tomorrow evening. And apologize to Frode and Else about the car. If they have to go anywhere, ask Lewis to take them in the bus. He's just sitting around with nothing to do. And tell Harriet that I'm going to follow up on my meeting and not to worry."

Chapter Twenty-Three

June 25

Seth Ludington slept fitfully even though he had pulled down the blackout curtain in his hotel room. Most Orkney bedrooms were so equipped in order to darken them during the weeks of white nights. He lay in the double bed on the second floor of the Kirkwall Arms awake with anxiety, not about his safety, rather wakeful with guilt. Fiona had named guilt one of his two default emotions, although he felt "guilt" was too weighted a word to accurately name what so often haunted him. Self-reproach might to better, or most accurately, the Apostle's spatial image of "falling short." Fiona said his other default emotion was "pathological curiosity." He was not sure that curiosity was an emotion, but he knew that what she said about him was true. He felt guilty for using Shelly Waterson. He felt guilty about not telling Fiona, Harriet, or Isbister about his planned rendezvous with Ronald Linklater. If he did, he knew they would have tried to put a stop to it. He felt guilty about his critiquing the precision of Fiona's observations about his default emotions. But mostly he felt guilty – maybe responsible was the better word – for having made decisions that led to Phil Desmond's death – the decision to come to Orkney in late June despite what had happened in late June of the last two years. Exhaustion finally conquered guilt or whatever it was that often kept him up at night and he fell into restless sleep, only to wake at seven-thirty without benefit of his iPhone alarm. He showered, but could not shave, having crossed to Mainland with no intent of spending the night.

He sat on the end of the bed and used the remote control to turn on the small television set perched atop a chest of drawers. He flipped through the several iterations of BBC and ITV until he came to a morning news broadcast. After a weather update, he heard the newscaster say, "And now to a rebroadcast of yesterday's news conference with Police Scotland officials in Kirkwall, Orkney."

The only official on camera was Detective Chief Inspector Alistair McCormick. As the man approached the podium, he straightened his tie, cleared his throat, looked solemnly into the camera and said what amounted to nothing, "We are following several leads…. Yes, we believe it likely that the person responsible is probably the same person responsible for the murders of the prior years. Yes, we have been monitoring all persons leaving the island of Hoy on the ferries. No, we are not prepared to disclose the identity of the victim, as family are still being notified."

Ludington knew this last statement was untrue. Desmond's family in the States had all been called. Harriet had been with Penny when the calls were made. McCormick was simply averse to announcing that an American tourist had been murdered in Scotland before he had made an arrest.

A young woman reporter asked the obvious question without raising her hand to be called on, "Was this victim also a member of the clergy?" McCormick hesitated and answered, "Yes, we believe so." He obviously did not want to field any more questions and turned from the reporters and toward Magnus Isbister who was standing behind him and almost off camera. He pushed Isbister ahead of him and strode away from the gaggle of nettlesome reporters yelling questions at McCormick's retreating backside.

Ludington had not been near a television when this truncated news conference had aired live the day before. This was the first time he'd seen it. But it now made it clear to him how Shelly and her little hearth—indeed all of the U.K.—knew that it was indeed another clergyman who had been murdered in Orkney. The news conference had disclosed that fact, though little more. Harry Mulholland had once told him that the police are often strategically guarded about disclosing the details of crimes they were investigating. He had said, "It's important not to let suspects or any witnesses out there know what you know…, or let them know what you don't know."

Ludington's cell phone rang at 7:55. It was Isbister. "Seth, I'm in the lobby. It's okay to come down."

Magnus Isbister shook Ludington's hand as they met and said in the soft way of Orcadians, "I think some breakfast is in order, Reverend Ludington, and some words as well." They settled into the tea room off the lobby of the Kirkwall Arms. Both selected scones with butter and orange marmalade. The pimply young waiter apologized for the lack of clotted cream without noting it was the English way to enhance scones. Isbister chose tea with lemon; Ludington a cappuccino.

Isbister began, "I told McCormick that you were on The Mainland and that you had met the Waterston lass and her peedie pagan club. He's furious, furious with you and furious with me. He suspects that I might have suggested you do what he wouldna' permit me to do. The man may be stubborn, but he's not thick. He wants you on the next ferry back to Hoy. I do as well, for that matter."

Seth nodded but said nothing.

Isbister took a bare sip of his tea, not cooled enough to drink, "But there's more, Seth. I'm going to tell you this because your meeting has got us onto something. I told you that the name—Ronald Linklater—sounded vaguely familiar. I ran a records check early this morning. God bless computers. 'Linklater' came up in connection with a suspicious death twenty-one years ago. I was on the force then, but a merest constable. I recalled a bit about the case, but vaguely. This is what came up in the records."

He pulled out his little spiral notebook and looked at it to jog his memory of the details, "A woman from Stromness named Hilda Linklater died under circumstances that led to a formal investigation. Age forty-two she was, the wife of one John Linklater and mother to our Ronald. He was age seventeen at the time and their only child. Tumbled down the cellar stairs and broke her neck, she did. The death was investigated thoroughly, not only because it was accidental, but because the local constable had twice been called in previously—by Hilda. "Domestic disputes" the earlier reports said – "disputes" with the husband that is. Not the son. Anyway, the obvious suspicion was that Hilda had perhaps been pushed down those cellar stairs in another 'domestic dispute' with her husband." Isbister put "domestic dispute" in air quotes as he said the words, his voice sodden with irony. "Nothing could be proven, of course. John, the father, died in a road accident on the Kirkwall-Stromness Road two years later. Single vehicle at the Bridge o' Waithe. Car nose down into the Loch of Stenness. Alone he was. Alcohol involved. No seatbelt. Ronald would have been nineteen at the time."

As he listened to this tale, Ludington could only imagine what a hell the Linklater marriage must have been. A hell that had shaped a boy into a man who slit the throats of pigs on the night of the winter solstice. In contrast, he thought of his own marriage and how it had somehow worked to make him an incrementally better human being. Or so he hoped. He had once told Fiona that though she loved him as he was, her acceptance nudged him to be more than he was. He thought of Harry and Georgia, Harriett and Margaret, Penny and Phil. Marriages really can go either way.

Isbister interrupted his musing. "Seth, you with me?

Ludington nodded and took a bite of scone. Isbister continued, "After I read the report, I made a phone call, just now. The minister of the Church of Scotland congregation in Stromness is a friend. We're on a Presbytery committee together. She's a Stromness native, lived there all her life. Knows the place like only a long-standing pastor in a small place might know it. Anyway, I asked her what she knew of any Linklaters in Stromness. I told her about the deaths of the parents and I mentioned the son, Ronald."

"She knew of the family, though she didna' know them personally. The two deaths had made them only too notorious in Stromness. The boy had dropped out of trade school after his father died. He worked off and on, but changed jobs all the time. There was a rumor in town that he had tried to take his own life. She lamented the sadness of it all. Then she said that Hilda, the mother, was a church-goer, not her Church of Scotland kirk, but a little fundamentalist congregation, not Wee Frees, but yards to the right of them. She said they used to meet in a rented hall in Stromness. Called themselves "The Bible Kirk" as if the others weren't. I asked her why she said 'used to meet.' 'Are they out of business?' She went silent for a moment, a bit surprised that I had not made the connection. She said, 'Magnus, their minister was the first one killed. Two years back, by your Sod Stuffer. The peedie kirk was all about him, so when he was killed, they just disbanded.'"

Ludington took a sip of his coffee and wiped cappuccino foam from his unshaven upper lip. He said, "Coincidences that are so unlikely often betray truth. You've told McCormick I assume."

"Of course. He's still onto his pedo theory, but he's now fit the Neo-pagan thing into it. He has it in his head that the Bible Kirk minister was an abuser. Abused the boy. So, maybe the kid turns to paganism, which he fancies to be the antithesis of Christianity. That's not enough, so seventeen years later, he murders his abuser and parks the body in a pagan site. McCormick thinks the next one was probably a pedophile as well, even though he admits that the killer could hardly have thought that of Desmond. No way for him to know. Our Detective Chief Inspector McCormick is guessing that the man merely widened his hatred to all clergy. Maybe he enjoyed the first killing and wanted another rush, same time next year on your pagan holiday." He paused and said, "Then he killed again this year. Serial killers usually enjoy it. It's like a release for them." Ludington winced at the thought.

Isbister put the notebook down and picked up his phone. I did a bit of internet research last night. Couldna' sleep. I found the same list of serial killer characteristics on a couple of sites. Seems the list was put together by one of your American FBI agents, guy named Ressler."

He read it to Ludington from his phone.

"1. Over 90 percent male

2. Tend to be intelligent.

3. Do poorly in school, have trouble holding down jobs, and often work as unskilled laborers.

4. Tend to come from decidedly unstable families.

5. Abandoned by their fathers as children and raised by domineering mothers.

6. Families often have criminal, psychiatric, and alcoholic histories.

7. Hate their fathers and mothers.

8. Psychological, physical, and sexual abuse as child is common—often by a family member.

9. Many have spent time in institutions as children and have records of early psychiatric problems.

10. High suicide-attempt rates.

11. Many intensely interested from an early age in voyeurism, fetishism, and sadomasochistic pornography.

12. More than 60 percent wet their beds beyond age twelve.

13. Many fascinated with starting fires.

14. Involved in sadistic activity or tormenting small creatures.

A sad list it is. Little as we know of Linklater, I count him fitting at least half of the characteristics on the FBI list."

"So, what's your guess, Magnie?"

"It fits, Seth, but I've double-checked, and Ronald Linklater definitely wasna' on any ferry off Hoy after Desmond's murder. I thought maybe he could have used a false ID, but it doesn't look like it. All the gents anywhere near his age that were on the boats check out. But we're going to haul him in for questioning anyway, and McCormick is confident it's enough for a search warrant for his place in Stromness. Both are in the works. We're heading out there in an hour. I thought you should know. No arrest, at least not yet. Not nearly enough for that. Unless he confesses or we find something totally damning in his place, we'll have to release him. Without an arrest we can hold him for twelve hours, no more. But it's something. Between you and me, Seth, 'thank you.' Now get yourself off this island and back to your bonnie wife."

Chapter Twenty-Four

June 25

When Detective Chief Inspector Magnus Isbister phoned Seth Ludington later that morning to let him know that they had brought Linklater in for questioning, the first thing he said when Ludington picked up was, "Where are you"?"

"Here in Kirkwall."

"Seth, you've missed at least two ferries back to Hoy. Why are you still here, man?"

"I feel quite safe, Magnie. Now that you've got him in your hands. But I'm going to catch the next boat."

"Good. Seth, we hauled him in alright, but we'll almost surely be releasing him. We can only hold him twelve hours without charge and arrest. But since you're still here, I would like for you and me to talk again before you go back to Hoy. I'd like to tell you what there is to tell, one bit of it is very intriguing. Let's meet at the Strynd Tea Room. It's on Broadway, up from the harbor very near the Cathedral. I'll be there by eleven."

Ludington wandered Kirkwall for an hour, finding himself increasingly anxious that the cops' evidence against Linklater would indeed prove insufficient for an arrest. He imagined that he might yet have to keep his evening assignation with the man, should they release him in time. Perhaps he could lure Linklater into some incriminating statement, or maybe even an incriminating act. His thoughts wound themselves into tangles as he poked his nose into St. Magus yet again. He sat in a back pew this time, perspiring despite the cool, fixated as he considered murders and what justice for them might mean, justice for murdered St. Magnus centuries ago and for murdered Philip Desmond four days ago.

He left the church and found the Strynd Tea Room. It was a fussy lace-curtain, church-lady kind of place. It was at the opposite culinary and aesthetic pole from the Viking Bothy. It served no beverage more arch than tea and coffee, the latter offered with a hint of disapproval. But there was a grand assortment of cakes, biscuits, scones (with clotted cream, oddly) and crust-free cucumber sandwiches. He ordered a sandwich and hot tea. He would have preferred iced tea, but had come to understand that such was close to heresy in Scotland.

Isbister arrived and sat opposite him at his window table as the young waitress set a fine-looking ham and Orkney cheese sandwich before Ludington with a smile and a "Here you are, sir." As she did so, he recalled the first time anyone had addressed him as "sir." It had been four years ago, when a young man had chased him through the lobby of a Broadway theater. "You forgot your umbrella, sir." Ludington, mid-thirties at the time, had been stunned to silence at being called "sir." He had not even managed to sputter out a "thank you."

"Seth, you'll be on the 3:15 from Houton, right?"

Ludington nodded and took a sip of his tea, still a bit too hot for comfort. He said, "What can you tell me about Linklater?"

"McCormick would be enraged at my talking to you, but I no longer care. We found Linklater at his home just before 9:00 this morning. He still lives in his parents' place in Stromness. Peedie house, old gray stone place right in town. Neat as a pin inside. In bed he was. Seems he works a night shift as a delivery driver with Streamside these days. He stone-walled when we got him to the station, wanted his lawyer, not that he had one. Arms crossed, all the while crying police harassment. Answered only one question we put to him. McCormick, as you might guess, is a less than subtle interrogator. Frankly, I'm not sure I'd talk to him myself. But when McCormick was grilling him here in Kirkwall, my constable and I were free to conduct a good search of his place without him being there and complaining. Found a veritable library of pagan and neo-pagan books and internet articles he'd printed out. One or two of them seemed not merely pagan, but decidedly anti-Christian. We have his computer and we're guessing we'll find more of the same when the crew from Inverness goes through it. But here's what really clicks. We found a bottle of Rohypnol in his medicine cabinet. Seth, you'll recall that traces of it were found in the first two victims. That's the date rape drug, the 'roofie" as they name it. Anyway, that's the question he did answer. Said he had been prescribed it for insomnia. 'The night shift messes up my sleep patterns,' he said. We called his physician. She confirmed having written it, just over two years ago. But the bottle was still half full. None of this is near enough for an arrest; it's all circumstantial. McCormick will be at him again this afternoon, but I doubt he'll crack. The man's gone quiet, but I keeked anger in him—livid anger, boiling under the quiet. I looked back at the report of his mother's death. When they went back for more questions the day after she died, they found that the cellar door was all boarded up. Linklater – the son, that is – said he had done it. Out of fear the same thing might happen to him, I'd guess."

"So, you think it's him, Magnie?"

"Well, McCormick is convinced. Probably right, he is… Probably. We're going to hold him the twelve hours. Like I said, McCormick wants another go at him. But there's still the big question—how did the man get himself back to The Mainland after Desmond's murder to mail his piece of correspondence to us? Desmond was killed late the evening or night of Friday, June 21. The letter was posted from Stromness the next day, late that day it seems. Like I told you this morning, he was not on any ferry. I'm confident of that. A boat of his ain? Maybe. But he doesna' seem to own one himself. No boat registered to him anyway. Andy—my constable—is asking around about boats in Stromness harbor and down the coast. But Scapa Flow was all churned up after that great screever we had. Would have been a scary crossing in a peedie vessel. But possible."

Ludington noticed that Isbister's accent thickened as his thinking deepened. "So, we're asking the media to run notices inquiring after any boats—

large or small—that have gone missing on Hoy or been found on The Mainland. The television and Radio Orkney and this week's *Orcadian* are cooperating. But the prior question, before the matter of how he got himself off Hoy—the one that haunts me every bit as much—is why would he have come to Hoy without his own vehicle in the first place? I suppose he figured he could have nicked a car when he got there, of course. People on the out islands often leave their keys in them. The hotel's car perhaps? Seems it was free for the takin'. It was parked in front of the Royal, just where it belonged, the next morning. But how could he know he'd find a car—that one or another—if he went to the island without one? Why would he *not* have come in his car? It doesna' answer." He released a long sigh, "But maybe."

Ludington said, "He clearly could have read about our group visiting Hoy – a group that included a few clergy—in that article in *The Orcadian* and seen his chance. Maybe he knew the storm was coming and was worried he'd be trapped in Hoy."

"Maybe," Isbister nodded. But the ferries so rarely suspend service, especially the Houton-Hoy service. Scapa Flow is relatively protected. One of the world's great harbors, they say."

Ludington altered the focus from this imponderable and said, "And there should be cut-up magazines somewhere, right Magnie? Left from creating his note to you. What did he do with them?"

Isbister smiled for the first time in their conversation, "You are the detective, aren't you Reverend Ludington?" He nodded his head in congratulatory regard and said, "We looked, of course. Went through his rubbish bins. The several rubbish bins inside and the one out. Even looked for paper ash in his stove. Nothing. I checked on the rubbish collection schedule for his street. Once a week on Wednesdays, so it would have been collected two days before the murder and won't be again till late tomorrow."

Ludington gave his head a nod in recognition of Isbister's thoroughness. The Orkney cop gulped down the last of his cooling tea and said, "I'm off to visit the Stromness postmistress in a bit."

Seth put down his ham and cheese sandwich and said, "How about nearby trash bins? Public ones, or ones outside other houses or businesses? The man may have been clever enough not to leave the remains of decimated magazines in his own trash or burn them in his stove."

Isbister looked Ludington square in the eyes. "Didna' think of that." He smiled and added, "But neither did McCormick."

Chapter Twenty-Five

June 25

Ludington thought "Ro Ro" to be an especially satisfactory acronym. He judged it so as he rolled the Peugeot onto the Houton ferry at 3:00, knowing he'd roll it off at Lyness on Hoy in ninety minutes. This would be a longer run than usual, as the timetable noted they would be stopping at the in-between island of Flotta. The day had yielded to a fine rain, more a mist actually, as it seemed not to be descending from above but emanating from the engulfing gray wet. Ludington had had to fiddle with both steering wheel stalks before he found the wipers.

The weather matched his mood, and the longer trip was just as well. He felt the weight of what he could only deem failure after his fruitless foray into the hearth and the planned meeting with Linklater that would not happen. The cops had picked him up, they guessed him guilty, they were holding him the twelve hours they could, but unless McCormick coaxed something out of the man, they would probably be releasing him late that evening. Ludington had little confidence in the coaxing powers of Detective Chief Inspector McCormick. And Fiona would not be waiting for him at the Royal when he returned. She and her grandmother had been granted liberty by McCormick to leave the confines of the hotel to have dinner in Rackwick with friends of Ingrid's. She was eager to show off her granddaughter, who was beautiful, bright… and pregnant. Fiona said they would aim to be back by ten. So why hurry?

Ludington was pleased, though curious, that the authorities had decided the group's quarantine could be loosened. As long as they swore to stay together. They were actually to be allowed a sojourn to Mainland the next day. Even a night at the Lynnfield Hotel that had been on their original itinerary had been restored. The ever-efficient Harriet van der Berg had been able to rescue the booking that Ludington had cancelled out of anxiety a week earlier. Constable Munro was to accompany them on the bus and stay with them in the hotel—a shepherdess to corral any stragglers as they toured Kirkwall. When Isbister told him that they were free to travel a bit, the man had sucked in his breath as Orcadians are wont to do when hearing or saying something weighty, and said, "We canna' keep ye locked up in that peedie hotel forever." Ludington had a hunch there was something he had not been told. But he trusted Isbister. The man had shared a remarkable amount of information, but perhaps not everything.

After the short stop at Flotta, they docked at Lyness pier a few minutes before five. Ludington carefully rolled the borrowed Peugeot off the ferry and drove the six miles to Longhope more slowly than needful. There was no reason to hurry. When he arrived and got up to his room, he decided to shave before dinner. The dark stubble of two days itched. Fashionable as it might be and even through Fiona liked the look, it made him appear as bedraggled as he felt when he encountered his face in the small mirror dangling over the sink in his room.

The tour group, now totaling nine minus Fiona and, of course, Phil Desmond, were already seated at three tables when he came down for dinner and entered the dining room. They were more animated than he had seen them since the morning they had learned of Desmond's death. People always modulated their affect in the wake of tragedy, assuming a decorous sobriety, but they can only manage it for so long. The prospect of the impending trip to Kirkwall had enlivened the mood, even though they were still practicing a modicum of emotional discretion. This was especially the case at the table he chose to sit at, for it included the widow of Philip Desmond. Penny sat opposite him, Harry and Georgia Mulholland on either side of her. Harriet van der Berg was to his right. At another table sat the students—Sarah

Mrazek, still as morose as she had been for the last four days, and Alex Buskirk and Hope Feely, shamelessly giggling over something. At the third table, the seminary trustee, Al McNulty, and bus driver Lewis Ross were engaged in a lively conversation, though not exactly a conversation, as Ross alone was talking, unwinding some interminable narrative to a silent McNulty, a dolorous victim of the man's expertise in almost everything.

Facing Penny across the table over lamb chops she had barely touched made Seth feel positively miserable. How he had failed her. When Frode stopped at their table to ask how the lamb was, Seth asked him for a Scotch, "Make it a double, neat." "A preference, Reverend Ludington?" "Well, Highland Park I suppose." Ludington was not a Scotch drinker. He usually gravitated toward red wine, French or Italian mostly, and in moderation. Harriet looked at him quizzically after he asked for the whiskey. He said, "When in Rome."

Every time he looked across the table at Penny Desmond, she refused to catch his eye. She looked at her untouched plate or said something softly to Georgia, but never returned Seth's glances. Whether it was there or not, he sensed reproach, certainly judgement, perhaps even the razor edge of rage. He had thought to switch to wine with dinner, but ordered another Scotch. "Double again?" asked Frode. "Why not?" he answered.

Both Harriet and Harry were watching him, watching his drinking to be more exact. Neither said anything, of course. There was really nothing they could say, and Seth didn't care. He was half way though his third Scotch, which Frode had made a lean single, when his cell phone pinged an incoming text message. He picked up his drink, excused himself, and made his wobbly way out the front door into the dove gray Orkney evening. He pulled out his phone, dropped it into the grass and picked it up, noting the time as he did so – 9:15. He fumbled his way to his texts and found the one that had just come in. It was from Isbister. *"Releasing him in fifteen minutes. Insufficient evidence. Sorry."*

Ludington staggered to the side of the hotel facing the water, sat on the stone bench overlooking the narrow bay called Long Hope and began to work his way through the remains of his Scotch. He was more than

154

miserable; he felt as though he were unwinding, unraveled by the picky fingers of culpability, undone by Phil's widow's refusal to even see him. He downed the last of the Highland Park and managed his way back to the dining room.

Everyone save Harriet van der Berg and Harry Mulholland had adjourned either to the lounge for cards and puzzles or up to their rooms to rest for the next day's touring. Harry saw Seth come through the front door and rose to meet him before he tried to mount the stairs to his room. "Seth, got a minute?" He took his pastor's arm and escorted him to the table where Harriet sat, an anxious mien on her usually imperturbable face.

Harry said, "Seth, I haven't seen you like this since the steeple imbroglio." Ludington guffawed at the mention of the affair of the steeple. He remembered the night after Old Stone's trustees had made their lamentable decision. A few months before, he and Fiona had deliberately overpaid the church for the five-story brownstone on 84th Street that had been the church-owned ministers' manse for half a century. They had done so in order to enable the church to restore its crumbling steeple, bringing it back to its erstwhile Gothic-revival glory. Instead, the congregation's five-man (and they were all men) Board of Trustees had voted to replace the old steeple, which had been wrapped in scaffolding for the last decade to save 82nd Street pedestrians from falling bits, with a truncated, mass-produced economy steeple – "The Coventry 1400," a prefabricated ersatz steeple manufactured by Aluminspire, Inc. of Lima, Ohio. The considerable money thus saved would be used to establish an endowment fund to maintain the church's building in future years.

In the meeting, Ludington had laughed out loud at the word "Aluminspire." He knew he was something of an architectural purist and he found himself furious about the decision. He had left the meeting without a word just as it adjourned. Then he did what he never did, at least almost never did— drink heavily and alone. One of the trustees was worried enough about the manner of his departure from the meeting to phone Harry Mulholland. Mulholland was the Clerk of Session, and was assumed to be a friend of the pastor. After a brief search, Harry had found his pastor on a bar stool in

Ryan's Daughter on East 85th Street. They had talked till nearly midnight.

Harry did not drink with Seth. Indeed, he did not drink at all, having once drunk way too much for way too long. Harry Mulholland knew an alcoholic when he saw one, and he knew a binge drinker when he saw one. Seth was not the former, he had told him. But he did tell him—emphatically, in the manner of an *in loco* father—that drinking away disappointment doesn't work. "That's really something you ought to understand, Seth." A few days after that evening in Ryan's Daughter, Harry told him with a wry smile that Seth had rambled on that night—derisively and with great conviction, about "bean counters" and "Philistines."

These memories quickened in Seth as Harry and Harriet jointly prodded him as to what was amiss this time. Seth merely said, several times, "It really is my fault. I mean, it *is*. I could have cancelled Orkney. I should have cancelled Orkney. What in God's name was I thinking?"

Both friends offered the predictable bromides, "You couldn't have known...." "You took the proper steps...." "Phil Desmond was a grown man, he made an unfortunate decision...."

But for Seth, their attempts at consolation did not answer. "Somebody has to do something. Harry, they think they know who it is, I mean the cops. Isbister and McCormick seem to be convinced. They even picked him up. But they let him go. 'Insufficient evidence...'. And now he's free as a bird." As he said this last, he realized he had used a tired simile he never would have sunk to when sober.

Harry the ex-cop said, "I doubt they're done with him." Harry the friend said, "Let's get you to your bed before Fiona gets back."

Harry led him up the stairs to his room, a worried Harriet at their heels. He sat him on his bed, and helped him with his shoes, the laces of which seemed the Gordian knot to Seth. Harry helped him with his jacket, pants and shirt, and then tucked him in like a child, the child he and Georgia had never had. He offered a "good night" that Seth did not answer and went off to bed, offering Harriet wordless raised eyebrows as he passed her, still standing in the open doorway.

As Harry left the room, Ludington's cell rang. He managed to find it in the pocket of his blazer that Harry had draped over a chair next to the bed. A U.K. number scrolled across the screen of his Apple 6s. He pushed the green button and said, "Hello."

"James, is that you? Ronald Linklater here. Sorry to miss our meeting earlier. I was... detained." He guffawed as he offered this vague excuse.

Ludington was cogent enough to play dumb. "Sorry to hear. I waited at the Viking Bothy for an hour," he lied.

"Well, my apologies. So, how about tomorrow night? Same time, same place."

Suddenly, even in his Scotch fog—or maybe because of it—Ludington knew what had to be done. And he knew who had to do it.

"Perfect," he said. "I look forward to it. Meet you there."

Seth did not see Harriet watching him from the doorway as he lay the phone on the bedside table. Then she pushed her tongue into her cheek and closed the door to Seth's bedroom, very softly.

Chapter Twenty-Six

June 26

"Seth, you're snoring like a lumberjack. It's time to be up and at 'em, my love. It's going on nine."

He considered asking his wife what she knew about lumberjacks and how they snored, but thought better of it. He sat up in bed, ran his hand through his hair to get it out of his reddened eyes, managed a coy smile and said, "Morning, my dear."

She said, "You look awful. Was a day of being grilled by the authorities that trying?"

The excuse he had offered for his overnight trip to Mainland the day before had been "that Isbister and McCormick want to ask me more about Desmond, and they insisted we talk in person." He had told her nothing about seeking out Shelly Waterson in the fish and chips restaurant, snagging an invitation to a Neo-pagan hearth, nor about scheduling drinks with its senior member that evening. Better she not know.

So, he said, "Just rather a long day, I guess." In truth it was a long day—one of nagging self-recrimination followed by an evening of too much Highland Park.

"Well, Lewis wants us on his bus by ten and I'd like some breakfast. And you look like you need coffee. Lewis will wait on us, but the ferry won't."

Their tour of Kirkwall marched from one pile of antique stone to the next – St. Magnus Cathedral, the Bishop and Earl's Palaces, then the Tankerness

House Gardens, the Orkney Museum, most of which sites Seth had seen on his own while killing time between his visit to Shelly Waterson's restaurant and the hearth meeting two days earlier. Each was worth a second visit, but he felt guilty pretending to his wife that he was seeing them for the first time. Wordless lies, but lies none the less. The group was deposited at the Lynnfield in time for a late tour of the nearby distillery before it was back on the bus and off to dinner at the Shore Restaurant near Kirkwall's harbor.

The restaurant was tucked into the ground floor of the little beige stucco hotel by the same name. The place looked modest inside and out, but the food was fabled. Seth and Fiona each ordered a petit filet mignon with Béarnaise, an indulgence not available at the Royal. Her appetite had finally eased its way back. Today it was Seth who picked at his food, fine as it was. He was no longer battling the worst of his hangover, but was struggling to imagine what excuse he might offer his wife when he left her sitting with the Mulhollands so he could keep his eight o'clock rendezvous with Linklater at the Viking Bothy just up the hill. He decided to capitalize on her observation, mentioned several times during the day, that he looked "awfully tired." Little did she know that "awfully tired" was actually the remnants of "hungover."

"I'm not feeling myself, Fiona. I'm going to grab a taxi back to the hotel." He looked down at his half-eaten steak as if it bore witness to his condition. She insisted on coming with him, but he insisted with equal force that she stay and have dessert. "I'll be fine. I just need to lay down. Please Fiona."

Harry Mulholland, who knew a hangover when he saw one, assured Fiona that her husband would be fine. "Have yourself a crème brulee with me and Georgia."

She was finally persuaded to stay, but only reluctantly. Seth tried his best to look even more unwell than he was as he excused himself and set off for the short walk to the Viking Bothy. As he left the dining room, he turned to see Harriet van der Berg watching him out of the corner of her eye.

He walked quickly through the lanes of old Kirkwall, arriving at the bar at ten minutes to eight. Unlike two nights earlier, the place was nearly full. And it was as noisy as it had then been quiet. A flock of fit young men in green and white jerseys emblazoned with "Kirkwall Thorfinn Football Club" was gathered around the television hung over the bar. BBC was broadcasting a game between two Scottish rivals that evoked passion even on these islands, ambiguous as they were about being part of that country. Ludington found a small table at some distance from the bar and around a corner from the door.

He ordered a gin and tonic, "with next to no gin, please, in fact none at all" and waited for Linklater.

"We got no limes," the miffed waitress declared.

He shrugged a "doesn't matter" in response, "So tonic water straight up."

He planned to stay perfectly sober this evening. He wasn't simply hoping to pry information from a man he assumed to be a serial killer. Egged on by his unrelenting guilt, Ludington decided to attempt to bait Ronald Linklater, offering himself as a potential victim. And to avoid actually becoming a fourth victim, he knew he needed to be in possession of every one of his faculties. As a cheer rose from the soccer fans, he turned to look at the television over the bar. Then he glanced back in the direction of the front door of the Viking Booth. It had opened to admit several people, but the door was around the corner from his table and he couldn't see much through the Kirkwall Thorfinn crowd. He assumed Linklater would find him when he arrived.

Which he did, at five minutes after eight. The man was dressed in black jeans and a dark anorak, gray or navy. It was hard to distinguish the color in the dim bar. He smiled and offered Ludington his hand before he sat.

Ludington found it hard to return the smile. He nodded and said nothing.

"Well, James, your interest must be keen. Here you are again. Sorry about last night."

Ludington shrugged his shoulders and said, "It's simply that I've become fascinated with pre-Christian religion. I know that Orkney was late to Christianity; the old paganism lies more at the surface here. Or so I'm guessing. So, here I am, come to the source. Thanks for meeting. I can tell you know your stuff"

"The old religion here was Norse, of course." Linklater seemed to enjoy the rhyme. He then launched into an intelligent exposition of the religious system of the Scandinavians who had begun to settle the islands in the late eighth century. He spoke knowledgably of Odin and Thor, Freya and Loki. "I'm not sure if the old Orcadians really believed they actually existed. I really don't think I do. Any more than I believe that Moses or Jesus actually existed. All religious figures and their stories are mere narrative incarnations. They form a collective myth system to explicate their respective moral systems, their virtues, if you will, the great virtues of the old religion in one case, and the lamentable ones in the case of the Christianity that came later."

Ludington asked, "And what would you identify as the great virtues? Of the old religion, I mean."

Linklater took a sip of the dark ale the waitress had set before him without his having to order it. He dabbed a spot of foam from his upper lip delicately, and said, "You know, or maybe you don't. Those great virtues were—and they still are—personal strength, courage, valor, honor, heroism, loyalty to kith and clan. The truest virtues."

Linklater proceeded to expound on Thor, red-bearded, hammer wielding, slayer of endless enemies, and father of assorted lesser deities by his several women. "He is an embodiment of the things we are trying to resurrect—bravery, power, virility. Whether he really exists or not hardly matters."

Ludington judged the man to be well-read, intelligent, and very passionate. He sensed he would be easy to goad into a reaction.

Ludington asked, "What of compassion? And self-giving, and dare I say the word, what of love?"

"Ah, the Jesus shite virtues, the saccharine poison that polluted our deep old wells, here and across Europe. Then it spread everywhere. Thank God it's faltering." He paused for a moment and said with a smile, "It's retreating back to the dark hole it rose from."

Ludington was jolted by both the invocation of the Deity and what he heard as an allusion to Resurrection, accidental as both might have been. He also sensed that the man was rising to the very deliberate provocation he was attempting. "You say the old religion valorized loyalty, fidelity to your own, I mean to your family, your tribe. Is there nothing to be said for a universal love, I mean for humanity, one that transcends just your own?" He thought of the eight men of the Long Hope Life Boat Station who had set out in a force 9 gale to save the lives of strangers aboard a foundering Liberian freighter. He had to bite his tongue to keep from quoting the Sermon on the Mount, the scandalous bit about loving enemies and not only your family, "as the pagans do" Jesus had said.

"You're going to blather on about the virtues of serving next. Or self-sacrifice. It's not normal. I mean the whole business of living for others, loving them like you love yourself. As if it's even possible. James, it sounds to me like you've not quite sloughed off that ordination you spoke of. "

Ludington decided it was time to set the hook. "You say the Christian virtues are not possible. Maybe that's exactly the point. Aim for the impossible and you might manage a near miss. I guess I'll never rid myself of it. It's seeded itself too deep in the soil of my soul. It has captured me, for better or worse, netted me with the impossible possibilities. Ronald, your old religion is a curiosity, but I have to tell you, I am not really that curious about it. I actually know it well enough. Yes, I was ordained as a minister. In fact, I am still a minister, minister of a church in New York. And I'm as content in it as one might be."

And I'm guessing your name is not James, is it?"

Ludington raised his glass of tonic water, barely touched, and said, "It's one of my names."

"So then, James-is-one-of-my-names, why did you want to meet me?"

"I thought I might interest you in the new religion." The barb of the hook was set.

As he whispered those words, a roar rose from Kirkwall Thorfinn and their hangers-on gathered before the television. Aberdeen had scored. Glasses were raised, beery hugs offered and backs patted. As you must at such a moment, Seth could not help but turn to see the excitement. He looked away from both Linklater and this gin-less tonic.

When he returned his attention to Linklater, the man said, "So try to convert me, reverend. Why don't you give it a try? I've got the time and I'm all ears."

Linklater raised his beer glass into the air for the waitress to see, a wordless request for a re-fill.

Ludington doubted that Ronald Linklater was convertible. Though he was a minister, he was not much accustomed to personal evangelism. He merely told Linklater his own story, a long winding saga that led through despair and ended in seminary and a dog collar around his neck. He sipped away at his tonic water to quench a thirst born of talking. He unwound his story slowly and injected into it as much Jesus as he could in order to provoke Linklater. As he talked, he began to feel off, not hungover, not exactly drunk, but increasingly and vaguely euphoric, somehow pliable. When Linklater said that the Viking Bothy was too loud for serious conversation and suggested they move on to another place he knew.

"It'll be quiet there, James, very quiet."

As Ludington rose to his feet, they seemed to disappear from under him. He steadied himself by laying both of his hands on the table, knocking his empty glass to the floor as he did so. It did not break, but all eyes turned to him as they do when something hits the floor in a tavern. Linklater took his arm like an usher at a wedding and steered him toward the door that led to the street.

Chapter Twenty-Seven

June 27

As he slowly came to the next morning, Seth Ludington was unsure of where he was. It was no familiar place and the first face that looked down at him was equally unfamiliar. He sensed a hand on his wrist, holding it tightly. It seemed to be taking his pulse. The face spoke, "Back to normal, almost. Looks as though someone slipped you a roofie, handsome, probably a double roofie. Put you out for the night, it did."

Fiona rose to stand beside the no-nonsense nurse in the Balfour Hospital Emergency Room who was indeed taking his pulse. When the nurse stepped aside, she took her husband's hand and said without a smile, "I was worried, now I'm furious. What the hell were you thinking, Seth?"

He was still too groggy to attempt a cogent explanation. He merely said, "Somebody had to do something."

His last minutes at the Viking Bothy began to arrange themselves in his crippled memory. He recalled that a moment before he and Linklater reached the front door, he had heard a familiar voice echoing above the din of the television and the happy banter of the Kirkwall Thorfill Football Club. It was an imperious voice, accustomed to both giving instruction and having those instructions being obeyed. "Do not accompany that man, Dominie. I mean Seth. Do you hear me?"

He seemed to remember Linklater suddenly dropping his arm and bolting for the door, Harriet van der Berg at his heals. He remembered slumping to

164

a bench by the door as she swept past him into the street, shouting, "Stop right there! You are to stop, young man, immediately. I mean it."

As the nurse pushed the curtain of the emergency room bay aside to leave, Harriet—inches taller than Fiona—rose from her chair in the cramped bay, "I followed you to that tavern. I overheard your telephone conversation with that person the night before last, in your room at the Royal. When you left the restaurant last evening, I decided to tail you, as they say on *Magnum PI*. I was sitting at a table across the room from you in that disreputable establishment, hiding behind my travel guide to Orkney. Then I saw that person stir something into your drink when you looked away—the soccer hullabaloo, you know. And some time later you unwisely decided to follow him. You were in what appeared to be a compromised condition. I had to intervene. I could not but call out, as loudly as I could. I must say, we caused quite the sensation."

Ludington winced at his carelessness and said, "And what of 'that person?'" He meant Linklater.

It was Fiona who responded, "Yes, he bolted out the door when Harriet screamed. And he ran right into the arms of Chief Inspector Isbister. They'd been following him since they released him. But Isbister had no idea you and Harriet were in the bar. You'd both gotten there before Linklater. Isbister told us the story last night when he stopped by to check on you after they had arrested him. He also said that their surveillance of him was the reason they felt they could free us from our quarantine. Seth, why didn't you tell me what you were doing?"

She asked her question and then leveled a glare at Harriet, who she knew was equally guilty of keeping her husband's sleuthing a secret.

He answered with the obvious and insufficient, "I didn't want you to worry."

"My husband is out baiting a serial killer and I'm not supposed to worry?" Her face reddened when she was angry, hiding the freckles as it always did.

The awkward edge of the moment was interrupted when Chief Inspector Isbister pulled back the curtain and entered the bay. He looked down at Seth, shook his head, and said, "Stupid. Really vera, vera stupid."

He sat in the chair near the bed and said to Ludington, "You may be stupid, but we do need to talk." He glanced up at Harriet and said, "I'm guessing that Mrs. Ludington could do with a cuppa."

Both women took the less-than-subtle hint. Fiona bent down to plant a kiss on her husband's lips and whispered, "Back in a bit. Doctor says they're starting the paperwork for your release."

After they left, Isbister stood and peeked through the privacy curtains on either side of Ludington's bed. When he was confident that the small emergency ward of the Balfour was empty except for the two of them, he sat back down and said in a soft voice, "He's confessed. To all three murders, the two before, and Desmond."

Isbister reached into his tweed jacket and pulled out his notebook. He hardly needed to look at his notes, but wanted to omit no detail. "It was actually his attempt on you that broke him. The lab in Inverness is analyzing the glass you drank from in the Viking Bothy last night. We're confident it'll confirm Rohypnol. We told him we had already done the analysis. He had a baggie of pills on him, roofies no doubt, and a syringe and a vial of what's doubtless fentanyl. McCormick pressed him with everything we had, and he broke."

And what is all that you have?"

"We looked in trash bins near his house in Stromness." He didn't need to add "as you suggested." They both understood as much. "We found three glossy periodicals in a big dumpster behind the Tesco a couple of blocks down the road, all cut up, the right letters missing. They were definitely used to prepare the last note. We told Linklater that we found his prints all over them. Which was not true. They were either wiped clean or handled with gloves, but he fell for it. Must think he missed some pages. And the Stromness postmistress recalls him mailing an envelope last Saturday afternoon. He didn't have to buy stamps for it, but she saw him working to stuff it in the slot. Seems it barely fit. She's a nosy type, watches everything. Said she knows him, or at least knows who he is. We went back with a photo and she confirmed it. And then I called the delivery company where he works. Seems he keeps a locker there. McCormick just searched it and called me. Found another syringe and several more vials of what will doubtless also prove to be fentanyl. But Seth, it's still all pretty circumstantial – the envelope, the magazines, the anti-Christian stuff in his house and on his hard drive, even the drugs. Strong circumstantial evidence, but I dinna' believe it would convict had he not confessed."

"Anyway, McCormick told him we had him for attempted murder... of you. I doubt that would stick either, but we do have him for drugging you and for possession of a controlled substance. Isbister looked away, contemplating the folds in white curtain opposite him, "I hate to say it, but he broke because of your stupid stunt." He's proud and arrogant, aches for the attention. Seems he reasoned he might as well take credit for the murders and bask in homicidal glory."

Ludington nodded, relieved, saddened, but still unsure of what he was hearing.

"Did he say why he did it, the murders?'

"The interview last night went to three hours. When McCormick threw his pedophilia theories at him he got defensive and angry. His first display of anything like emotion. Then he became loquacious, actually very loquacious. As I said, the man's arrogant and defensive, brimming over with what I can only imagine is self-pity. It's not really the Neo-pagan business that motivated him to target Christian clergy. Oh, he hates ministers, hates Christianity as a whole, but that's not the source of the rage. You'll recall what happened when he was a teenager, with his parents, I mean."

Seth said, "An accident you said. Or a maybe accident. Abuse by the husband, then a fall at home, down the stairs."

"That's what we knew," Isbister said. "But it's deeper, much deeper. When McCormick pushed his pedo ideas at him, the man was driven to tell the story, self-justifying as it is. Linklater said he had witnessed his father striking his mother multiple times in the years before that night, the night she died. He wasna' there that day, you'll remember. Well, it seems that right before his mother died, he'd gone to see the minister of her peedie fundamentalist kirk in Stromness. She'd often dragged the boy to the church, insisted that he attend with her, so he kind of knew the man. He had once told the boy that he could bring all his problems to God, meaning to the minister, I guess. So, Linklater told the guy, Duncan Taylor was his name, told him about his fear for his mother. He told him that he had seen his father strike her. He told us that Taylor's answers were a rubbish heap of platitudes about how the man was to be the head of the household, that Scripture teaches wives to be subservient to their husbands. Linklater says that when he told him that his mother was suffering, the man blathered on about suffering sometimes being needful in life, said that the woman is called to self-sacrifice. He told him he should try to understand his father's frustration. Linklater says the man even said that corporal discipline is sometimes essential to keep order in the home. All this is etched in Linklater's memory, as it would be I suppose. He grew livid just telling us the tale last night."

Ludington groaned, "Religion can grow so malignant. And when it does, it can deal in death."

Isbister nodded reluctantly, "Well, only a week after that visit to the minister, his mother was dead at the bottom of the cellar stairs. Linklater was not there when it happened, but it was he who found her. He blamed his father, of course, but his father was soon dead. Then he blamed Duncan Taylor. Then he blamed all ministers. Finally, he blamed Christianity and settled into what he imagined to be its nemesis, the Neo-pagan stuff. He talked about the righteousness of vengeance, the need for retribution in order to set things right. I guess there's a great helping of that kind of thinking among the old Norse gods, or so he said. Lots of pay-backs. But remember, it was 17 years after his mother's death that he killed Duncan Taylor. The man's rage had burned hot in him for years. He told us he went back to Taylor all those years later saying he wanted some counseling. He drugged the man's tea, then injected the fentanyl. Seems he found moral justification for murder in his twisted reading of the old pagan myths. That's the reason for the solstice and the old heathen sites to deposit the bodies. He said the first murder satisfied him, that it brought him peace, that it felt good and right, so he did it again, twice. The next one, the year after the first, was Halston Hughes. He picked him up in a bar here in Kirkwall, or maybe Hughes picked him up. Linklater dinna' know him, but Linklater knew he was a minister, knew so by local rumor. Then he said that last week, when he read the story in *The Orcadian* about your group on Hoy he saw his chance for this year. He had figured that local clergy were being watched, which was quite true. Said he went to the wedding reception on Hoy and found Desmond. And then he admitted—with a shit-faced grin—that last night he was about to add a fourth."

"And the sod stuffed in their mouths, what did he say about that?"

"McCormick speered him about it. "To shut them up," he said, "to stifle all the claptrap about suffering and submission.""

Seth winced and said "Exactly as he said in the notes—'Another apostle of lies silenced.' But Magnie, why me? Why a fourth murder if he had gotten his annual satisfaction with Desmond?"

"I asked him that. Said he was worried that we were maybe on to him and he wanted one more just in case it was the end."

"But Magnie, why did he change drugs, and what did he say about how he got on and off Hoy and back to Stromness in time to post his note?"

"To the first question, he said, 'I like variety.' To the second he said, 'I flew' and then he laughed. We've not had any calls in response to our queries about missing boats, but McCormick is sure one will turn up."

"And Magnie, did you ask him how he knew Desmond was a minister? He wasn't wearing his dog collar when we found him. Did he tell you how he knew? And did he tell you why he used Ambien on Desmond, not the roofie and the fentanyl?"

"That's when he clammed up and asked for his lawyer. Not that he needs one. He's confessed and has been formally charged with the three murders and with drugging you.

McCormick is on his way back to Inverness this afternoon. He says it's all in the box, wrapped up neat and tied with a bow."

"What do you think?"

The Chief Constable of Orkney looked uncomfortable, sucked in his breath, and said softly, "I do wish the bow were better done."

Chapter Twenty-Eight

June 27

After being told by the startlingly young physician who had treated him the night before that his stomach had been pumped—not once, but twice—Ludington was discharged just after noon. He, Fiona, and Harriet took a taxi from Balfour Hospital the several blocks to the Lynnfield, even though Seth swore he would be fine with walking. Arriving back at the hotel, the members of the tour group gathered in the lobby knew that their leader had spent the night in the hospital, but were discreet enough to ask questions no more detailed than, "Are you okay, Seth?" They had asked each other what they thought, of course. And they soon tried, with subtle stratagems, to extract information from Harriet, but without success. Her years as a Wall Street Executive Secretary had taught her how to keep her counsel close.

They all piled back on Lewis Ross' little bus for the twenty-minute drive from Kirkwall to Houton to catch the afternoon ferry back to Hoy. Even Ross was uncharacteristically quiet, offering Ludington no more than "Afternoon, Reverend" as Seth climbed onto the bus. Fiona was sound asleep before they reached Houton. Harriet, seated across the aisle said to him, "Seth, your pregnant wife was up and awake, at your bedside without fail, all through the night. She's exhausted."

The bus eased onto the ferry and then the ferry eased its careful way from the Houton pier and turned south toward the high hills of Hoy, barely visible below the low summer sun. It struggled with little success to break through the heavy cloud which lay close enough to earth to hide the top of Hoy's Ward Hill. Seth turned to Harriet and said that he needed some air. He folded up his jacket and tucked it between his sleeping wife's lovely head and the window of the bus. Harriet followed him onto the deck of the small ferry. He wiggled his way between several cars to the bow of the boat, van der Berg following right behind him. He leaned his forearms against the rail and watched the uninhabited little island called Cava rising before them just off to port. Harriet stood next to him, pulling the collar of her woolen coat about her neck. They were silent for a long minute.

He said, "McCormick says we're free to leave now. I'll call the agency and get them to book us home as soon as possible. And Isbister told me that Phil's body has been released. Booking a dead body home seems to be more complicated than booking live ones, but he's been helpful. Penny's alright with flying home now—with us—and waiting a few days for Phil if she has to, waiting for his body I mean."

"So, it's over." Harriet said.

"McCormick told Isbister it's all wrapped up and tied with a bow. But Isbister says he wishes the bow were more neatly tied. I think he has his doubts about Linklater having killed Phil. Harriet, I have to tell you that I have my doubts as well."

Van der Berg looked away from Cava and to Ludington as the little island slipped by and said, "What's your reluctance?"

"Same as those Isbister keeps hinting at. Like him, I have no doubt that Linklater killed the first two, and maybe he actually did murder Phil. He could have simply gotten lucky—us arriving on Hoy at just the right time of year. It's so very unlikely, but if that's what really happened, the fact is that it was I who put the pieces in place for him by bringing us here. He's confessed to all three, but... some loose ends are still hanging loose."

Harriet van der Berg was a clever enough woman to guess at Ludington's loose ends, but she asked anyway, "Such as?"

"Well, first off, how did he get himself off Hoy in time to mail his note late Saturday, the day after they found Phil? The ferries weren't running till noon, and the police checked everyone getting off them after they started up again. Linklater simply was not on any of them. Isbister is sure of it. A small boat of his own, or maybe one he borrowed or swiped? Maybe, but Scapa Flow was still rough, and Linklater doesn't seem to have owned a vessel of any kind and none have been reported missing or found. Isbister has made public queries. No responses. McCormick says the boat will turn up. He may be right."

Van der Berg said nothing, leaving silence sit so that her pastor could unload his litany of qualms. "And Linklater was late in mailing his note this time, later than before. I suppose it could have taken him some time to get back to the magazine stash at his place in Stromness. But the point is, he actually mailed it right after news of Phil's murder broke in the media."

He paused for but a moment and pushed his hair off his forehead, "Isbister said that Linklater's confession was remarkably detailed, totally candid, nothing held back. So, why won't he tell them how he got off Hoy? And why won't he say why he switched drugs when he killed Desmond? I mean, he dosed me with Rohypnol and he had his fentanyl at the ready last night, just like the first two. But Phil died of an Ambien and alcohol overdose. McCormick says that serial killers change their M.O. I'm sure they do, but why won't Linklater say it?" He was eager enough to blurt out every other gory detail."

Ludington's worries waxed even as he articulated them, "And not only that. How did he know Desmond was a minister when he picked him out at the wedding? Penny said he may have taken his collar off when they left the village hall. When she left him to go off to bed and he wandered away alone, he was just a guy in a blazer and a dark shirt, a clergy shirt to be sure, but they aren't that much of a giveaway. Of course, he could have seen him wearing his collar earlier, during the reception. And then there's one last thing, Harriet."

He paused, as if for effect, and looked away from her and then back at the retreating south side of Cava, "Why did he want to kill me if he'd already had his kill for the year? Isbister said they asked him exactly that. He said he was worried that they were on to him and that he wanted to get one last one."

She said, "Seth, I judge Chief Inspector Isbister to be an intelligent man. He is quite aware of all these concerns. What does he think?"

"That McCormick says they have their confession. That the man can't wait to get himself away from Orkney and back to Inverness. He's as much as told Isbister to stand down."

"And you, Seth Ludington, what do you say?"

"I say that Ronald Linklater is a consummate narcissist. That he's a man to crave attention for any and every murder he might claim, whether he did the murder or not. And I say these questions are haunting me. And I think they haunt Magnus Isbister as well. But he's been ordered to ignore them, for now at least."

Ludington said no more as the oil terminal on Flotta rose to view, a rude trespass of industrial modernity into a landscape little altered in centuries.

After the silence had rested long enough, Harriet stated the uncomfortable obvious, "If that man did not kill Philip Desmond, somebody imitating him did. He—or she—chose the solstice date, chose the Neolithic site, and, of course, the sod." She could not bring herself to say "stuffed in his mouth."

Ludington shook his head despairingly, "A Sod Stuffer wannabe? Another crazy on this serene little archipelago where almost nobody ever gets murdered?"

"Perhaps." Harriett hesitated before continuing, "But perhaps someone else—someone astute and quite sane—used this disturbed serial killer and the convenient date as a—what do they say?—as a cover. Someone who saw an opportunity to commit murder for quite another motive and to cast the blame upon that man, a despicable villain who has turned out to be quite happy to take the credit."

Both stared over the slack gray waters of Scapa Flow toward the ugliness of the oil terminal that sullied green Flotta. Rising in their imaginations, they both saw the ugliness of what Harriet's observation suggested.

Ludington said softy, "That would be someone who knew Phil, not a stranger. And it would be someone who knew him and was on the island of Hoy five days ago. I count ten of us."

He gazed at looming tanks of the terminal, "Evil at a remove is a very different matter from evil come proximate, when it 'crouches at your door' as they say."

Harriet picked up on the reference and said to Seth, "Just what the Almighty said to Cain, before he took his brother's life, if I recall my Scripture. "Sin crouches at the door." As a child I found it a terrifying image. I imagined a great smelly beast breathing softly outside my bedroom door."

Seth looked her in the face and said softly, "The original *bête noir.* "

Van der Berg pondered the unhappy direction in which their conversation had wended, nodded her head and said, "I think I have mentioned before that my Margaret was a great fan of detective stories. She attempted to induce me to read them, but I prefer history and biography. Never autobiographies, however. They are inevitably dishonest – self-serving even when they feign not to be. Anyway, just after she had slammed a particularly satisfying mystery novel closed, I recall her telling me that there are only four motives for murder, and that they all begin with the letter 'l'. I suggested to her that only four sounded like oversimplification, reductionism at best, but she insisted. 'And what would they be, Margaret?' I inquired. Well, as they all did indeed start with the letter 'l', I can recall them. She said, 'loathing, lust, lucre, and love.'"

With no hint of a smile, Ludington said, "Naming money as 'lucre' to get the 'l' is rather a contrivance."

"Perhaps. So, what was that man's motivation, I mean Linklater? Was it loathing?"

Ludington answered, "It was loathing for certain, but perhaps also love. For his mother."

Chapter Twenty-Nine

June 27

As Ludington stepped off the tour bus in front of the Royal Hotel, his cell jolted him with both its vibration and piercing old phone ringtone. He had offered Georgia Mulholland his hand to help her down the steps. Harry, ever the gentleman, was behind his wife and the last member of the group to disembark.

Georgia heard the phone and said, "You'd better take that, Seth."

He pried it out of the front pocket of his blue jeans and recognized a Philadelphia number. He turned to walk around the hotel toward the water side and out of earshot of the tour group. He gave Fiona a 'don't worry' wave as he rounded the corner.

"Hello, Seth Ludington here."

"Seth, it's Henry Barkman returning your call… finally. Sorry to be so slow in getting back to you."

"It's no problem, Henry. Just glad you've called."

Ludington didn't know Henry Barkman well enough for first names, but he followed the man's lead. They had met only once, at Phil Desmond's retirement dinner a few months earlier. Barkman was the retired CEO of something and the long-standing chair of the board of Philadelphia Theological Seminary. He knew Ludington was the current minister of the congregation Desmond had once served. He also knew him as a "potential supporter of the seminary"—development office code for sympathetic persons able to write large checks. It was Barkman who had sent Desmond the email marked "urgent" right before the man was killed. That message and its several attachments had been found on the dead man's phone. Isbister had forwarded it to Ludington, knowing it to have originated in America and judging the matter to be unrelated to his investigation of the man's death.

"Kitty and I have been at our place in Cape May. Just got back to Philadelphia and picked up your message on the land line here. Kitty makes me leave my cell at home when we go to the shore. Says I'm an iPhone junkie. 'What could be so urgent?' she says. 'And if it is, they'll find us.'"

Ludington hesitated for a bare moment before relating his genuinely urgent news. It was clear that Barkman did not know that the former president of the seminary was dead. It was not the kind of story to make national news in the States, but he thought the *Inquirer* would have perhaps run something, or that the seminary grapevine would have found Barkman in Cape May. Then he recalled that when Penny had phoned her daughters with the news of their father's death, she had asked them not to go public with it until she got back and funeral arrangements had been made.

"Henry, Phil Desmond is dead. He died five, actually four, days ago, here in Scotland."

Barkman knew about the tour and was aware that Phil and Penny had signed up to go on it. Desmond had announced Ludington's offer of tour scholarships at a board meeting where Barkman had been present.

The phone was silent for a moment as Barkman took in the news. "I can't believe it. I'm flabbergasted, Seth. He seemed to be healthy enough. I mean, he had slowed down a lot, but don't we all. I can't tell you how sorry I am to hear this. How is Penny doing? Poor woman. When will she be back?"

"In a couple of days. But Henry, you also need to know that Phil was, well,…" He could not help but hesitate before he said the word, "murdered."

"Oh my God. I mean, Oh my. Murdered? I can't believe it. Murdered? What happened?"

"A suspect has confessed, actually confessed to a series of murders up here in the Orkney islands where we are, two before, and now Phil. Deeply disturbed man. A local. It's all so profoundly sad."

Ludington decided it was not the moment to offer either the details of Desmond's death or to mention his reservations about the confession of the "deeply disturbed man." But he did want to mention one curious detail, "Henry, you're probably not aware of it, but Al McNulty is here. He signed up for the trip, signed up at the last minute."

Ludington was reluctant to tell Barkman that McNulty and Desmond had quarreled several days before he died. Both knew that McNulty was chair of the seminary's investment committee, the man who would have been responsible for overseeing investing some portion of the seminary's considerable endowment in those three socially responsible investment firms whose prospectuses had been attached to Barkman's urgent email.

The phone went silent again after Seth informed Henry Barkman that McNulty was on the tour.

"Henry, are you still there?"

"Yes Seth, still here. It's all such a jolt. I mean Phil being killed and Al right there. But you say they got the guy?"

"So it would seem. But I have to ask… Henry, why were you so eager to talk to Phil? You said you thought he might have been 'right about something.' And you attached those three investment fund prospectuses. You said it was urgent."

"I can't believe any of this, Seth. The reason for the urgency needs some back story. Couple years ago, way before Phil retired, the board decided it would be appropriate to reinvest some of the seminary's endowment, actually a decent hunk of the endowment, with socially responsible funds. Some students and alums were pressuring the board on the issue. McNulty's committee was asked to do it, of course. Not much of a committee, mostly him and a couple of pastors who can read some Greek, but not spreadsheets. Well, about a year later, Phil had seen an article in some magazine about what they call 'greenwashing.' It seems that there are some asset management outfits that say they are ESG – sensitive to environmental issues, social issues, and governance issues—ESG—but they really aren't, or at least not very. They actually invest in stuff like oil and Chinese coal, booze and tobacco, all the putatively bad stuff, but they keep it on the downlow. That's what they call it, 'greenwashing.' Phil was worried that it might be the case with the investment firms Al had gone with. He had looked through some of the paperwork and had talked to Al, but wasn't quite satisfied with the answers he got. Frankly I don't think he ever much liked the guy. Phil could always read people like a book. Anyway, Phil talked to me about it again, a couple months ago. So I asked a friend from my old firm, our comptroller, to look through those prospectuses, the ESG ones. The guy called me the week before last and said—this is a quote—'greenwashing could be the least of your problems. You need a thorough audit.' Well, that's what we're doing, doing it now. I wanted Phil to know that he was probably onto something."

"Henry, if greenwashing is the least of it, what's most of it?"

"Not sure, not until we get the audit report. It surprises me that Al would sign up for a European jaunt with Phil and Penny when this was brewing."

"Surprises me too. Well, thanks for the call, Henry. Looks like we'll be back in two or three days, Penny included. As soon as they can book us a flight together. I'm sure Penny will announce the arraignments soon. In the meantime, probably best to keep his death under your hat. Let her and the girls take the lead."

Ludington ended the call and looked out at the wet fog wafting west to east over Long Hope bay. He could see nothing of the hills of Hoy, not even the near shore of North Walls across the water. When he turned around he could barely make out the façade of the hotel. He found his way around the building to the front door and entered. As he did so, he glanced at his watch. It was nearly five. The lobby was empty; everyone had retreated to their rooms for a preprandial lie down, everyone except Al McNulty who was seated alone at the bar, sipping something iceless and amber. The two men glanced at each other, but offered no word or gesture of greeting.

Ludington went to the Royal's lobby and called through the open Dutch door to the tiny office, "Frode, Else."

The former appeared promptly and said gravely in his Norwegian-accented English, "It is so good that they have captured this man and that he has, what is the word, 'confessed.'" He pronounced the last word as if it had three syllables.

"Yes, it is. Frode, could I borrow your laptop for a minute?"

Frode returned with his bruised MacBook Air, asked no questions, and said, "The password is 'saga.'"

Ludington sat down alone in the dining room. Before he opened the laptop, he texted Fiona who was upstairs in their room. "You okay?" She texted right back, "Having a rest, down in an hour."

After some wandering around the Gmail site on Frode's laptop and successfully remembering his own password for a change, Ludington was able to access his personal email account. He scrolled down through dozens of emails to find the one Isbister had forwarded to him several days earlier, the email the cops had found on Desmond's phone, the one from Barkman marked 'urgent' with the three attachments of the three prospectuses from the three ESG firms in which McNulty had invested seminary funds.

Unlike most Presbyterian ministers, Seth Ludington could not only read some New Testament Greek and a little less Hebrew, he could also read a spreadsheet and decipher a prospectus. He did not directly manage his own wealth, but he kept a close eye on those who did. He poked away at the laptop, working his way through the three documents, the first from "Plowshares for a Better Future," the second from "Invest for Tomorrow," the third from "The Giving Back Fund." "What cutesy names," he thought to himself.

He methodically explored the three documents. He noticed that some of the firms whose stock was listed as a part of each fund's assets were indeed questionable as to their ESG *bona fides*. But he saw nothing else untoward until he happened to notice that the first page of each document did not include what the first pages of prospectuses routinely include – a list of names identifying the managers and directors of the investment firm. Each prospectus simply noted that the holdings were managed by MBA Financial Services, LLC. No names. This was probably what Henry Barkhorn's friend from his old firm had also noticed. Ludington closed the three attachments, then the email, and returned Frode's laptop.

He went to his bedroom to find his wife sleeping. He sat in the ladderback chair in the corner of the room and fished out his cellphone. There was barely enough battery to make the one call he needed to make. He went to contacts and found the cell number for his only New York broker who always picked up. "Bill, Seth here." They had long been on a first name basis. "I'm going to email you three fund prospectuses. None of them list managers, directors, or board members. Just a management firm rather generically named, something called MBA Financial Services, believe it or not. Odd, of course. The firms have got to be on file somewhere. See what you can find out."

William Queen knew better than to ask questions, "Be back to you tomorrow, Seth."

Seth Ludington lay the phone on the windowsill and looked out to see that the day was still as opaque as it had been when they returned from Mainland. Nothing visible but a thick gray. He emitted the slightest guffaw as he thought how often it's true that even though we go through life looking for answers, in the end the answers often find us.

Chapter Thirty

June 27

After he ended the call to Bill Queen and tucked his phone back in his jeans pocket, he turned to see that Fiona had awakened and was propped up on the bed and again reading *Hawkfall*, George MacKay Brown's collection of brooding Orcadian fables.

She looked at him, recognizing the worry on his face. She decided not to ask, but said, "Brown really gives you a feel for the islands, he does, at least as they used to be. It was a hard place, I mean a century ago. But he's got a quirky spiritual edge. Grams lent me the book. She gave me another one of Brown's. It's about the death of St. Magnus, the murdered earl they named the cathedral for. She said he compares his murder to that of Dietrich Bonhoeffer, the pastor the Nazis killed, you know. Two martyrs eight-hundred years apart. You might want to read this one."

Reading about murders was the last thing Seth Ludington was eager for at the moment. A very real and immediately present one lay before him, and unlike those of Magnus and Bonhoeffer, this one was less than satisfactorily resolved.

"Maybe on the flight home. Looks like we're going to be booked back out of Edinburgh, not the day after tomorrow, but the day after that."

Eager as he was to be home, the thought of getting off a plane at JFK without answers to the questions about Desmond's death that were haunting him made his stomach turn. He wiped the anxiety from his face and said,

"You ready for dinner, my love."

Fiona smiled and laid the paperback book face down on the nightstand. "I am. In fact, I'm actually quite hungry again."

She followed her husband down the narrow stairway, a hand laid softly on his right shoulder as they descended. They sat down with Harriet at a table set for four. The Mulhollands were seated with Penny Desmond, who was still wan and silent. The younger seminarians, Ted and Hope, were seated together, tight next to each other at a window table for two, holding hands over the table and gazing into each other's eyes. Al McNulty was not in the dining room.

As Seth pushed in Fiona's chair for her, he could not help but see that her pregnancy bump was growing, as it should with twins coming. As he turned to sit, he noticed Sarah Mrazek alone at a table pushed into the only windowless corner in the dining room. She had chosen a chair facing the wall rather than one looking into the room. Seth walked over to invite her to join them. She looked up at him as he rounded the table. Her eyes were swollen and red. Runs of unattended mascara trailed down her cheeks.

Like the rest of the group, she had learned of Ronald Linklater's arrest right after they arrived back on Hoy. Frode had the little television in the lounge tuned to BBC news which was rerunning the brief news conference that McCormick had presided over late that afternoon. It had been short and direct. The Inverness detective simply announced the arrest of one Ronald Linklater for three murders, charges to which he had confessed. McCormick had assumed a grim visage, more than a bit stagey, as he announced the "signed confession." He then spoke obliquely of what he named "substantial corroborating evidence." But he did not mention the attempt on Ludington nor the fact that the man had been charged with it as well. He refused to answer the obvious questions about motive that the gaggle of reporters shot at him as he turned from the camera, shepherding a sober-faced Isbister away before him.

Sarah did not respond to Ludington's invitation to join them. She was silent for a moment, then looked up at him and said, "I can't believe he's actually dead. He had so much to live for. A new chapter in life was before him."

Seth sat in the chair next to her, laid his elbows on the table, and assumed his best pastoral demeanor. He hesitated, then nodded and said, "Yes, you mean a new life in retirement, retirement after such a grand career."

Sarah looked at him and said, "Yes, well, that I suppose."

Though he was unsure of the meaning of what he had heard, he responded in the classic Rogerian manner in which he had been trained, "I hear you."

"No, you don't," she spat back. You'll never understand. Never. Nobody does. I need to be alone."

Dinner was baked chicken breasts with a dollop of butter, a lemon wedge and several sprigs of rosemary tucked under the crispy skin. Fiona's appetite had waxed even as Seth's had waned since his first experience of having his stomach pumped. It was as much the thought of the procedure as it was any residual discomfort that compromised his appetite. He could only assume that his stomach was as empty as it had ever been, though it didn't feel that way.

As Fiona picked up her knife and fork to greet the chicken breast, she sneezed gently. She excused herself and reached for her purse which she had slung over the back of her chair. She pulled it unto her lap and reached into it, fishing for the little packet of tissues she always carried. She found it and pulled it out. With it came an earring lodged in the open slit of the tissue package.

She held it up to the light and said to everyone at the table, "Forgot all about this. Else gave it to me before we left yesterday. She said Frode found it in the car, their Peugeot. On the floor, she said. She figures it belongs to somebody in the group. They cleaned the car before we arrived and it wasn't there then so it probably belongs to one of us." She handed it to her husband.

He took it between his thumb and index finger. It was oval in shape, perhaps half an inch wide and three quarters high, intricately fashioned of what looked like both gold and silver in a tapestry-like pattern. As he looked more closely, he saw a stylized bird, perhaps a tern, with its wings pulled to its side hidden in the delicate pattern. He said to his wife, "It's not yours then?"

"Seth Ludington, we have been married for over a decade. Have you not noticed that I have pierced ears? This is a clip-on. And would you not have noticed this piece of jewelry if it were mine?"

"Well, yes, of course I would have. So, who's might it be?"

Harriet spoke in a voice just above a whisper, "Anybody but Fiona's or Ted's. They're the only ones on the bus with pierced ears. I bet Hope's are too, but I haven't noticed. Most young women these days have had their ears pierced."

Ludington handed it to van der Berg, who examined it closely, turning it around in her hand several times. She did not look at Seth when she spoke, "It's a cunning piece of jewelry—old, but not that valuable, I shouldn't think. It appears to be vintage Damascene." She quickly set it down on the table. "And no, it's not mine either, though I've never had my ears pierced, of course."

After dessert was served, Ludington returned to the table where Sarah Mrazek sat alone, a small glass of some yellow-colored aperitif set before her. Not her first dinner drink, he had noticed. He sat down and opened his hand to reveal the earring. He nodded to it. "Could this be yours, Sarah. Frode found it."

She looked at the earring and then at him. She reached up to touch her ear, unpierced Seth noticed.

"No, I don't think so." She downed the yellow liquid in a single swallow, looked at the piece of jewelry again and said, "It's definitely not mine."

When he returned to his table, Harriet asked if she might see the earring again. She rolled it over in her hand without comment and returned it to Seth, a quizzical look rising on her face.

As the group adjourned to the lounge for puzzles or outdoors for fresh air, Seth told Fiona he wanted to ask Frode some questions. He went to the Royal's office door, the top half of which was always open, and called out the Norwegian's curious name. The man appeared, drying his hands on a blue dish towel. "How can I be of help to you, Reverend?"

Seth held up the earring, "Fiona said you found this in the car. She said you think it must belong to one of us."

"Yes, because it wasn't there before you arrived. I cleaned the car that morning, very thoroughly. I would have found it."

"Where in the car did you find it?'

"On the carpet to the right of the driver's seat. In that little crack space down there by the door. I almost vacuumed it up."

"Frode, has anybody besides me borrowed the car? I mean anyone in our group."

"We leave the keys in it and I offer it to everybody, so I don't know. Chief Inspector Isbister asked the same question of me. I also told him that I didn't know." Frode looked at the earring, then at Ludington, and said, "But I guess somebody did."

Chapter Thirty-One

June 27

Frode tossed the dish towel over his shoulder and retreated back to the kitchen and the pile of dinner dishes waiting to be washed. When he closed the door from the little office to the kitchen, Ludington quietly opened the bottom of the Dutch door separating the hotel's entrance hall from its office and entered. He knew where to look, as he had seen which drawer Else had placed their passports the day they had arrived at the hotel. Informal as the Royal was, they maintained the Continental practice of collecting and keeping guests' passports during their stays. He pulled the drawer open quietly and saw the row of dark blue American passports lined up neatly.

It took him only a moment to find McNulty's. He opened it to see the man's sober visage staring at him. His middle name was Bruce. That made his initials "ABM." Ludington had guessed at the possibility. He closed the passport and put it back in its place in the drawer. He needed to talk this over with Harriet, but not until he spoke to his broker about whatever he might have been able to ferret out about the MBA Financial Services and the funds they managed for Philadelphia Theological Seminary. But before he bounced these thoughts off her—his worries about financial mismanagement at the seminary—he wanted to talk to van der Berg about earrings.

Fiona had gone up to their room and back to George MacKay Brown's Orkney tales. Seth found Harriet sitting still alone at their table, the only person in the room, sipping a cup of tea gone cold and looking pensive, a rare mood for someone as purposeful as she.

He sat opposite this woman who was his volunteer administrative assistant at Old Stone Church, who had become first a friend, and then his confidant in sleuthing, another iteration of which had again been thrust on him by some quirky providence.

"I showed the earring to Sarah," he said. She says it's not hers. She doesn't have pierced ears, though. I'm guessing you've noticed that."

"I saw you asking her about the earring. I have to say that there is something familiar about it. One can misremember such things, but when I held it in my hand at dinner, I seemed to know it. I'm confident that I've seen it somewhere before."

Ludington nodded and said, "Sarah's coming unhinged, Harriet, I mean more unhinged. I'm worried."

Painful as it was to him, Seth knew it was time to name names. "Frankly, I worry not only about her mental health, but I also worry about what she might have been capable of doing. You know that she was fixated on Phil. We've talked about it. And I think she probably came on the trip only to be close to him. She didn't sign up until after he and Penny did. Since Phil died, she's become even more morose and solitary. But I can't help but wonder, Harriet. I had a talk with Harry about stalkers. He has experience with them from his NYPD days. She fits the bill. Honestly, she impresses me not only as being repressed, but, well, maybe delusional. She could be projecting a part of herself that she hates on Linklater."

"Love and lust? Two of the 'l's.'" Harriet had spoken the two words slowly, as a question.

"Maybe an admixture of both, then steeped in delusion."

Harriet took a sip of her cold tea and said, "Phil Desmond clearly went willingly to the Dwarfie Stane that night. Nobody, not Linklater nor Sarah or whoever, could have carried him out there."

There was indeed yet another "whoever"—another possibility haunting Seth, but he would not name him to Harriet until he talked to William Queen about what he might discover about three curious ESG investment funds managed by MBA Financial Services.

Rather, he simply said, "Phil had said he wanted to see the Dwarfie Stane. It's the kind of thing that would have fascinated him. He had drunk too much that night, both at the wedding reception, even before we went to the church. He might have gone off with anybody who suggested a drive up to Rackwick and a walk out to the Stane in the summer twilight. But, of course you're right, the fact is that he was driven there by someone. No car was left there, of course. He was way too drunk to drive himself anyway."

He paused before adding, "And now Frode has found an earring on the floor of the Peugeot, an earring lost on the door side of the driver's seat. And he swears that it was not there when we got here, so it was lost in the last few days. That car could have driven Phil up to the Dwarfie Stane. Harriet, that earring has a mate somewhere."

Van der Burg looked into her tea. The milk had not entirely dissolved and had shaped itself into a pattern, a graceful counter-clockwise swirl in the amber liquid. She examined it as if she were reading tea leaves and said, "Two things to consider, Seth. First, someone could have planted the earring to deflect suspicion away from him or her. "Planted"—that's the agrarian term they employ on *Investigation Discovery*. Secondly, when a woman loses an earring, she usually keeps the other, at least for a while. In hope that the lost one may be found. I have several single earrings. I am a very hopeful person."

Van der Berg picked up a spoon and stirred her tea. Ludington's cellphone vibrated. He had silenced it for dinner. He pulled it from his pocket and recognized Isbister's number.

"Seth, it's Magnus. Toxicology report finally came back on that empty— actually not quite empty—whiskey bottle we found in the Dwarfie Stane. Traces of zolpidem—Ambien—in the whiskey. No surprise there, but I thought you'd want to know. No prints on the bottle. Must have been wiped clean. Have you booked yourselves back to the States yet?"

"Yes, in a couple of days. We'll leave Orkney the day after tomorrow. Then down to Edinburgh and home."

"Not much time for tying neater bows on boxes, is it?"

Ludington did not respond to the question and its suggestion. He said only, "Thanks for calling, Magnie."

He told Harriet about the traces of Ambien in the bottle of Highland Park that had been left in the Dwarfie Stane the night of Desmond's death.

She nodded and said, "To be expected. And you'll remember that Frode believes he was missing a bottle in the bar the next day. I supposed Linklater could have entered the hotel and purloined the whiskey."

"As could several other people. I've got a call to make, Harriet."

He went outside and around the hotel to the stone bench that overlooked the water of Long Hope and dialed William Queen's 917 cell phone number.

"Evening, Seth, at least evening there. I was worried that it was too late so I was going to wait till morning to get back to you. Glad you called. So, it's really fishy. Those three funds are all definitely greenwashing. I mean, they're really quite well-invested, nicely diversified, but save for a couple of small holdings in some intriguing little third-world projects, there's nothing special about them in terms of ESG—environment, social consciousness or governance. Actually, their yields should have been pretty spectacular these last few years. But here's the clincher. Nobody knows who MBA Financial Services LLC is. Not registered with anybody anywhere. Looks like a ghost to me, Seth."

Ludington sighed and said, "I have a hunch who the ghost is. Thanks for the digging, Bill. And don't worry, I don't have any money in any of them. It's a friend, an institution actually."

"Well, tell them to get out. Quick. Your guess is as good as mine, but I'd hazard somebody is skimming, or charging ridiculous management fees. It could even be outright embezzlement. Somebody needs to get in touch with the SEC."

As Ludington ended the call, he silently mouthed another of the "l" words, "lucre."

He knew that the somebody who would be calling the Securities and Exchange Commission would be Henry Barkman. But his call to Barkman could wait a day, maybe two.

Ludington rounded the Royal and entered the front door to find van der Berg descending the stairway, hiding something in her clenched hand and wearing a triumphant look on her face. She walked to the door and whispered conspiratorially to her pastor, "Let's talk outside, Seth."

He followed her around to the back of their empty tour bus and out of sight and earshot of the hotel.

"Well," she began, "I was just now walking back to my room, and as I did so I necessarily passed by Sarah's room, of course. The door was cracked open and I knocked. As I anticipated, she did not answer. I had seen her set off on a walk after dinner. "

Van der Berg looked sheepish as she continued. "The door was open a little. I confess that I opened it a bit more. As I did so, I couldn't help but see it laying right there on the unmade bed in her room. Really, I cannot believe people leave their beds unmade. Anyway, there it was, half tucked under the pillow as if it were intended to be hidden, but I could see it. I felt I was quite justified in entering and retrieving it, considering the events of these last few days and the responsibilities that have been forced upon us by these events."

She opened her hand and showed Ludington what it held. It was a clerical collar, an open white circle of soft plastic that would have attached itself to a black clerical shirt with little brass collar buttons, a sartorial anachronism maintained only in corners of the Christian church.

Seth took it in his hands and read aloud the words printed on the inside, "Clericool 16 ½ made in Italy," and then he said, "That's a fairly large neck size. Too big to be hers.""

Harriet wrinkled her brow, "Is that really the name of a brand?"

"It is, Harriet. It is. And we both know who's Clericool collar it is. Or was.

Chapter Thirty-Two

June 27

"Let's have us an evening stroll, Harriet. I think better when I move." Ludington and van der Berg walked from the hotel, turned left at the road that ran along the shore of South Walls and ambled slowly, side-by-side, east toward St. Columba's Kirk. They found it locked, as it should be so late on a weekday evening. There was no bench outside the building on which to sit. The church was not even surrounded by a graveyard that might offer a tombstone to perch upon while reflecting on murder. So, they sat on the threshold stone laid at the dour little kirk's front door, even though it was set way too low for comfort. Seth had to help Harriet down. Proud of her agility at her age, she accepted his arm grudgingly.

Ludington turned the clerical collar she had given him over in his hands as he told her about his conversations with Henry Barkman and William Queen. "He suspects financial malfeasance, Bill does. Actually, more than suspects. Al McNulty is surely in some very deep trouble. My guess is that he knows Phil was on to him, that he's known it for a while. I'm guessing it's what their argument in Braemar was about. I bet Al knew about Phil's suspicions when he signed up for the trip. Probably why he signed up. He told me he was interested in seeing County Antrim where his McNulty ancestors came from. Antrim is in Northern Ireland."

"So, what do you think he meant to accomplish by coming along?"

191

"Maybe he only wanted to sidle up to Phil and offer his excuses. Perhaps he thought he could convince him that he'd make up whatever his scheme had cost the seminary. I read somewhere that a lot of embezzlers honestly imagine that they're loaning themselves the money and that they'll eventually pay it back."

"Do you think he actually tried to talk to Phil about such financial matters while we were on our tour. You are imagining that Mr. McNulty asked him to eschew, or perhaps delay, reporting what he was suspecting so that he might have time to repay the funds he had diverted to himself? We had a somewhat similar situation at the law firm right before I retired. A junior partner was billing rather more hours than he spent on certain of the cases he was working. They covered it up, the firm did, but he never made full partner, of course. He was eased out a year later. All very polite."

"McNulty may have tried to work something like that with Phil, but my guess is that if he did, it didn't go well. I mean, that was quite the quarrel that night in the bar at the Fife Arms. I overheard snatches of it, including the word 'improprieties.' McNulty didn't know I was at the bar."

"But Seth, do you really think that Phil would have voluntarily gotten into a car with that man and gone off on a twilight excursion to visit the lonely Dwarfie Stane? That is to say, would he have done so with such a matter lying between them?."

"As you well know, Harriet, Phil Desmond was a gracious soul, always quick to forgive, maybe too quick. And he was drunk that night, and he really wanted to see the place. So maybe. Yes, I can imagine it."

"You are conjecturing that perhaps Phil then refused Mr. McNulty's pleas, that Phil told him he intended to suggest an audit of the seminary's endowment funds upon his return home, and that the man then took another course of action... in order to silence him?"

Ludington shrugged his shoulders, looked at his feet, and said, "It's only too possible."

He then raised the clerical collar he was fingering so that it was directly before their eyes, and changed the vector of their speculations.

"Where and how did she get hold of this, Harriet? It's got to be Phil's. I can ask Penny, in fact I plan to, but I'm pretty sure it's his. He'd be about sixteen-and-a-half. It's too big to be Sarah's. And she's not ordained, so it's unlikely she'd even own a clerical collar. And we know that the one Phil wore that night is missing. It wasn't on him when they found him, and it hasn't shown up. It's painfully obvious, Harriet. I mean, you found it tucked under her pillow like a keepsake. Good grief, the woman was sleeping with it."

"So, I put the parallel question to you, Seth. Would President Emeritus Phil Desmond have gotten in a car with a female student studying at his erstwhile institution late of an evening in order to visit a distant archeological site on a remote island? He was, as you know, a man of the highest moral integrity."

"Same response, Harriet. He'd had way too much to drink and he wanted to see the Dwarfie Stane. No one would ever need to know he'd gone with her. And we don't know whether he had any idea that she was so fixated on him."

"So, if she is a murderess, what would her motive have been? To kill a man with whom she was hopelessly infatuated? I suppose one might surmise that she had made intimate advances to Phil at some point in our tour. He would have rebuffed them, of course. We both know that. One might then imagine that her love translated itself into rage. Love is sometimes wont to do just that. So, come the night of a wedding, one might imagine that she offered him a ride to the Dwarfie Stane and along the way gave him whiskey laced with sleeping drugs from the bottle she had purloined from the bar at our hotel?"

"We think perversely alike, Harriet van der Berg. Again, your scenario is possible, too sadly possible. After all, like McNulty, Sarah didn't sign up for the trip until after Phil did. Maybe she planned to make her move when she had him close, just like Al. But she would have planned to make a very different kind of move. In either case, the move went hopelessly wrong. Then one would have to conjecture that either one of them would have decided—perhaps in advance or maybe at the last minute—to mimic the Sod Stuffer. We'd been hearing about him since we arrived in Scotland. It was the right date, June 21, the solstice, just like the two years before. A serial killer was handy, a serial killer who, as it turned out, was only too eager to take the credit for a third murder."

Ludington stuffed the clerical collar into his jacket pocket and said, "And the earring, Harriet?"

"Well," she stammered, "It could have nothing to do with the matter we are considering. Anyone of us—or even someone else on this island of generous lenders and ready borrowers—might have used the car at any time for an innocent reason and lost an earring while driving it. There's really no reason to think it is necessarily related to Phil's death in any way. Or some person, a person both clever and nefarious, might have planted it there, precisely as I suggested to you previously. To cast blame away from herself." She quickly added, "Or from himself."

Ludington looked at her questioningly, then gazed down at the path before them that led to St. Columba's front step where they sat, a path worn into the earth over the centuries by a thousand feet bearing souls come to face the Great Mystery. He said slowly, "Then why is no one claiming it?"

Van der Berg glanced away and did not answer his question. He stood and helped the older woman to her feet.

"Thank you." She dusted off her knee-length woolen skirt even though it bore no trace of dust.

As they walked along the road back to the hotel in the dim, she said, "I have told you that my Margaret was a great reader of mystery novels. She especially favored what she called "the English ladies" – Agatha Christie of course, and Dorothy Sayers, and more recently P. D. James. But she insisted that her favorite was an author named Josephine Tey. Margaret labored tirelessly to induce me to read them. I did enjoy them, but I rather tired of weekend country house parties. But I digress. Our current dilemma brought to mind the game of *Clue* that Margaret also so enjoyed. For a time, we invited Greg and Brian, the two younger gentlemen who lived in 4F, for evenings of *Clue* and cosmopolitans. 'C and C evenings,' we called them. I must say, we did have a merry time before they moved to Indiana, of all places. At any rate, in the game of *Clue*…. Have you ever played it, Seth?"

"No, sorry. I'm a cribbage man."

"Well, in the game of *Clue*, each player attempts to deduce which of the weekend guests has committed yet another tiresome country house murder, and not only who did it, but which of several deadly implements was used in the crime, and in which of the house's several rooms it took place. The solution has been sealed in a little envelope placed at the center of the board before play begins."

"I think I'll stick with cribbage."

"Wisely perhaps. At any rate, here is my point, Dominie. I mean Seth."

Ludington had come to understand that when she was excited or distracted, Harriet still occasionally relapsed to calling him "Dominie."

Only half aware of her slip, she continued, pointing her finger at the air in front of her as she walked and spoke, "When one of the players believes that he or she knows the solution to the crime, they make what is called 'an accusation.' He or she says, for example, 'Professor Plum, with the candlestick, in the conservatory.' All very juvenile, frankly. Margaret used to stand and raise her cosmopolitan glass in the air whenever she made an accusation. But, here is what has occurred to me, Seth. I think that you—and I—have perhaps come to the point of making such an accusation, or maybe two accusations. Though perhaps 'confrontations' is a better word. I don't mean to frame the gravity of the matter before us with a silly game, but it makes my point."

"And after we do so, Harriet, I mean after we confront someone with an accusation, where do we find the little envelope telling us whether we were right or wrong?"

There was no answer to that question, so he asked another. "You still miss Margaret?"

Seth asked the question as the Royal rose to view a few hundred yards down the road, though the hotel was barely visible in the dim light of near-midnight.

"I always shall. Everything seems to bring her to mind. This sleuthing business of ours does so, though murder and its detection were always fictive for her, a fireside entertainment. I cannot imagine what she might have done with a real one."

"How long were you together?"

"Fifty-four years, two months, and let me think, seven days."

"A long time, Harriet, half a century plus."

"Oh, it was not always the proverbial bed of roses. We really did have—what do they say—our 'ups and downs.' She was often flighty, Margaret. She called it 'being playful.' She was always saying, 'Oh, lighten up, Harriet.' In time, I came to understand that it was so good for me—she was good for me—sober old Dutchwoman that I am. You might say we complimented each other."

"Any counsel for a guy in a younger relationship who is about to become a father?"

She walked a few more steps in silence, stopped in the middle of the road, and turned to face her pastor. She was nearly as tall as he, and still stood straight-backed.

"Love is not a mere feeling, Seth. Oh, it's that, but it's more. It has to be more. Feelings, our emotions, they have their sweet days and they have their foul days. That's how we are. So, love has to be more than how we happen to feel at any given moment. It also has to be a choice you make, an act of will, I guess you could say. You really do decide to love. It's not a disease; you don't just catch it one day and then get over it the next. You choose it, and then you choose to do it. You choose to do it every day."

She turned and took his arm and walked him toward the hotel. He and Fiona had always said they "fell in love" that summer on the archeological dig in Israel. "Fell," was the word they used, as if they had been walking along and tripped on something that they had not seen in front of them. He had to confess that it was probably more lust than love, at least at first. But over those memorable months that followed, it had soon rested into love. In retrospect, he knew that they both probably did make a choice to love each other, at least it had become their choice by the time autumn had come and they left Mount Herodium, together.

He said none of this, only, "I guess it's accusations time come morning, Harriet. 'Confrontations,' at the least. It'll be less than pleasant. I think you and I should speak to Sarah first. Better the two of us. I'll talk to McNulty

196

alone."

She nodded and then sighed.

Seth found Fiona in bed but not yet asleep, her nose in the last few pages of *Hawkfall*. He assumed that she knew he had been with Harriet and had surmised that something was brewing. She asked no questions, but he decided she had every right to know. Not precisely a right to know. Rather, it was something he could no longer keep from his wife. All marriages have their secrets, but this one did not fit in the box, especially if it exploded into something very large and dangerous, as it well might. He had kept a secret from her once before, one much closer to the bone than this one, and had come to sorely regret having done so. He undressed and put on the oversized Michigan tee shirt that served as his nightshirt. He looked at his wife's book and waited until she had read the last page and closed it.

"Fine and moody tales Mr. Brown tells," she said. "Did you know he became a Roman Catholic late in life? I Googled him."

It was time to tell her. "Speaking of acts of insurrection, Harriet and I have been talking, well, more than talking, speculating about Phil's death." He told her about the email with the attached prospectuses that had been found on Desmond's phone. He told her about his calls to Henry Barkman and Bill Queen and their suspicions of financial malfeasance. He told her of the quarrel between Desmond and McNulty he had witnessed in the bar in Braemar where that word had been spoken. Then he showed her the clerical collar Harriet had found tucked under Sarah Mrazek's pillow.

He finished by saying, "So, I'll be having a little talk with both of them tomorrow morning."

She sighed and lay her book face-down on the duvet. "It'll be more than a little talk, my dear. The police really ought to be doing this, not you and Harriet."

He told her that McCormick considered the case solved and had ordered Isbister to cease any further investigations.

But Seth, you're going to be accusing each of them of murder. At the least you'll be suggesting to one that he's an embezzler and to the other that she's a madwoman. Of course, I've sensed that you and Harriet had your doubts

197

about the Sod Stuffer having killed Phil. But this is such a risky business. Before you talk to either of them, do me a favor. At least talk to Harry. You need a professional's counsel. Please. Talk to Harry."

"Okay, if you insist."

Seth eventually fell asleep with half-formed prayers on his lips.

Chapter Thirty-Three

June 28

Ludington woke early after another fitful night. Fiona was already up and dressed in a St. Andrew's sweatshirt, camo jeans and hiking boots. He knew that Ingrid was picking her up in her Land Rover at 7:30. The two of them had planned a final day together—first a stop at the Scapa Flow Museum in Lyness with its bits of sunken warships, then up to Rackwick for lunch with yet another of Ingrid's friends. The woman loved showing her granddaughter off, something Seth completely understood. Then – weather permitting – the two women planned a hike out to the headland that overlooked the giant sandstone sea stack that was the Old Man of Hoy. They promised to be back to the Royal in time for the special dinner Frode and Else had insisted on presenting to their guests before they departed. The itinerary had originally named it "A Festive Final Dinner." After Desmond's death, the notice posted on the bulletin board to the left of the office door had renamed it "A Farewell Dinner." Still an unfortunate choice of words, Seth thought.

Seth crawled out of bed and headed for the shower. Fiona gave him a peck on the check and said by way of explaining her absence on their last day in Orkney, "Don't know when I'll see Grams again. But we'll be back for dinner. Stay out of mischief if you can." Seth guessed she might have been relieved not to be around the Royal for the two awkward conversations he and Harriet were planning

Seth knew that Harry Mulholland was an early riser and hoped he might catch him at breakfast. Georgia on other hand—so Harry had told him—often slept in, so he'd hopefully find the man alone. Indeed, Seth found his Clerk of Session sitting solo at a window table, a full breakfast and yesterday's edition of *The Scotsman* spread out before him.

"May I join you, Harry?"

"Of course, of course." He pulled the newspaper off the place setting to his right and tapped the table to indicate that Seth should sit.

"Front page," he said. "This guy—Linklater's—confession. Perverse character, but then he's a serial killer. They're all crazy."

"Did you ever work any serial killer cases when you were NYPD?'

"No, but I certainly remember the big one. The Son of Sam case in the City? Do you remember it? No, you wouldn't. Way before your time."

"When was it?"

"Late seventies. I guess you weren't even born. Satanic cult stuff. He confessed just like this guy, but he kept changing his story."

Frode came by the table with a pot of his lamentable coffee. Ludington asked for a scone with butter and orange marmalade."

"The sausages are superb, Seth, and the eggs are nice, too. Frode's scrambled something in there, thyme, I think. Anyway, Son of Sam... The other day, I told you that we—we cops, I mean—sometimes keep details about cases from the public, do it for a bunch of reasons. One I didn't mention to you is in order to trip up false confessions. That was a question with Berkowitz, the Son of Sam guy. Oh, he did some of them. Question was always whether he did all of them. I was pounding a beat in East Harlem in '77, so I had nothing to do with it. But we all followed it. The whole city followed it. Even today, there's still some question about whether there were other crazies involved."

"So, Harry, do you think there's any chance that Linklater's confession might not be legit?'

"I doubt it, Seth, I really do. But you can bet that Isbister and what's-his-name—McCormick—you can bet they know stuff they're keeping quiet.

Seth thought to himself, "Indeed they are – Ambien, an empty bottle of

Highland Park, ferry passenger lists and small boats." But he said nothing as he buttered his hot scone. He decided not to speak with Harry about either Sarah and the collar or Al and the money. Harry would only try to warn him off. He'd surely tell him to call Isbister, even though McCormick had effectively tied the man's hands when he had retreated to Inverness after declaring the case closed. But Seth had kept his promise to Fiona that he would talk to Harry, even if he had not talked to him about quite everything. So, they drank coffee and discussed the long drive back to Edinburgh the next day and their return flight to the States the day after that.

Seth saw Harriet descending the stairs and quickly downed the last of his coffee. He excused himself, left Harry to the last of his sausages, and went to intercept her at the foot of the stairway. He said softly, "Let's talk to Sarah first, Harriet. Together, in her room. I don't think I should be alone with her." A decade in ministry had taught him when it was unwise to be alone in a room with someone, especially if they were of the opposite sex. You never knew what they might say later about what transpired.

Sarah Mrazek did not answer their knock. Seth called out through the door, "Sarah, could we have a word? Harriet and I?"

"Go away." The command was resolute, though soft and muffled.

Harriet turned the door knob. No doors in the Royal locked. She gently pushed it open far enough to stick her head into the room. Ludington, just behind her, could see that it was almost pitch black in the room. The heavy summer sleeping shades were drawn and the lights were off, but Seth could make out the human lump in the bed. Harriet opened the door all the way and strode in.

"Young lady, taking to the bed will not solve your problems. We are here to talk, whether doing so pleases you or not."

Harriet flicked on the bedside lamp and motioned for Seth to enter. She moved to sit at the foot of the bed and motioned to Seth to take the single chair in the room. As he pulled it across the wooden floor, it made a startling screech. Sarah heard it, rose in the bed and turned and stared at the two of them, anger in her swollen red eyes, her hair a tangled mess of magenta.

"I said go away."

Seth drew the clerical collar from his pocket and held it in his hand for her to see.

She pushed herself farther up in the bed, "So, *you* stole it. I want it back." She lunged for it as Seth pulled it out of her reach.

He said softly, "Sarah, Where did you get this? I know it's not yours." He then retreated to the passive voice to spare van der Berg and said, "It was discovered here in your room."

"I found it." She whispered, and reached out her hand for it again.

He pulled it farther away. "Where, Sarah? Where did you find it?"

"On the road. It was just lying there, in the middle of the road."

"When?"

"The night of the wedding."

"Exactly when that night?"

"Late, after everybody was leaving the reception at the hall. Give it back. It's all I have left to remember him."

Harriet nodded at Seth in a way that said, "Ask the unpleasant question."

"Sarah, did you and Phil go anywhere that night, in the car?" Then he said—to van der Berg's surprise, "Sarah, I heard Phil say something strange to you in Edinburgh, at the National Museum that day. His words are hard to forget. He said, 'I have told you before. It will not work. We have to rethink this.'"

She was a bright young woman and immediately understood the implication of his question.

"What?" she screamed. "You can't think…. He was talking about my doctoral dissertation. I've been exploring a womanist reading of the Song of Solomon. He didn't think it would work. I told him I thought it could, but he insisted that it was a bad idea. He was on my committee."

She suddenly sprang from the bed and lunged at Ludington, again attempting to retrieve the clerical collar. He stood up and backed away. She was fully dressed in the jeans and tank top that she had obviously slept in. Seth held the collar above his head, out of her reach. In failure, she collapsed back in the bed and leaned her back against the headboard.

Then she grabbed her knees in her arms and began to rock back and forth in the bed, silent save for sobs. She began to shake her head back and forth violently, the classic gesture of a furious child, as she screamed, "No, no, no!" even though they had asked her no more questions.

"Stay with her, Harriet. Would you?"

He left the room, thinking that Sarah Mrazek was either entering a deeper phase of a psychological break or that she was a consummate actress. Ludington was inclined to believe it was the former. If it should come to it—though he was still quite unsure of her culpability—an insanity defense would probably be credible.

The second confrontation that lay before him that morning promised to be awkward as well, but less potentially unpleasant. He didn't like Al McNulty, and had little doubt that the man was guilty—guilty of financial crimes at least. Seth had printed out the three prospectuses on the hotel's printer the night before and was holding them in his hand when he knocked on McNulty's bedroom door. The man had not been in the dining room when he had left Harry half an hour before. McNulty, he had noticed, was a late riser when given the choice.

Al McNulty opened the door to the knock and grinned at Ludington, "Seth, you're up and about bright and early."

"Could you take a walk with me, Al. We need to talk, you know... privately."

That last word always communicated urgency. Ludington saw McNulty glance at the papers he was holding in his hands.

He hesitated for a moment, forced a smile and said, "Let me throw some clothes on. I'll meet you out in front of the hotel, by that bench there. Nice view of the water."

Seth sat on the familiar bench and waited for ten minutes, haunted by the absurdity of the situation. He decided to walk back to the lobby to find McNulty. He rounded the corner of the building just in time to see the man dash out of the hotel's front door and climb into the Peugeot. He saw him grope for the keys on the dashboard, start the car, back it out of the parking lot and kill the engine as he struggled with the manual transmission. He started the car up again, shifted into first gear and managed to shoot a little gravel from the front wheels as he bolted past Ludington and west toward the Ayre and to Hoy proper where – or so Ludington assumed – he would catch a ferry off the island to somewhere else, anywhere else.

Seth took his cell from his pocket and called Isbister. He picked up on the first ring. Seth began by reminding the detective of those attachments to the email Desmond had received a few days before he was killed, correspondence that McCormick had deemed unrelated to his murder.

"I made some calls about those documents, and it seems McNulty's up to something fishy with seminary money. I was going to confront him with it and he bolted. He took the hotel's car and raced off. I imagine he'll catch the next ferry and try to get himself out of Orkney."

Isbister was silent for a good ten seconds, "Two questions, Seth. Are there any criminal charges on this financial stuff in the States yet? Something we could detain him for. And a second question." He paused, and lowered his voice before he asked, "So, ye think there's a chance this money business might be related to Desmond's death?"

"Magnie, the answer to the first question is no. No charges yet, and I can't imagine a case being brought in Pennsylvania for days or weeks. The answer to your second question is that I simply don't know. Maybe. All I have is my Calvinist's capacity to imagine the wretched things mortals are capable of, especially when they're cornered."

"Well, I can't detain him for your suspicions about his fallen human nature. But you said he took the hotel's car, right?"

"Yes, but they lend it to everybody."

But I don't know that, do I? And you've reported it stolen, haven't you? I could arrest him for theft of a vehicle, couldn't I? '*Vol de voiture,*' as the French would say. Peugeot pilfering. I think I'll do just that."

Ludington thought to himself, "The man even plays with words in French."

Chapter Thirty-Four

June 28

Later that morning, Harriet found Seth sitting in one of the two worn overstuffed chairs in the Royal's lounge. His hands were folded, index fingers forming a little steeple with which he was frantically tapping his lips. He often did so when he was thinking.

She said, "I've phoned Jilly Wilson, the nurse. She said she'd come have a look at Sarah in an hour or two. Maybe there's something she can give her to calm her down."

"She's a fragile young woman, Harriet. Let's just get her home in one piece and then make sure she gets the help she needs."

The lounge was empty save for the two of them, so Seth and Harriet moved to sit facing each other across one of the several card tables covered with half-completed jigsaw puzzles, this one with the thousand-pieces of Skara Brae.

Seth fingered a pair of loose puzzle pieces. "Sarah's had a breakdown and Al's bolted." He related the details of his brief encounter with the man and his panicked flight in the hotel's car. "He must have recognized the printouts of the prospectuses I was holding." He told Harriet about the call he had then made to Isbister. "They can hold him for twelve hours on the car theft and then he's free to go wherever. Who knows?" He rolled his eyes. "Paraguay maybe."

Van der Berg took in this news and nodded her understanding. "What do we do now, Seth?"

"I do want to talk to Penny. I need to ask her if Phil may really have lost his collar that night like Sarah's implying. And I'd like to see what she might know about Phil's relationship with McNulty, if anything. He may have said something to her about his suspicions, before or after he got the email from Henry Barkman. Not sure where it will get us, though. I don't know what else to do."

Van der Berg's face was flat, expressionless, "Yes, do talk to Penny, you alone. She's in her room, up and dressed. I just knocked on her door and poked my head in. I'll ask her to come down and have a chat with you."

Ludington managed to fit three puzzle pieces while he waited for Penny Desmond. The two women entered the room together as he tapped the third piece into place, a chunk of steel-gray Orkney sky.

Penny was dressed in jeans and a white Harvard sweatshirt. One of their daughters had gone there, he recalled. He sensed that the widow was growing increasingly composed. She was not, he knew, a woman to wear her heart on her sleeve. Her grief was deep, but it was hers alone, hers personally. She was hardly one to display it to the world. Both Harriet and Penny sat with him at the card table, the latter after setting her purse, a large and colorful cloth bag—probably Vera Bradley, a brand Fiona sometimes favored—on another card table behind her.

"Harriet said you wanted a word."

"Yes, well, I wanted you to know that I just got an email from the travel agency. They've been able to arrange for Phil to be on our flight home."

"Phil's body, you mean."

"Yes, sorry. Phil's body. Is one of the girls going to meet you at JFK?"

"All three of them will be there." She said the words with a hint of a smile – that of a mother proud of her daughters' attentiveness, Seth guessed.

He reached into his jacket pocket and retrieved the collar that Harriet had found tucked under Sarah Mrazek's pillow. He gently laid it on top of the uncompleted puzzle. Penny stared at it and gasped. The slightest intake of air. As she did so, Harriet excused herself and rose to leave them to talk privately. Seth was startled when he saw her step behind Penny and carefully lift Penny's Vera Bradley bag from the nearby table and leave the room with it, hiding it in front of her as she left. She looked back at Seth and raised her eyebrows at him. It was an expression that confused him at first. He was barely able to conceal his shock at what van der Berg had done. He finally surmised that she was telling him to keep Penny occupied for a moment.

He turned back to Penny, who had taken the clerical collar in her hands and was turning it over to look at the size noted on the inside.

He asked, "Is it Phil's?"

She slid the collar between her thumb and index finger, veritably caressing it. "Yes, it has to be. It's his size and the brand he always bought."

"You said you think he may have taken it off after you left the wedding reception that night. What did he do with it? Do you recall?"

"Honestly, I don't. He often took it off if it was irritating him. He was so deliberate about when he wore it and when he didn't. He usually only wore it when he was functioning as a minister – weddings and funerals, hospital calls and the like. He never put it on to attract attention."

She smiled at the memory of how thoughtfully her husband had approached his role in life. She said, "He only wore his collar that night because he had not thought to pack a dress shirt and a tie. When he did wear it for some reason, he would often take it off right afterward. He might have done so that night. If he did, he probably would have just stuffed it in his jacket pocket."

Seth looked down at the Clericool collar. "Someone said they found it that night. On the road between the village hall and here."

"That's possible. He may have tried to get it into his pocket, but missed and dropped it. I'm only guessing. I don't really know. Why are you asking me this, Seth?"

He brushed the obvious question away with an ambiguity, "Well, just to make sure of things. And I wanted to return it to you."

She moved to give him the collar back in spite of what he had said.

"No, really. You should have it, Penny. You should also know that Al McNulty has left, on his own."

He told her about the emails found on her husband's phone with the curious ESG prospectuses attached to them, his subsequent calls to Henry Barkman and his broker in New York, and finally his attempt to confront the man that morning over his suspicions of financial wrongdoing. He did not mention either his hunch that the man might be a murderer or the panicked nature of his flight in the hotel's car.

"Phil didn't much like Al McNulty. He never said anything to me about him. Seminary presidents have to like everybody, but I could read Phil like a book. What you're saying doesn't much surprise me."

Seth nodded. "I heard the two of them having quite the quarrel when we were in Braemar. In the bar that night. I asked Phil about it, but he brushed it off."

Penny smiled. "That's what he would do. At least it's what he would do until he was ready to pounce."

"Do you think he was ready to do that, pounce I mean, on Al?"

"If he knew what you're telling me you suspect, yes. But he wouldn't have done it until we got back to Philadelphia."

Harriet van der Berg entered the room, walking softly, her face drawn, her usually fastidiously organized French twist oddly askew. Penny Desmond's back was to her, but Harriet was holding something behind her own back anyway, hiding it in case the woman might turn around. As she neared them, she withdrew the large Vera Bradly cloth bag and set it back on the table from which she had taken it five minutes earlier. Seth was careful not to look up at her as she obviously did not want Penny to see that she had returned it. Harriet then quickly raised her right hand just above and behind Penny's head to show Seth an earring she held between her index finger and thumb. It was identical to the one in the pocket of Seth's blue jeans, the earring Frode had found in the Peugeot. Seth was barely able to keep the shock of her find and its implication from registering on his face. Harriet then dropped the earring back in the Vera Bradley bag before clearing her throat to announce her presence. Seth Ludington now understood that there was one more thing he needed to discuss with Penny Desmond.

Harriet sat down at the puzzle table between Seth and Penny. She looked at Seth, who reached into his pocket, and said to Penny, "Oh, and one last thing…"

He pulled the earring from his jeans pocket and laid it on top of a nearly completed part of the Skara Brae puzzle and said, "This has got to be yours."

Her face was expressionless as she reached for the earring, took it in her hand and then set it back down.

She began to say, "I don't think…" when Harriet interrupted her. "Oh Penny, I remember those earrings from way back, from when you and Phil were at Old Stone." She offered a theatrical smile, poorly done. She was so obviously acting. "He gave them to you for Valentine's Day one year. You showed them to me and Margaret."

Penny was silent for a moment, then took the earring off the table and said, "Thank you, Seth. Wherever did you find it?"

"Actually, Frode found it. A few days ago. On the floor of his car, to the right of the driver's seat."

Penny Desmond looked at the piece of jewelry and said, "That makes sense, I must have lost it that morning, that morning when we got the news about Phil. I was so distraught. I tried to drive off on my own, to get up to that place where he was. But I never learned to drive a manual shift car. I was so frustrated and upset. You had to drive me up there. Remember? You have been so consistently supportive in all this, Seth. Thank you."

Ludington nodded in acknowledgement, but neither he nor van der Berg said anything in response. He knew they had just been lied to. He sensed that Harriet knew it as well, but perhaps not for the same reason. Two lies, not only one, had just been told.

Chapter Thirty-Five

June 28

"Well, if you'll excuse me." Penny Desmond pushed her chair away from the card table in the lounge, and rose to her full dignity. "I need to call the girls to let them know about the arrangements. They'll have to see about a hearse at JFK when we land. Do you have any recommendations, Seth? Funeral directors in the City, I mean. You're the New Yorker."

"I would try Campbell's on Madison. I'd be happy to phone them if you'd like. I know some of the staff there." Campbell's was the City's celebrity funeral home, not cheap, but he figured the Desmond's could manage the cost and would value the discreet service that was the place's specialty.

"Would you, Seth? I'd so appreciate it."

"Of course, of course. I'll phone as soon as they open." He looked at the Shinola Runwell on his wrist. It was late morning Orkney time. Somebody ought to be in Campbell's office in four or five hours.

Penny rose and smiled languidly at Ludington and van der Berg, further discomforting them with her easy grace, both of movement and dissembling.

Seth looked at Harriet after Penny had left. He was not sure whether she was ready to talk about what had just unfolded, but he knew he was not. He said, "I need to go for a walk, to think a bit."

"Yes, you should do precisely that. I have an unpleasant matter I need to attend to as well."

Ludington decided that the old Martello Tower in Hackness at the east end of South Walls was as good a destination as any. As he passed St. Columba's Kirk, he worked over the memory that had rattled him a few moments earlier when Penny told her story about losing the earring, an earring he sensed she was about to deny owning had Harriet not interrupted with her memory of the pair. But what had shaken him more was when Penny had told them that she had never learned to drive a car with a manual transmission. It was, of course, a credible possibility. Most people in this age of automatics cannot manage a stick shift. But as she said it, he had suddenly remembered the photo he'd seen on Phil Desmond's desk in his seminary office several months earlier. It was a happy shot of slightly younger iterations of Phil and Penny seated in a lovely vintage MGA roadster, British racing green, the top down. Phil had said it was a 1960 model, his gift to his wife on her fiftieth birthday. Her dream car, he had told him. Penny, in big sunglasses and a kerchief tied over her head, was in the driver's seat, an exploding smile spread across her face. Seth Ludington knew European cars, and he knew full well that no 1960 MGA had ever been manufactured with an automatic transmission. He also knew that working a clutch and running through the gears of a manual transmission was like riding a bicycle. It's a motor skill that stays with you. He had no doubt that Penny Desmond was lying about not being able to manage the stick shift in the hotel's Peugeot. Not only had she lied to him about it a few minutes earlier, but she had put on quite a little performance of feminine ineptitude the morning after her husband's death when she had gotten into the car to drive herself to the Dwarfie Stane. But why the deception? All answers to that question were painfully awkward, especially if she was trying to demonstrate that she could never have driven the car to the Dwarfie Stane and back.

The door of the Martello Tower was open when he arrived. He entered and climbed to the top of the shortish round stone structure, built to defend Orkney from Napoléon, who never came. That year, 1813, he had turned his ambitions east, to Germany. Ludington had majored in American history in college, but the little French general's ambitions had had ramifications on his side of the Atlantic as well.

The day's gray was finally clearing, scudding clouds racing west to east. The view from the tower was stunning. The island of Flotta lay to the north, across Switha Sound. Its unsightly oil terminal was hidden from view at this angle. He could make out an interisland ferry in the distance moving across the chop, probably toward Flotta and then on to Mainland. Al McNulty might well be on it, quite unaware that Magnus Isbister would be waiting to arrest him for auto theft when he docked. To his right was little Switha, and beyond it the much larger island of South Ronaldsay, now connected to Mainland by the Churchill Barriers and the road built over them. Ludington turned around to gaze at the low deep green of South Walls, a fertile patch of rich black earth blessed with long summer days and generous rainfall. He could see grim little St. Columba's and the village hall, the two places where Phil Desmond had spent his next-to-last hours. And very happy hours they had been, Seth thought – a joyful wedding ceremony at which he didn't have to officiate, a piper to lead them to a feast of local fare, drink aplenty and mad dancing. And all the while, he had a wife of fifty years at his side, still a beauty at seventy-whatever.

He asked himself again, actually mouthing the words, "Why did she just lie to me and Harriet?" He had first thought to challenge her with his memory of the photo of her and Phil in the MGA. But then he had decided it would be wiser to first conduct a hunt for the one thing that was still missing, the one thing that might illumine the truth hiding behind all the obfuscation.

He walked back to the Royal from the Martello Tower much more quickly than he had walked there. Summer rental cottages were on his left, the shore on his right. He noticed several small boats pulled up the steep bank. He approached the hotel from its back, the east side of the building where the rubbish bins were discreetly hidden behind a high wooden fence that had been freshly painted the off-white of the hotel's trim. Behind the fence, through its wide pickets, he could make out a figure who was apparently already doing what he planned to do—rummaging through the several trash cans inside. He opened the latch on the gate to the trash enclosure as softly as he could.

"Dumpster diving, Miss van der Berg."

"Oh, Dominie, I mean Seth." She stood, startled and holding a head of wilted lettuce in her rubber-gloved hands. "This is so very distressing. This entire matter is so consummately distressing. Have we not opened Pandora's proverbial box with our snooping?"

Harriet Van der Berg leaned against the gray stucco wall next to the door that Seth assumed led to the hotel's kitchen. Perhaps she did so to support herself, or maybe to save herself from an impending swoon. The smell was stomach-churning.

"We may have done precisely that," he said. "I mean opened Pandora's box. So, Harriet, no earrings are missing, the collar is found, and the police have the whiskey bottle—almost empty save for a half shot of Highland Park laced with Ambien. What are you looking for?"

She hesitated in answering, but finally found her voice and declared boldly, "Penny Desmond would never wear such jewelry in the morning while dressed informally. I mean, she was wearing blue jeans that morning, Seth. It's just not done. Not the blue jeans, but such formal earrings worn with blue jeans. I know her. She would not have worn those earrings that morning. I would surely have noticed such a *faux pas*. I also believe that before I interrupted her this morning, she was about to deny that the earrings were hers. I did not mention this to you earlier because I was still unsure, but I thought I recognized them yesterday. As I reflected further, I became confident that they were indeed the pair Phil had given her on a Valentine's Day so many years ago. I regret to say this—I regret it with all my being—but the objective facts lead me to conclude that Penny was misdirecting us in our conversation this morning."

"As do I." He told her his reason—the photo of Penny in the driver's seat of the vintage MGA that he had seen in Desmond's office. He said, "She has to know how to drive a stick."

He looked down at the large rubber gloves on van der Berg's hands and asked again, "So what are you looking for, Harriet"

"You know precisely what I am looking for."

"Well, we might as well both do it. We seem destined to search for hidden things together."

She nodded to the door leading into the kitchen. "There's another pair of rubber gloves laying over the sink. Frode uses them for dishwashing." Examining the decaying head of lettuce in her hand, she said, "You'll be wanting them. I asked Else if I might borrow these. I told her that I may have lost a credit card, that it might have slipped off my bedside table into the trash basket in my room. I must say that I do regret speaking such fabrications, even if they be in the service of truth. The ends justifying the means, as they say. My greater regret is that they seem to be growing ever easier for me to utter. Do you think I need to confess them in my prayers?"

"No, Harriet, not unless it would make you feel better." Then he said, "Though it happens less often than we think, the ends sometimes do justify the means. But it's so very difficult to discern exactly when."

Ludington went into the kitchen and found the pair of rubber gloves. As he attacked the second of the three garbage bins in the enclosure he said, "Harriet, if I know you, you've already asked Else when the garbage was last collected. That obviously matters."

"Of course I did. It was collected last Friday morning, the morning of the day of the wedding. The trash collection truck comes but once a week."

For some forty minutes, the two of them rummaged through a week's worth of the Royal Hotel's garbage, some of it fully-aged and revolting. They systematically laid out the contents of each bin on the gravel floor of the enclosure, then sorted through it like a pair of archeologists before placing it back in its bin. Their search finally yielded exactly what they were looking for and exactly what they feared they might find. It was Harriet who found it. She extracted it from the toilet paper that had been wound around it, looked at it closely, and then held it up for Seth to see. Her face barely masked a mixture of confusion and sadness. It was a medium-sized amber-colored plastic prescription bottle. The top of the label read "Ambien (zolpidem tartrate) 5mg, take one tablet immediately before going to bed." The note at the bottom of the label indicated the quantity—"Qty60TAB." It had been filled by a CVS in Philadelphia and was dated three days before they had left on the tour. The name on the prescription is "Penelope W. Desmond." It was empty.

Chapter Thirty-Six

June 28

In a sober silence, Ludington and van der Berg dutifully returned the trash they had strewn about the gravel to the three plastic bins, all of it except the little amber prescription bottle. Seth stuffed that into the pocket of the suede jacket he had put on for his hike to Hackness.

"I'll put the gloves back in the kitchen, Harriet."

When he emerged from the kitchen door after doing so, she looked at her pastor, not a hint of affect on her face, and said in a flat voice, "I wish to be there when you talk with her. I've known her for fifty years. I simply cannot imagine what this means, but I shall be present."

Harriet van der Berg had spent much of her long career as an executive secretary on Wall Street getting her way with powerful people by the subtleties of indirection. She rarely gave such direct orders as this, but when she did, Seth understood that you attended to them.

"Of course. I want you with me, Harriet." He actually did.

Seth knocked on the door of Penny Desmond's room, but it was Harriet who answered Penny when she called out a loud and questioning, "Yes?"

"Penny, The Reverend Ludington and I would like a moment, please."

In Harriet van der Berg's understanding of the world, moments of gravity demanded arch formality.

"Come in then, the both of you."

They found her packing—blouses, sweaters, slacks, two dresses and a pair of jeans, all neatly folded and laid out in two rows on the bed. Her hard-case roller bag was yawning open and set atop a folding wooden luggage rack, waiting to receive two weeks's worth of carefully chosen travel clothing. She had not overpacked.

Penny looked up from her work and said, "I can't decide what to do about Phil's clothes. It seems utterly pointless to drag them home, but just as odd to leave them here. Maybe Frode could use them. What do you think?"

Ludington finally spoke for the first time since entering the room, but he did not answer her query about Phil Desmond's clothes. "Could we sit down, Penny?" He looked at Penny's clothing covering the bed and then to the single chair pushed up to the small writing desk.

"Well, certainly."

She cleared enough room on the bed for her and Harriet to sit next to each other and pulled the chair away from the desk for Seth. Always the perfect hostess, he thought. That—and raising three daughters—had been her chosen career. She had done both very well. The two women sat side-by-side on the bed—close but not touching. Seth pulled the ladderback desk chair with its cane seat closer to the bed. He was less than a yard from them when he sat. His knees almost touched Penny's.

He looked at them and held his silence for a long moment before he spoke. He faced two women, both elderly and of studied dignity, remarkable intelligence and great accomplishment. He liked and respected each of them. Had she been born a decade or two later, van der Berg would have probably gone to law school rather than done secretarial training. She would have made a formidable attorney. Perhaps Penny would have attended seminary herself. She had become a tenacious mother, and good pastors are actually rather mother-like. He was deeply troubled by the questions that providence was now calling him to put to one of them. He decided that he would ask without words. He reached into his jacket pocket and withdrew the empty Ambien prescription bottle. He opened his hand and held it for Penny to see. Harriet looked sideways at her friend, hoping to discreetly gauge her reaction without obviously staring.

Penny Desmond did not gasp, nor did she reach to take the bottle. "Where did you find that?"

"In a trash bin behind the hotel. Wrapped up in toilet paper."

She did not respond at first. All three of them understood that the context and mood of this encounter carried awkward questions at the least, an allegation at the most. Seth could only guess at the thoughts tumbling through Penny Desmond's mind as she looked at the prescription bottle in his hand. She had to understand that he had searched the hotel's trash. She had to know that he had done that for a reason. And now he was showing her what he had found, and was doing so in a carefully staged interview with Harriet present.

"I threw it away," she blurted. "After I emptied all the pills down the toilet." She glanced over her shoulder to the bathroom as if for confirmation. "I was taking too many of them. I decided it was dangerous. I thought it best to rid myself of the temptation."

He wanted to believe her. He imagined that van der Berg wanted to believe her. But the coincidence of her empty prescription bottle of Ambien and a man—her husband—dead with an overdose of the same on a small island was too much even for the most hopeful and sympathetic credulity.

Ludington hated to say what he said next, but it was necessary. "Penny, I know you can drive a manual transmission car. Phil once showed me a photo of the two of you in the MGA he gave you. You were in the driver's seat. It was a stick shift, of course. They all were." Then he asked his second question, this one with words. "Why did you say you couldn't manage a manual? You said as much that morning when you went to drive yourself out to the Dwarfie Stane in the hotel's car and you said it again this morning."

Harriet van der Berg looked down at her hands, clenched tightly in her lap as if in prayer, and said, reluctantly at first, but then decisively, "And Penny, you could not have lost the earring that morning. You weren't wearing them. Not at that hour, not with blue jeans. Had you been, I would have noticed." Harriet looked at her friend of half a century and then back at her hands, "Penny, I think you attempted to deceive us, to deceive me. Why ever would you do that?"

A blade of anxiety began to pierce Penny Desmond's scrim of calm as she answered, speaking more loudly than before, "I don't know what you're talking about. I was too wearing them and I have just forgotten how to drive a stick. What on earth are the two of you suggesting?"

Seth Ludington decided it was time to press her with a prevarication of his own, "Magnus Isbister called. Penny, they found your fingerprints on that whiskey bottle, the one inside the Dwarfie Stane. He has some questions he wants to ask you."

"What? That's simply not possible. I wiped it...." The words were spoken before she had time to contain her shock at Ludington's fake news. He knew that her fingerprints on the whiskey bottle would not really have been that damning even if they had actually been there. She might well have handled it before it ever went to Rackwick. But the thought that they were on the bottle had jolted her, and with one errant word—"wiped"—she realized that she had betrayed herself. She was an intelligent woman, but Penny Desmond was not a practiced liar.

She suddenly seemed to melt before their eyes. From her body movements, Ludington thought she might lean sideways into van der Berg, even lay her head on her friend's shoulder. Instead, after rocking one way and then the other, she leaned forward and put her face in her hands. Harriet laid her arm over her friend's shoulders and began patting her back rhythmically. With her other hand, Harriet reached to the bedside table for a tissue, but held on to it when she saw that no tears were coming, at least not yet.

Instead of weeping, Penny bolted up, sitting ram-rod straight, and looked Seth in the eyes. Their faces were not three feet apart. "Phil had ALS. Lou Gehrig's Disease. He was diagnosed a year and a half ago. Do you know anything about ALS? Everybody dies, but not until they spend months, sometimes years, locked inside a body that doesn't work. Your brain works, but you can't speak, you can't eat, you can't drink, then, finally, you can't breathe and you suffocate. Can you imagine? It's hell, perfect hell without a cure – except for death."

She rose from the bed and took a few steps to the writing desk behind Ludington. She picked up a small book with a tattered dark blue sleeve from where it lay on the desk's corner. It was the book Seth had seen Desmond

218

reading and jotting notes in several times during the early days of their travels. It was, he knew, John Baillie's classic *"A Diary of Daily Prayer."* Penny returned to her place on the bed beside Harriet and began to page through the book.

As she searched, she said, "I was a bit surprised by Phil's affection for Baillie. It's not exactly contemporary devotional literature with all the faux-Elizabethan thees and thous. And it's so heavily confessional, but Phil had been praying his way through it, twice every day. Maybe he thought his illness was a failing that needed confessing. I think he started using it right after the diagnosis."

She stopped leafing through the book when she found the page she was searching for. She turned it toward Ludington. The page was labeled "TWENTY-FIRST DAY, EVENING." He knew that the book was set up so that the prayers for the day—one for morning, and on the following page, the one for that evening, filled the right hand side of each page of the book. The left side was left blank for a reader who might want to make notes. She handed it to Seth. "Read it," she said forcefully. He took the book from her. The handwriting that filled the left side of the book was wobbly, sometimes difficult to decipher, but Seth could make out the date Phil Desmond had noted when he had made the entry on the blank page opposite Baillie's prayer. Phil's entry was dated, "May 30."

Penny whispered, "Handwriting deteriorates with ALS, along with everything else, except for cognition. Do you want me to read it?"

"Please."

Seth handed her back the book. She read what her husband had written, read it very slowly, though from the way she looked into space more than down at the page as she did so, Ludington sensed she had the words memorized. *"I do not fear death, but getting there by this path terrifies me. I no longer pray to be cured. I know that is not to be. But I pray that I could somehow be spared what lies between now and my end. I have considered taking my life, but could never do that to Penny and the girls. Suicide still bears such stigma. I do pray that I might fall asleep one night and not wake the next morning, at least not here."*

"I read that the first time a few days after he wrote it. I'd not been sleeping well and I picked up the book from Phil's side of the bed in the middle of another sleepless night back in Philadelphia. He actually could sleep, fitfully perhaps, but better than I did. The Ambien was prescribed for my insomnia."

She reached behind her shoulder to hold Harriet's hand, still draped over her. "You have to understand that I have loved Phil Desmond from the first day I laid eyes on him. I guess it was school girl love then, but it seasoned well, so very well. For fifty years, I have ached to make him happy. And he wanted little more than to make me happy, big ego though he was. They say marriage is a school for the soul. Torrance said it at the wedding that night. Well, they're right. He was right. It taught me that my happiness was all wrapped up in his. And I think it taught him the same. Marriage – when they make it anyway – pulls you out of yourself. After I read the note he wrote on Day 21, I began to imagine how I might bring him happiness in this horror, how I could somehow answer his prayer. I mean the last line in that entry, the one about just falling asleep and not waking up here. But I had to do it in a way that wouldn't saddle our daughters with a murderess for a mother. I imagine you believe in providence, Seth. I think I do."

He nodded, not so much in agreement, but to give her permission to continue. Harriet's arm was still draped over Penny, though Penny had pulled hers away and the patting had ceased.

"When we were in Edinburgh last week, I read the story in *The Scotsman* about the clergy murders here in Orkney. It seemed providential, this despicable Sod Stuffer and all the pills I had been prescribed tucked in my suitcase. And then there was the fact that Phil had been drinking rather more than in the past, quite a bit more, actually. Who could blame him? My physician had cautioned me about Ambien and alcohol. I think he actually used the word, 'deadly.' It seemed to fall into place—the serial killer, the Ambien and the alcohol. It was like it was meant to be. The two killings on the same date in the past two years could offer me cover. And I found such solace knowing that Phil would never be aware that death was coming, and that it would come to him before he was locked up in the ALS dungeon. It would be exactly what he prayed for. I was a bit worried that this serial killer might actually claim his own victim the same day. But maybe he would choose two this year."

Ludington and van der Berg listened in stunned silence to the unfolding confession. He nodded at Penny ever so slightly, an acknowledgment that he understood her thinking, even if he was unsure he could agree with it.

"Right before dinner on the night of June 21, the day of the wedding, I suggested to Phil that we should visit the Dwarfie Stane that night, after the reception. He had actually asked me about it before we ever got to Orkney, and then he had talked about it after we got here. He said he wanted to make sure we saw it. It was the kind of thing he loved."

Penny smiled, but barely. "I remember the afternoon before the wedding. We were dressing, up here in our room, about to go down for drinks before we went to the church. He was having trouble fastening his clerical collar. I had to help him with it. I'll never forget the look in his eyes as I had to do what he had always done for himself. His motor skills were deteriorating so fast, just like they said they would. He hated being pitied. I could see it in his eyes as I did the buttons and the collar. He knew—and I knew—that this was only a foretaste of what was to come."

Ludington sensed that Penny's telling of the story bore some measure of release as she unfolded its details.

"I had crushed all the Ambien the night before when he was sleeping, forty, fifty-some pills, I think. Smashed them into a powder with a spoon and a soup bowl I'd taken from the kitchen. And I had filched a bottle of whiskey from the bar the night the seminarians went missing. I put a lot of the powder in the bottle that night, but I saved some."

"We had our drinks at the hotel before we went to the church and then more at the party afterward. I slipped some Ambien into every one of his. Not into that cog they passed around, of course. You saw us leave, Seth. You were standing outside waiting for the nurse. So yes, I borrowed the Hotel's Peugeot. And yes, I can drive a stick." Defiance was rising in her voice. "We still have the MG." She paused and corrected herself, "I mean, I still have the MG he gave me."

"I drove north to the Dwarfie Stane that night. I was afraid he might fall asleep in the car, but he was excited and managed to stay awake. The place was utterly abandoned when we got there. I don't know what I would have done if someone else had been there. It's a bit of a walk from the road out to the tomb itself, but you know that. Phil was exhausted; he was getting drowsy. He was pretty loopy by time we arrived."

"He barely managed the walk. I had to hold him close, our arms wrapped around each other the last third of the way. It was still fairly light. The longest day of the year, but you know that. The storm had been forecast, but it was waiting, blessedly. When we finally got to the Dwarfie Stane, I suggested we crawl inside. We sat there hunched low in the dark of the place and we drank – actually he drank – the better part of the bottle. I remember him saying, "A fine old Orkney whiskey in a fine old Orkney tomb." Then he laughed. I said I thought we should lie down in those two carved niches for a minute. Phil always had a sense for the playful. It is—was—one of the things I loved about him."

She paused, turned to Harriet, smiled weakly again, and looked back to Seth.

"We lay there, side by side, holding hands. In a few minutes, Phil fell asleep. Before long, he was more than asleep. When I knew for certain he was gone, I lay there beside him. I lay there for an age, probably a couple of hours, just looking at him. I whispered a prayer, not for forgiveness, mind you. It was a prayer of thanksgiving—for him, for our life together, and for a good death. Then I kissed his forehead. He was starting to grow cool by then. I crawled out of the tomb and scooped up a handful of wet dirt and grass and went back in. Then I gently put it into his mouth. It was like I was feeding him. I kissed him again, on the forehead. I drove back to the hotel through the dim. I shed some tears along the way. I don't know how I did it, the drive I mean. When I got back, I came up to this room and I sat in that chair you're sitting in, Seth. I sat and stared out at the water till morning and watched as the light came back. I didn't weep anymore. I never had a second thought about what I did. I still haven't."

Chapter Thirty-Seven

June 28

There was nothing more to be said, at least nothing that might be said in the presence of Penny Desmond. So, without a word, Seth left the room to the two women. They were still sitting close to each other on the bed covered in folded travel clothes waiting to be packed. Tears had come at last, come to both of them. Not open weeping; such overt display was hardly the accustomed manner of either. But as he stood, he did see silent tears, wet in the corners of reddened eyes. He turned back to them as he opened the door to leave and saw Harriet dab her eyes delicately and then hand the tissue to Penny.

He found that he could not quite bring himself to phone Isbister and tell him about the confession he had just heard, a confession substantiated by an empty Ambien bottle, a photo of Penny in the MGA, and a lie about the earrings. At least he could not make the call quite yet. He had to think things through first – exactly what he might say and how he would frame it. And he definitely wanted to talk to Harriet before he did anything. He walked down the stairs and out the front door of the Royal, blessedly encountering no one in the tour group. He walked quickly around to the water side of the hotel and sat on the stone bench. It had become something like a pew for him, not a pew facing a church's chancel, but an outdoor pew facing the water of Long Hope and the hills of Hoy rising green-gray on the other side. As he sat, he sighed and thought of the deep valley beyond the hills and the empty tomb they called the Dwarfie Stane that lay in its fold.

He realized that he was hesitating to make his call to Magnus Isbister because he could not help but imagine what he would want for himself if ever in his life he would come to countenance something like ALS. What would he want? What if it were his wife or his mother or father? What would he do if they asked him for a kinder death than what ALS and its likes offered? Yet murder was murder. He assumed the law was clear about it – no exceptions for mercy killing. What would Isbister do when he made the call? He impressed Seth as a man who might look the other way, the kind of cop who would err on the side of agnostic mercy. And if he called Isbister, and if the man did arrest Penny, would a Scottish jury really send a seventy-four-year-old widow to prison for something done out of love? But prison or no, the scandal of it would rock the Desmond family – those three lovely daughters and the umpteen grandchildren. And the press would never let it go. He could imagine the headlines in the tabloids—*society preacher's wife murders dying husband.*" Yet he could not but ask himself, "Who was Penny Desmond to play God?" Phil might have had a few more good months in him. She took those from him. And what about a miracle cure, or even a healing miracle? Ludington thought that he believed in miracles. They happened... sometimes.

He turned around to look up at the window of Penny Desmond's room. He didn't expect to see anything, but it was where the woman was, the woman whose fate providence had laid in his hands. His zeal to know the truth about Desmond's murder had gotten him in this moral quandary. Suddenly, he saw Harriet van der Berg come to the window of Penny Desmond's room and look down. She saw him, as if she expected that she would see him on the familiar bench. She did not wave, nor did he. But a few moments later Harriet van der Berg was sitting at his side on the stone bench.

She looked across the water at Hoy, not at him, and said, "She asked to be alone. You have phoned Chief Inspector Isbister, I assume."

"I will. I guess I have to. Then he said, perhaps to explain his delay in calling, "Fiona has been reading George Mackay Brown. The famous Orkney author. She mentioned a novel Brown wrote about Bonhoeffer, at least partly about Bonhoeffer."

Van der Berg looked away from Hoy and at her pastor, "The minister the Nazi's executed?

"One of them. I've been sitting here, thinking about him, what he chose to do. You know he took part in a plot to assassinate Hitler. Murder for a higher good. They figured killing him would save countless lives. My point is that they played God, or at least they tried to. Their plot failed. But most everybody today would say they did the right thing. I know I would agree."

Van der Berg said, "Well, killing a monster like Hitler for the greater good is not the same thing as taking the life of a good man, even if he was facing horrific suffering. Cannot suffering deepen the soul, pastor? Could Philip not have provided a witness, a demonstration of Christian courage perhaps."

Ludington could not tell whether her question was real or if her moralizing was by way of baiting him.

"Deepen his soul for what? He had a few months to live. I've seen ALS. A friend of my father's died of it. How can you witness if you can't speak or move a hand to write?"

She laid her hand on his knee and said, "But murder is wrong, Seth. Always and simply wrong. The sixth commandment."

"What about Bonhoeffer?" he said.

"Well, that was different. Hitler was a demon. Phil was a saint. I have always liked Penny, and you know I adored her husband. I wither to imagine where this will lead, what it will mean for her and the girls, but the way is clear. If you don't phone the authorities, I guess I will."

"Are things always so very clear, Harriet? I've been at a few hospital bedsides where I guessed that death had been hastened along, welcomed with some form of action or inaction. Done mercifully and surreptitiously. A bit too much pain-killer in the IV. The feeding tube withdrawn. The oxygen mask removed. Isn't that playing God?"

Van der Berg did not answer his question, rhetorical as it was. Instead she began to weep, her shoulders shaking. Ludington was stunned by the woman's sudden wave of descending emotion. She pulled the wad of tissue she had offered Penny Desmond from the pocket of her cardigan and dried her eyes. Then she blew her running nose. This was a disclosure of vulnerability, an overt demonstration of passion unlike anything he had ever seen in this stubbornly self-disciplined and self-contained woman.

Seth could only guess that these tears were not for Penny Desmond, or even for Penny's dead husband. They were wept for something closer, closer to the bone. He said nothing, but placed his hand atop hers, still resting on his left knee. He knew her well enough to understand that she would feel the need to explain this uncharacteristic loss of composure.

She sniffled and sat up straight on the stone. "I never really knew exactly what happened when Margaret died. She had been in Sloan Kettering for six weeks. She was mostly unconscious the last few weeks. They had to administer a great deal of morphine to keep her comfortable. When her doctor asked me about a medical directive, I said that Margaret had never done one. Not even when she was first diagnosed with the cancer, breast cancer it was, advanced by the time they caught it. Then they asked me about withdrawing the life support measures. They assumed I was her sister. I explained that we shared an apartment, but were unrelated. You know that she and I were together for half a century, but we never married. We could not do so, not in New York until quite recently. The law only changed just before she died. So, I had to phone her brother, her younger brother, Roger. Sweet man, but ineffectual, or so I had always thought. He lived out on Long Island, in Nassau County somewhere. He had come to visit Margaret in the hospital several times in those dreadful weeks. But he never stayed long. When she was still awake, he reminisced with her about their childhood, which was kind. She enjoyed it, but every time he left the room, he merely shook his head and said, "so unfortunate." When I phoned him that day, I told him that there was a decision to be made, the decision about the life support, I mean. He came into the City the next morning and spoke with her doctors. I was not a part of the meeting. I was *persona non grata*, just the roommate. Margaret died two days later. I was with her. I never asked Roger what he decided, what he told the doctors. I didn't want to know. But I guess I do know. The IV with the pain medication was still there after his visit, but the feeding tube was gone that night. She slipped away over the next two days, slipped from sleep into death. It was, what do they say, 'peaceful.' Such a curious word for death. But here's the truth, Seth… I was actually relieved that I did not have to make the decision, the decision that mousey little Roger made. And I was ashamed of not wanting to make it. I am still ashamed. Frankly, I do not know what I would have decided."

Seth pivoted to face her on the stone bench and took her long skinny frame in his arms. It was awkward, but she did not resist his embrace. "Forgive yourself, Harriet," he whispered in her ear. "How dare you be less merciful than God."

Then he reached into his jeans and took out his iPhone. He stood, turned away from van der Berg and walked a few paces toward the still, blue-gray water of Long Hope. He looked back at her and said softly, but loudly enough for her to hear, "I have a call to make."

Chapter Thirty-Eight

June 28

"Magnie, it's Seth, Seth Ludington." If the Chief Inspector of Orkney's iteration of Police Scotland was surprised by Ludington's afternoon phone call, his voice did not betray it.

"What can I do for you?"

"We're leaving tomorrow morning from Stromness on the *Hamnavoe*. There's some unfinished business I need to take care of before we leave Orkney. Magnie, I need to see Linklater. Today. I need to see him in person. Can you make that happen? I assume you're still holding him in Kirkwall."

"Aye, he's still bidin' in our peedie lock-up. He's off to Inverness for more long-term accommodations the day after tomorrow. The trial and sentencing will be down there as well. Glad for it, I am. I detest having him here."

"So, could I see him? I mean in a few hours? Alone?"

Isbister did not answer immediately. He finally said, a question hanging over his answer, "Well, if you wish. He's entitled to visitors. He's not had a one. He hasna' even got himself a solicitor. Stands by his confession, he does, even with the holes it has in it. Still won't say how he got himself off Hoy, nor will he name the drug he used on Desmond."

"Think of it as a spiritual issue, more for me than him. Something that needs to be cleared up. I'll borrow the hotel's car and take the Lyness ferry to Houton."

"A spiritual issue, you say? That's a fresh one, Reverend Ludington."

Eager to change the subject, Ludington said, "Frode and Else are pleased you got the car back to them so quickly. How did you manage that?"

"Andy and I were waiting for McNulty in Houton when he pulled off the Ro Ro. I arrested him and I sent Andy right back to Hoy with the car. He just returned."

Ludington said, "I'm guessing that Frode and Else didn't press charges for theft, so what about our Al McNulty? I assume you've released him."

"Not yet, but I'll have to. But I dinna' know where he's going to be able to go, Scot free as he is." He chuckled at his feeble witticism before continuing. "The man forgot to grab his passport when he dashed off. The hotel still has it, I imagine. Not sure he'll want to be fetching it until you lot have left the place. Perhaps you can bring it along when you come."

Ludington smiled at the thought of Al McNulty abroad without a passport. Without it, he'd need to get himself to the American consulate in Edinburgh or the embassy in London and endure the horrors of numbered forms, proofs of identity, and then endless waiting. Perhaps the waiting would be long enough for an American arrest warrant to greet him on his return to the States.

He punched the red button to end his call and walked back to the stone bench where van der Berg was still sitting, the tears vanquished, her usual resolute demeanor regained.

He did not sit, but looked at her and said, "Check on Penny, would you Harriet. I've got to go to Kirkwall for a quick visit." He did not say whom he planned to visit.

She guessed. "Chief Inspector Isbister, I assume. Are you sure you want to do this? I guess you must."

"In a world of imperfect choices, we have to make the best ones before us, flawed as they may be. You surely understand that. Let's talk when I get back."

Harriet van der Berg had come to trust the man, though she had known him for little more than a year or two. She trusted him enough to ask no more of him before she stood, straightened the pleats of her flannel skirt, and returned to check on Penny Desmond one more time.

Seth found that neither Frode nor Else were in the office, so he opened the door that led from it into the kitchen. He saw that Frode was busy with dinner, laying out salmon filets on several wooden planks.

"Frode, may I use the car for a few hours. I'll be back with it by dinner." They had been told that their last meal at the Royal would be an hour later than usual, and that it would be special. In spite of one guest murdered and another absconded, the two hoteliers were determined to carry on.

Frode raised his rubber-gloved hands and said, "They smell of the fish. My hands. But you can find the car keys in the office yourself, in the drawer there." He pointed in the direction of the office door behind Ludington.

"No more keys left on the dashboard," Seth thought to himself as he returned to the little office and opened the only drawer in what served as a reception desk. He found the Peugeot's keys as well as the tidy row of American passports. He went through them quickly, found Al McNulty's, and slipped it into his back pocket.

He had forty minutes before he had to catch the ferry at Lyness. Instead of driving west to the Ayre and crossing it to Hoy and the ferry, Ludington drove east along the coast of South Walls for nearly two miles, almost to Hackness. When he had walked this road back from the Martello Tower earlier in the day, he had seen several small boats along the way, including a large sea kayak pulled up on the beach across from a small cottage, set alone and obviously vacant. The sign in front of it read "Holiday Let by the Week" and below the local agent's name and phone number. Seth pulled the car into the short gravel drive to the cottage and got out. He looked both ways, up and down the narrow road, to make certain no one was coming. He crossed the road and worked his way down the short, steep beach and untied the large plastic kayak from the post to which it was tethered by a yellow Nylon painter. Then he pushed it out into Switha Sound, pushed it hard so that it slid silently sixty feet out into the water where it was quickly caught by the rising west wind. He knew enough about wind and light vessels to hope that it might drift well out into the Sound of Hoxa, perhaps all the way to South Ronaldsay, by the next day.

He drove back across South Walls, crossed the Ayre to Hoy, and caught the ferry at Lyness just in time. The crossing was to be direct; no stopping at Flotta. He got out of the car ten minutes after the ferry left Lyness pier and wiggled his way between cars and trucks to the windward side of the vessel. He was the only person who had not either remained in their car as the west wind freshened or chosen to stand on the calmer, leeward, side of the ferry. He leaned on the painted metal rail, looked to his right and then to his left to be sure he was alone—the second time he had done so in the last hour. He reached into his back pocket and pulled out Al McNulty's passport. He took another quick look at it and let it slip from his hand and over the rail into the white horses rearing in Scapa Flow.

Ludington found the Kirkwall Police Station easily. It was an unfortunate attempt at modernism pretending to blend with the austere stone architecture of the old town. It was on Burgh Road near the town center, not far from the harbor. He had noticed it on his earlier foray into Kirkwall. He entered and was greeted warmly by Abby Munro, the young constable he had met five days and an eon earlier at Rackwick, the day they had found Desmond. She was expecting his visit, she said, "But Magnus, I mean Chief Inspector Isbister, isna' here. There's been a road accident up Finstown way. There are injuries, serious perhaps. He felt he had to go himself. Said he's sorry to miss you."

Perhaps the truth, Seth thought to himself. But it could also be that Isbister could not abide being in the building when Ludington and Linklater met. He clearly detested the man, and would just as soon not have to be present nor to speak to Ludington after his meeting with Linklater. He would not have to ask the obvious questions about the putative "spiritual matter" and exactly what had passed between the two of them. They were questions that Ludington would probably not answer anyway.

"You can sit with him alone, Reverend Ludington, but I'll be outside the door. There's a wire glass window in the door so I can see in. Andy will cuff him before he brings him in. Ten minutes, Chief Inspector said, no more."

Ludington sat alone in the small makeshift interview room for what seemed an eternity. The space was spartan, off-white walls, a small Formica-covered table and two oddly pink fiberglass chairs with metal legs facing each other across the table. He had visited young men in jail during his years at the ministry project he had worked for in Philadelphia before his move to Old Stone Church in New York. They were mostly cock-sure but terrified kids who had wound up in street gangs and done stupid stuff—sometimes harmless, sometimes anything but. The Philadelphia County Jail was nothing like this little lock-up in Orkney. No rows of plexiglass partitions here, no grimy old plastic phone handsets to talk into, no bored guards standing over your shoulder.

The young constable named Andy, the one with the unfathomable Orkney accent, led Ronald Linklater, hands cuffed before him, into the room. Andy nodded to the empty chair opposite Ludington and said, "Sit ye there." Then to Ludington, "We'll be just outside." The door he had brought Linklater through from the lock-up had no window.

Linklater sat, a look of mystification on his stubbled face. He appeared not to have shaved since his arrest. Ludington reached into this jacket pocket and took out the small New Testament he had packed for the trip. It was a KJV, a King James Version, one of those onion skin editions with pages so frail you were afraid to turn them. He had thought an occasion might arise on the trip for him to offer some sort of group devotions. The death of one of their number might seem to have been such, but no one had asked, not even Harriet or Harry, and he was loath to press it.

Linklater looked at the little Testament and sneered, "Come to save me, have you?"

"Saving you is possible, but it would not be my doing."

"Well, you can forget it. I have no regrets. I did what I had to do. And I would do it again."

Ludington heard his words and thought to himself, "A second murderer confessing to me in the same day, also with no regrets." But he knew that a chasm of motivation separated the two murderers—mindless loathing on one side, mindless love on the other.

He opened the little Testament and found the small piece of paper on which he had written a few words and then slipped between the pages of the Bible. As he removed it, he saw that he had placed it in the pages that told Luke's story of the crucifixion, the Twenty-Third Chapter. The Testament was a red-letter edition, all of the words of Jesus printed in flaming red. As he pulled the piece of paper from the Bible, he saw verse twenty-four, screaming at him in red, *"Father, forgive them, for they know not what they do."*

He said nothing to Linklater, but looked over his shoulder to see if Constable Abby Munro was watching them. Even though his back was to the door and she could not easily see what he was doing, he wanted to make sure that she saw nothing of what he was about to do. Fortunately, her head was turned away as she talked on her cell phone.

Ludington handed the note to Linklater and looked the man in the eyes. Very softy, he said, "Read it, and give it back." Linklater took the piece of paper, unfolded it, and read what Ludington had written. A look of utter confusion passed across his face, followed by sudden comprehension. The man may have been evil, but he was clever—an all too common and inevitably dangerous combination of traits. Ronald Linklater handed the piece of paper back to Ludington. Then he smiled the most discomfiting smile Seth Ludington had ever been offered.

Chapter Thirty-Nine

June 28-29

Ludington had written just three words on the note: *"It was Ambien."*
He glanced at his watch as he pulled the Peugeot into its parking
spot in front of the Royal. It was 7:30. He would be late for Frode's
farewell dinner. He entered the hotel and laid the car keys on the counter
atop the Dutch door into the office. Underneath the keys, he placed an
envelope with a check made out to Frode and Else Andresen, a check for
twenty-five thousand dollars. It was the least he could do for them and their
marginal operation after what his group had put them through.

He entered to see that the dining room was less full than it had been
before. Phil and Al were both gone of course, and Penny had obviously
chosen to remain in her room. Lewis Ross, their driver, was seated with
Sarah Mrazek and the two younger seminary students, all listening patiently
as he regaled them with another of his packaged narratives. Harry and
Georgia Mullholland were sitting alone, holding hands across a table that
was covered—as was each of the three in the room—with a freshly pressed
white tablecloth. And a candle set in a glass base had been placed at the
center of each. Good for Frode and Else, he thought. Putting on the dog for
the occasion in spite of everything.

Fiona and Ingrid had returned from their day together up in Rackwick.
They were seated with Harriet, who was looking even more sober than usual.
They had saved a place for him at their table. He wondered if his wife and

234

her grandmother had made the hike out to the cliff that overlooked the Old Man of Hoy as they had planned. He kissed Fiona and asked the question, "Make it out to the Old Man?"

Ingrid answered for them, obviously proud that she was fit enough for such a walk at her age, "Indeed, we did."

Then Fiona said, "It was a lovely day for it. The wind didn't come up till we were headed back."

He gave her the "that's one" look, holding up his index finger so she alone could see it. Even now, in the throes of all this, he was counting them.

He assumed that Harriet had told Fiona where her husband had gone that morning. But neither woman wanted to ask about his visit to Kirkwall in the presence of the other. He would tell both of them later. He would tell Fiona when they went back to their room after dinner, tell her the whole story. But on the ferry from back to Hoy from Mainland, he had decided that he would not tell Van der Berg what he had chosen to do until they returned to New York, though it would be obvious he had not told Isbister of Penny's confession. He was himself quite unsure whether he had done the right thing. He would probably carry his doubts with him for the rest of his life. But he feared that Harriet van der Berg, who tended to see the world with crisp borders between right and wrong, would be even less confident about the ethical probity of his actions. Better she not know till they left Scotland, though when Penny Desmond boarded their Delta flight home, unbothered by any representatives of Police Scotland, she would probably guess at what he had chosen to do.

The conversation around the dinner table was awkward, with unasked questions hovering over the four of them. The salmon was excellent, though Seth ate little of it. When they returned to their room, Seth took Fiona in his arms, then released her and massaged the growing pregnancy bump. He smiled, kissed her again, and said one word, "Life." Then he sat beside her on the bed and told her what Penny had confessed. Then he told her the entire saga and what he had done. She nodded and wiped a few inevitable tears from her eyes after hearing the tale. Fiona Ludington was a lawyer, and a fine one, but she chose to offer no legal opinion, much less a moral one.

Seth said to her, "Fiona, would you do one thing for me? Would you go to her room and tell her that she doesn't have to worry? Just say it's okay. No details, only that. If I tell her, she'll ask questions that I don't want to answer. Questions I'm not sure I can answer. If you tell her and she asks questions, you can say you don't know the details, simply that I told you she doesn't have to worry." He paused, pulled her tighter to him and said, "Sometimes it's better not to know everything."

* * *

Magnus Isbister was waiting for them in Houton as the ferry docked in Houton the next morning, standing beside his parked Police Scotland Ford Focus Estate. To Ludington's relief, the light on its roof not flashing. A good sign. As the crew cast the mooring lines to the dock and secured the vessel, Ludington watched Isbister as he moved to the base of the pier where foot passengers would disembark after they had walked the short gangplank. He could see that Isbister was alone. Another good sign.

Ludington looked over his shoulder into the little tour bus. He could not see either Harriet or Penny, though he knew that they had sat next to each other toward the back. Everyone but he had chosen to remain on the bus for the crossing. The west wind that had risen to a howl through the night had still not laid down. Ludington caught Isbister's eye and offered a slight wave of his hand. Isbister nodded in reply.

The Chief Inspector of Orkney Police Scotland stood waiting for him at the end of the pier, looking every bit the stolid Calvinist he was. He did not offer Ludington his hand, but he did take Seth's when he offered it. Then he took Ludington by the elbow and ushered him away from the parade of vehicles rolling off the ferry to a quiet spot in the lee of the ticket booth.

"Thought I'd come by and offer you a farewell, Reverend Ludington. That, and a bit of interesting news." He sucked in his breath in the Orkney way of marking significance. "So, yesterday afternoon, Linklater was suddenly able to come up with the specifics of the meds he says he gave Desmond. Not

236

long after your peedie visit it was. Sorry to miss you, by the way. He told us that he just decided to change things up. From Rohypnol to Ambien, you know. And then it was back to the roofie business with you, oddly enough. And would ye ken what else has happened? You'll not believe this – a fishing boat bound into Stromness late last night came across a loose sea kayak drifting about off Hoxa Head on South Ronaldsay. They pulled it aboard and called it in. Said they had seen my notice about missing boats. It's registered to a name and address on South Walls, a few hundred yards up the beach from Long Hope and the hotel."

After sharing his news, Magnus Isbister raised an eyebrow and said, "How about that?"

Seth Ludington said nothing

Epilogue

New York, December 31

Dear Magnie,

  I write to wish you a "Happy Hogmanay," if that's the right wording, as well as to congratulate you on your retirement, though to congratulate a person at retirement does seem curious. It suggests that a career is a trial to be endured and that you're to be congratulated upon getting through it. I suppose this can be true at times, but I do know that your life's work was so much more for you.

  Which is perhaps why I felt driven to write this. When we left Hoy last summer, I sensed that you still shared my doubts—our doubts really, I mean mine and Harriet's—about Ronald Linklater's culpability in the death of Phil Desmond. You said as much more than a few times. I read it in your face and heard it in your words when you met us that last day at the ferry dock in Houton.

  You were right, of course. I know this for certain. I cannot say more, nor can I assure you that justice has been done. As you doubtless know from your work, justice can be a slippery thing. We talk incessantly about the need for justice, and rightly so. But doing the perfectly just thing is often elusive. Sometimes it's simply impossible. I can assure you, however, that something like the right thing has been done, or if not the right thing, what I pray to be the rightest thing possible. Magnie, I came to know you well enough in those few days to understand that this question would haunt you. It needn't. I hope this makes cents to you. (I recall your love for word play.) It would probably help for you to know that Phil Desmond was dying

238

of ALS.

And you might also be interested to know that a warrant has been issued for the arrest of Al McNulty and his accomplice, a woman with whom he was in a relationship who worked at the bank the seminary used. It seems that she was the insider facilitating the funds transfers into and out of those questionable accounts, the ones attached to the email you found on Desmond's phone. The Pennsylvania authorities have tracked them to Costa Rica. I understand extraditions are being arranged, but not for murder, mind you. Merest financial crimes.

Fiona sends her love. Her grandmother phoned again the other day and mentioned that the New Year's Day Ba' is to be played in Kirkwall tomorrow. Don't know if the Isbisters are "Uppies" or "Doonies." Those are the two teams, are they not? I only hope your boys win the thing. I am, sincerely,

Yours, Seth

PS. Fiona gave birth to the twins the day before Christmas. All three of the women in my life are doing famously. We have resisted any temptation to name them "Holly" and "Noelle." We finally settled on "Astrid" and "Ingrid" after their remarkable maternal grandmother and great grandmother. Both pagan Norse names of course, but still used in Orkney.

A Note from the Author

Note that Orkney, magical as it may seem, is a very real place and worthy of a visit, though getting there is a bit of trouble. Some restaurants frequented by our characters are also quite real, though the Viking Bothy in Kirkwall is not. Nor is the Royal Hotel on the island of Hoy. Orcadian readers will doubtless note that we played freely with the interisland ferry schedules, though they do alter frequently. The largest of the islands of Orkney is known by several names: Hrossey, Pamona, Mainland and The Mainland. As the last of these could confuse readers who might understand "The Mainland" to refer to Scotland, we chose to use "Mainland" without the article except when native Orcadians are speaking. Any resemblance of our characters to real Police Scotland officers is unintentional. The only real person in the narrative is Iain Torrance, officiant the night of the fateful wedding. We offer apologies to Neil Gardener, another friend and the actual minister of the Canongate Kirk in Edinburgh, for replacing him with Fiona's father. The ancient Dwarfie Stane and the assorted Neolithic sites in Orkney that find their way into the book all exist. The Vale of Rackwick is also real, though you may not think so should you ever make your way to it.

Acknowledgements

We offer profuse thanks to our patient spouses and children who endured our inattentiveness as this book was written. We express deep appreciation to our persnickety beta readers—Steve Tracy, Fred Hasecke, Terri Lindvall, Iain Torrance and Andrew Knox, the last for his native's knowledge of Orkney, as well as to Dr. Diane Celinsky, our pharmaceutical consultant. And thanks yet again to our tireless agent at Gersh, Joe Veltre, and to the fabulous editors of Level Best Books for their confidence in our work.

About the Author

M. M. Lindvall is a father-daughter writing team. Madeline Lindvall Radman is a writer, producer and director of non-scripted television specializing in investigative documentary series. Michael Lindvall is a published author of several volumes of accessible theology and two novels. He is the Senior Minister Emeritus of the Brick Presbyterian Church in Manhattan. Michael and his wife Terri make their home on the shores of Lake Michigan near Pentwater in the summer months and in Fort Wayne in the winter. Madeline, her husband Tom and their two children live in Takoma Park, Maryland.

SOCIAL MEDIA HANDLES:
M. M. Lindvall
Michael Lindvall

AUTHOR WEBSITE:
mmlindvall.com

Also by M. M. Lindvall

Ashes to Ashes, by M. M. Lindvall

The Good News from North Haven and *Leaving North Haven,* by Michael Lindvall

A Geography of God, by Michael Lindvall